The Clock
of the Centuries

The Clock
of the Centuries

by
Albert Robida

Translated by
Brian Stableford

A Black Coat Press Book

ISBN 978-1-934543-13-9. First Printing. November 2008. Published by Black Coat Press, an imprint of Hollywood Comics.com, LLC, P.O. Box 17270, Encino, CA 91416. All rights reserved. Except for review purposes, no part of this book may be reproduced or transmitted in any form or by any means, electronic or mechanical, including photocopying, recording, or by any information storage and retrieval system, without permission in writing from the publisher. The stories and characters depicted in this novel are entirely fictional. Printed in the United States of America.

Table of Contents

Introduction

L'horloge des siècles, here translated as *The Clock of the Centuries*, was originally published in book form in 1902, and is notable as the first full-length literary account of time in reverse. It was not, however, the first satirical farce Albert Robida had written and illustrated in which he had played tricks with time; his earlier story "Jadis chez aujourd'hui" (here translated as "Yesterday Now"), serialized in the children's periodical *Le Petit Français Illustré* between May 10 and June 14, 1890, provided the seed of the idea and a preface to its ideological development. I have, therefore, combined the two in this volume.

"Jadis chez aujourd'hui" is a cheerfully ironic celebration of the great Exposition Universelle which opened in Paris in 1889, and for which the Eiffel Tower was constructed. That ostentatious exhibition of technological and cultural prowess was one of a long series initiated by London's Great Exhibition of 1851, which had been sited in the Crystal Palace. Paris had been the first city to follow in London's footsteps in 1853, and when London had organized a sequel in 1863, Paris had dutifully followed suit in 1867. Robida, whose first novel had been a comic pastiche of Jules Verne, probably knew that Verne had taken considerable inspiration from the 1867 exposition; it was there that Verne saw the submarine *Le Plongeur*, which presumably assisted in the inspiration of the *Nautilus*—a machine that Robida borrowed for his own epic of exploration.

London's third Great Exhibition ran from 1871 to 1874—dark years in French history, following defeat in the Franco-Prussian war and the collapse of the Second Empire—and Paris again trailed behind in 1878. The 1889 exposition, however, set out to establish a new standard and could not be

7

written off as any mere imitation; it was not until 1925, in fact, that London managed to put on a fourth exhibition, by which time many other cities had got in on the act and World War I had wrecked Europe so comprehensively that the United States of America, which had already taken the lead in the race to be principal engine of world progress in the 20th century—economically and technologically, if not culturally—would henceforth be unchallengeable. In 1889, however, that title was still hotly contested, and the Exposition Universelle, with its iconic central tower, represented France's bid to establish itself as the *avant-garde* of technological as well as cultural progress.

The 1889 exposition was, of course, timed to coincide with the centenary of the French Revolution, which was regarded by many people—not all of them French—as the beginning of the modern era, the turning-point at which the stultifying past had been rudely toppled and the future given free rein. The Revolution had been undertaken under the banner of Progress as well as the famous slogan of "*Liberté, Egalité, Fraternité*," and it had been very widely assumed in 1789 that scientific and technological advancement was the groundwork of social advancement—that progress in knowledge and techniques provided the fertile soil in which liberty, equality and fraternity might flourish, and that the advancement of liberty, equality and fraternity would, in its turn, facilitate the further growth of science and technology.

The 1889 exposition was supposed to re-emphasize that faith and demonstrate that the associated historical agenda was proceeding apace; a degree of skepticism had, however, developed by then. The central thesis of the philosophy of progress had generated its antithesis, whose adherents considered technological advancement highly injurious to social well-being—with the result that not everyone reacted to the Eiffel Tower and the exposition's many other exhibits in the wholeheartedly admiring fashion that their makers intended. "Jadis chez aujourd'hui" is a breezily frivolous reflection of that skepticism, in which the antithesis does not appear to have the author's support. On balance, Louis XIV and his courtiers come off worse than the exhibitors, and the progressive future succeeds in outshining the blinkered and uncomprehending past.

Paris followed up the 1889 exposition fairly swiftly with one that marked the end of the 19th century, and it was presumably the exposition of 1900 that prompted Robida to revisit the ideas that had floated into his head while writing his caricature of the 1889 exposition. He had only been an interested visitor to the 1889 exhibition, but he was actively involved in the 1900 exhibition. Significantly, however, the exhibit for which he shared the responsibility was not a celebration of the impending future, but a nostalgic re-creation of the past: models and illustrations of "Old Paris" as it had been in the Middle Ages and the 18th century. Robida had been working on such illustrative re-creations for some time, the produce of his being endeavors reflected in several books, most significantly *Paris de siècle en siècle* (1895). These historical studies had appeared alongside, and intermingled with, his speculative illustrative works exploring the potential aspect of 20th century Paris.

Robida had produced a great deal of speculative work regarding potential technological developments, illustrating his own writings lavishly and also illustrating speculative items by several other writers. His ideas about the likely shape of the future had been shaped by his vocation as a caricaturist, which forbade him to take his inventions too seriously and thus inclined him to representations in which nothing works as intended, producing comical results—but the intrinsic ironic humor of his work grew much darker over the course of his career, and *L'horloge des siècles*, which constitutes a kind of interim report of Robida's judgment on the idea of past and future Progress, includes several inklings of a deeper pessimism to come.

Although the novel's jocular narrative voice cannot be taken entirely seriously as a reflection of the author's opinions, it is undoubtedly the case that the philosophy of

9

progress takes something of a caning in the course of the narrative, and the antithesis to its thesis is given extravagant scope to make itself heard and felt. The further the story proceeds, the more committed the narrative voice becomes to the notion that 19th century technological progress has been an unmitigated disaster, and that the world went seriously awry in 1789. There comes a point when the reader can no longer believe that the author is simply playing with ideas, and is encouraged to accept that the story's rhetoric as a heartfelt element. Robida's subsequent work, especially the work he did after World War I, confirms the fact that he eventually became mordantly pessimistic about the past and likely future effects of technological development on the quality of human life.

Despite the relative triumph of the 1889 Exposition Universelle and its central folly, the decline in the fashionability of the philosophy of progress was already reflected by then in the critical success enjoyed by a prominent *avant-garde* of Decadent literature, which took it for granted that European civilization and culture were tottering on their last legs. The narrative voice of *L'horloge des siècles* is markedly unsympathetic to the stylistic embellishments, flagrant moral skepticism and symbolist affectations of Decadent literature, but one did not have to be a literary Decadent to support the thesis that some kind of historical terminus was imminent, and that contemporary civilization was rotten at the core. Although 1900 was 100 years short of the calendrical Millennium, there is a sense in which *L'horloge des siècles* is a wholehearted Millennial fantasy; it is a frankly Apocalyptic narrative, in which the Supreme Clockmaker, having contemplated the progressive prospectus for the 20th century, decides that enough is enough and stops time dead in 1901, and then starts the human story in motion again—as much by way of prescribing an educative penance as granting amazing grace, one suspects—in such a way as to require people to review their history in reverse, with wryly-enlightened eyes.

The novel is, of course, a comedy, and Robida saw no need to be thorough in the extrapolation of his premise. He avoids even mentioning many corollaries of the premise that might be deleterious to the arguments his narrative voice presents, initially in a candidly cavalier manner. While extolling the virtues of growing every younger, he is careful not to require or invite his readers to contemplate what will happen to his rejuvenated characters when the time comes for them to re-enter the maternal womb, and he is similarly coy about specifying the process by which the dead return to life. He is also remarkably vague about the workings of forgetfulness and its relevance to the benefits of experience; although his narrative voice and his principal characters wax lyrical about their golden opportunity to "ameliorate" the past that they are bound to re-live, the author is careful not to go into detail about exactly what they might do and how, or what relics of the former future they will be able to deploy in the process.

The patchwork structure of the novel facilitates this kind of selective blindsight, but blurs the whole to such an extent that, were it a painting, it would be every bit as impressionistic as the works of modern art that the characters in the story are so liberal in denouncing. Despite this patchwork quality and selective vision, however, the work has some very striking passages as well as some pleasantly amusing ones, and it certainly offers a tongue-in-cheek challenge to the philosophy of Progress that was, at the time, novel and ingenious. Although modern critics—including Jacques van Herp, who supplied a "Postface" to the 1994 reprint issued by the Belgian publisher Grama—often compare *L'horloge des siècles* to Philip K. Dick's novel of time in reverse, *Counter-Clock World* (1967), the resemblances are slight because Dick takes a keen interest in the surreal quality of those aspects of reversed life that Robida omits or ignores—the reversed passage of food through the alimentary tract, the practicalities of un-death and re-birth, etc.—and is relatively uninterested in the kind of assault on the philosophy of progress that is

Robida's primary obsession. The literary work with which *L'horloge des siècles* actually has most in common is probably Archibald Marshall's satirical farce about a world in which the profit motive works in reverse, *Upsidonia* (1915), although its nostalgic element also links it in an interesting manner to such late 19th century retreatist Utopias as William Morris's *News from Nowhere* (1890). Its most revealing context is, however, Robida's own evolving oeuvre, especially those aspects of it that employed futuristic visions.

Albert Robida was born in "the year of revolutions," 1848, in Compiègne, a town with a long and august history stretching back to a Medieval heyday. In more recent times, Louis XV had built a fine château there, which Napoléon I had further embellished, but a much earlier French King, Louis I, nicknamed *le Débonnaire*, also had a significant connection with the town, having been deposed there in 1832. Jeanne d'Arc had been held prisoner there by the Burgundians in 1430, when the town suffered several sieges, about which Robida wrote an account. It was, therefore, a town whose natives were easily able to cultivate an appreciation of the vast changes that had taken place over the centuries in French political history.

Robida was the son of a carpenter, who might in an earlier era have been apprenticed to his father and inducted into the guild supervising and organizing that craft—an awareness reflected in *L'horloge des siècles*' comments on the virtues of such institutions. Instead, he was directed towards a legal career, but he did not complete his initial course of study. Instead, he undertook to develop and exploit his skill as an illustrator and caricaturist; he joined the staff of the *Journal Amusant* in that capacity in 1866. He went on to become one of the most prominent and successful French illustrators of the second half of the 19th century, second only to Gustave Doré. Whereas Doré became famous for his lavish illustrations of literary classics, however, Robida initially specialized in contemporary and historical themes. Unlike Doré, Robida was also a writer, and the texts he wrote in support of his work became increasingly elaborate, until he eventually embarked on a novel that would give his illustrative talents unprecedented opportunities for flamboyance and imagination.

The most popular French writer of the 1870s was Jules Verne, and Robida set out to write a five-part series of farcical adventures parodying Verne's romances of exploration, *Voyages très extraordinaires de Saturnin Farandoul dans les 5 ou 6 parties du monde et dans tous les pays connus et même inconnus de M. Jules Verne* [The Very Extraordinary Voyages of Saturnin Farandoul in the 5 or 6 Continents, and in all the countries known, and even unknown, to Jules Verne] (1879).[1] The five-story series was issued in 100 parts, each one handsomely decorated. With a blithe disregard for issues of copyright, Robida borrowed Verne's Captain Nemo and Phileas Fogg, giving them prominent roles supportive of his Tarzaneque hero, who is raised by apes on a remote Pacific island and returned to civilization as a kind of primitive superman. Jacques van Herp suggests that the hero's family of intelligent primates was also inspired by a minor Verne story, "Gil Braltar," which was reprinted in 1880 in *Le Petit Français Illustré*, along with a glowing appreciation by Robida of Verne's works. Fortunately, Verne found Saturnin Farandoul's adventures very amusing, and gladly gave his blessing to the appropriations.

Robida followed up the adventures of Saturnin Farandoul with another substantial text. Early in his career, Verne had written a novelistic account of Paris in the 20th century, which his publisher, P.-J. Hetzel, had advised him not to publish and which languished in oblivion until the end of the century in which it was set, when it was rediscovered and belatedly published. Robida was presumably aware of the existence of this suppressed novel, and set out to fill the gap that Hetzel's

---

[1] First part translated in the Black Coat Press anthology *News from the Moon* as "The Monkey King;" full translation forthcoming.

short-sightedness had created. *Le Vingtième siècle* (1882-83; revised book edition 1895; tr. as *The Twentieth Century*) was, like its predecessor, initially issued as a part-work, this time in 50 parts. Although it is cast as a farcical comedy, and shows the influence of its equally inventive and scathingly skeptical predecessor, Emile Souvestre's *Le monde tel qu'il sera* (1846; tr. as *The World as it Shall Be*), the novel's adventurous description of life in the 1950s shows far considerably more foresight than the other accounts of the future produced before that date.

The plot of *Le Vingtième siècle* is a tokenistic device facilitating a tour of the institutions, folkways and international relations of Paris in the mid-20th century—1952 in the book version. Its heroine, Hélène Colobry, has just left school and is instructed by her guardian, the billionaire banker Raphaël Ponto, to find a means of earning a living. She dutifully tries out careers in the law, politics and journalism, coming unstuck in very instance, before reconciling herself to the fact that she is so generally incompetent that she will have to face the ultimate ignominy of shopping around for a husband instead. Although the tone of the narrative voice is light satirical, the novel's feminist sympathies seem quite genuine, and its tacit rhetoric contrasts sharply with the off-hand condemnation of feminism offered by the narrative voice of *L'horloge des siècles*.

Although the politic situation in *Le Vingtième siècle*'s version of 1952 inevitably provides grounds for mockery, the general increase in liberalism featured in the novel is depicted as sympathetically as its feminist corollary, and although the dominance of aerial transport is shown to have its drawbacks, the general attitude to airships and other new technologies is broadly admiring. Viewed as a whole, the novel is very amiable as well as funny, and its satirical aspects are conspicuously good-humored. The part-work was, however, immediately succeeded by a much shorter text supporting a series of illustrations published in *La Caricature*, a periodical founded by Robida and Georges Decaux. This was a lurid account of *La guerre au vingtième siècle* (1883; with new text in book version 1887; second text tr. as "War in the 20th Century"—*sans* illustrations—in I. F. Clarke's 1995 anthology *The Tale of the Next Great War* 1871-1914).

Here, there was a much more evident contrast between Robida's convictions and his subject-matter, and the contemplation of the difference that more powerful engines of war might make to casualty figures inevitably gave him a gloomier view of the utilitarian potential of further technological advance. He had already exhibited pacifist sympathies in his earlier works, and the work he put into his illustrations of air fleets, submarine armies and gigantic tanks might well have helped to sharpen these sympathies into passionate conviction. The satirical tone of *La guerre au vingtième siècle* is much more acidic than that of its predecessor, especially in the second version of he text, which moves the principal action backwards in time, from 1975 to 1945, and locates its chief battlefields much closer to home; the war described in the second version eventually involves the entire world, having escalated from its local origins in 1937.

"Jadis chez aujourd'hui" was written not long after the original version of *La guerre au vingtième siècle*, and was rapidly followed by Robida's next substantial, but more specialized, survey of 20th century life, *La vie électrique* [Electric Life] (1890). He went on to add several other sidebars illustrating the future of transport, but none is very substantial. In "La locomotion future" [Future Locomotion], which appeared in the January 1895 issue of *Le Monde Moderne*, Robida's illustrations accompanied an essay by Octave Uzanne, a writer peripherally associated with the Decadent movement—he was later to illustrate *Les conquérants de l'air* [Conquerors of the Air] by the much more flamboyantly Decadent Georges de Lys. Robida provided his own brief texts for a pair of single-page depictions of "L'automobile en 1950" and "L'aviation en 1950," which appeared in *Annales Politiques et Littéraires* in the 1908 Christmas issue, but they must have been hackwork written to commission. The tone of all these works is upbeat; Uzanne concludes with the hope that better communications will allow much better political relations to develop between nations, and that new means of locomotion therefore constitute a great leap forward in social as well as technical progress. The sequence was, however, interrupted in more ways than one by *L'horloge des siècles*.

Robida's keen interest in exotic inventions was also reflected in an exchange of pseudonymous letters on that subject published in 1896 in *La Caricature*, in which Robida signed himself Théodule Assenbrouck of the Académie des Sciences de Flyssemugue, while Henri Mifrot (alias Henriot) signed himself Omer Garo, and Georges Colomb (alias Christophe) signed himself Polyxène Billentoque. The variety of opinions and arguments reflected in the argument probably added fuel to the increasing ambiguity of Robida's own attitude. By this time, he was also attempting to establish himself as a conventional novelist as well as a writer of texts in support of caricaturish illustrations. *Le mystère de la Rue Carême-Prenant* (1897) appeared with no illustrations at all, and succeeded a little too well in its determination to be unadventurous.

Robida's imaginative illustrations became more various after the turn of the century, when he made significant early contributions to the development of *bandes dessinées* in the Vernian periodical *Journal des Voyages*, including series devoted to *Les fleurs carnivores* [Carnivorous Flowers] and *La redécouverte d'Amerique* [The Rediscovery of Amrica]. The same expansion of interest was manifested in his longer prose works, such as the Swiftian satire *L'île des centaures* [The Isle of the Centaurs] (1912). Swift's *Gulliver's Travels* was one of the few established classics for which he produced a new set of illustrations comparable to those Doré had produced for such imaginative epics as *Paradise Lost* and *The Divine Comedy*. Robida returned to contemplation of the year 1950, however, following the outbreak of World War I, and continued his episodic series of contemplations with a novella-length serial in the children's periodical *Mon Journal*, "Un potache en 1950" [A Student in 1950], which ran from September 8 to December 22, 1917. The young hero of the story, Gustave Turbille, is the son of a wealthy industrialist who is eager to go into business on his own account as a sponsor of new technologies; inventions and discoveries flow thick and fast, but many of them quickly reveal unforeseen flaws or precipitate minor catastrophes, with the eventual result that Gustave has second thoughts about his vocation. Although it is a conscientiously light-hearted work, written with the youth of its intended audience in mind, it does seem to be underlain by a greater unease than the earlier elements of the series.

The mild unease of "Un potache en 1950" was soon complemented by a much more strident work for adults, whose rhetoric is far more vitriolic than the darker passages of *L'horloge des siècles*. If Robida had been compelled to remain diplomatic while the Great War was still being fought and censorship in force, he was fully prepared to say what he really thought once it had ended. *L'ingénieur Von Satanas* [Von Satanas—i.e., the son of Satan—the Engineer] (1919) is a hectic anti-war polemic tracking the effects of hypothetical technological inventions in the aftermath of the war, which must have been written in haste if it had not been on the shelf for some time; it appeared a mere four months after the armistice. In the story, humankind is subjected to an extravagant series of violent indignities by technological diabolism before eventually being put out of its misery by the invention of a "doomsday weapon" that obliterates civilization.

Robida adopted a more distanced satirical viewpoint in the Biblical fantasy *Voyages et aventures de la famille Noé dans l'Arche* [The Voyages and Adventures of Noah's Family in the Ark] (1922), which harks back to the last time that the Supreme Clockmaker allegedly called time on the human race, and wonders exactly how Noah fed his family while the Ark was afloat, given the necessity of preserving the greater part of his livestock cargo. *Un chalet dans les airs* [A Cabin in the Sky] (1925), on the other hand, published a year before his death, is the bleakest of all his futuristic fantasies, featuring a tour of relatively distant future world that has been comprehensively blighted and devastated. It is framed as a comedy, but its humor is almost bit as black and bitter as that in *L'ingénieur Von Satanas*.

If *Un chalet dans les airs* represents the final phase of Robida's pessimism and conservatism, as *Le Vingtième siècle* had represented the initial high point of his optimism and liberalism, then *L'horloge des siècles* can be seen as a kind of fulcrum, in which his attitude teetered and his mood see-sawed uneasily from the dourly sardonic beginning to more sprightly passages before eventually swooping back into an angry gloom from which he had difficulty extracting himself again. There is one particularly telling moment when he seems to have caved in, at least momentarily, to the corrosive pressure of an argument that he had previously been deploying in a conscientiously non-serious fashion. That break comes in Chapter XVII—which introduces two new characters who have reappeared in the backward-moving world "ahead of time" in Monsieur Le Coq de la Bénardière and his wife—and, more specifically, in the last paragraph of that chapter, where the humor abruptly gives way to a moment of understated poignancy. The husband, who had died in 1788, and is blithely enthusiastic to find out what the society of the mid-19th century is like, cannot understand why his wife, who died in 1815, is so depressed that she cannot even bring herself to reply to his questions regarding the fortunes of his children and friends following his own demise. The dark implication of that uncharacteristically quiet moment not only colors the remainder of the text but was carried forward into all Robida's subsequent reflections of the march of time, and all his future examinations of the blithe assumption that change is intrinsically progressive.

"Jadis chez aujourd'hui" will inevitably seem to the modern reader to be a primitive story, even if one discounts the fact that it was written for children and forgives its feeble conclusion on that account. At the time it was written, however, literary time travel was in its infancy and no one had yet figured out a narrative frame for such fictions that did not relegate them to the status of dreams or delusions. If Robida had made the effort of wondering exactly what kind of technology Célestin Marjolet had employed to bring Louis XIV and his Court into the year 1890, he might have anticipated H. G. Wells' invention of the time machine—a literary device of very considerable utility, although Wells only used it the once. If he had carried the story forward far enough to fish up representative specimens of much earlier eras, he would have been forced to broaden his perspectives in several new directions, and if he had gone even further, realizing Marjolet's initially proposal to bring about a "recommencement" of the entire world—markedly different, one assumes, from the perverse recommencement achieved in *L'horloge des siècles*—he might have achieved something even more adventurous. Alas, he was not ready to do any of those things, especially in a children's story; nor was anyone else, at the time. Modest as the story is, however, it did help lay the groundwork for more ambitious 20th century exercises in literary time-twisting, and Robida did eventually follow it up himself in a more robust fashion.

L'horloge des siècles was not the first fantasy of reversed time, but it was the most ambitious at the time it was published. Most stories of time moving backwards tend to reverse its flow merely in respect of a particular individual, who grows younger while the rest of the world proceeds in its normal course, as in Eden Phillpotts' *A Deal with the Devil* (1900) or F. Scott Fitzgerald's "The Curious Case of Benjamin Button" (1922). An image of that sort had been accompanied by more general speculations about time in "The Lieutenant's Daughter" (1847) by "Zeta" (J. A. Froude), but the notion of a general reversal of time briefly broached therein is not fully developed in the narrative.

Another significant predecessor of Robida's work, although he surely never read it, was Edward Page Mitchell's "The Clock That Went Backward" (1881); as in Froude's story, though, the tale's brief philosophical speculations about the possibility that cause and effect might work in the opposite direction to the order of their subjective perception is completely undeveloped in a rather weak and tentative narrative describing a simple timeslip. A more robust extrapolation of a philosophical argument had, however, been introduced into French speculative fiction by Camille Flammarion in *Lumen* (1866-69; in *Récits de l'infini* [Space Stories] 1872; separate book edition 1887), in a passage dramatizing the supposition that time would appear to run backwards to an observer approaching the Earth at a velocity greater than the speed of light.

Among the reversed events described by Flammarion is the battle of Waterloo, the author observing that the battle makes a much more edifying spectacle from that viewpoint, as the slaughtered dead and atrociously wounded are healed and fully restored to health. Given that Robida probably had read *Lumen*, this passage might have provided the inspirational seed for his own observations about the salutary effects of time-reversal, but a more immediate inspiration might have been provided by contemporary experiments in cinema by the former stage-magician Georges Méliès, who delighted in using such camera-tricks as running film-sequences backwards. Robida's reversion is, however, much more elastic than any straightforward sequence-reversal, and although the partiality of the reversal does not make much sense, it certainly lends itself more readily to speculative elaboration.

Although many more accounts of time reversal were published in between 1902 and 1967, when Dick's *Counter-Clock World* and Brian W. Aldiss's *An Age* (a.k.a. *Cryptozoic*) were published, it is arguable that none of them were quite as adventurous in their speculative range and verve as *L'horloge des siècles*, however tentative, vague and confused the latter might have been, and no matter what advantages its rivals may have enjoyed in terms of literary sophistication. For this reason, Robida's time-twisting fantasies are well worthy of translation into English, even at this long distance from their time of origin.

The following translation of "Jadis chez aujourd'hui" was made from the chapbook edition issued in 2000 by Apex. Although that edition is a facsimile, Apex editor Jean-Pierre Moumon states that it has been reproduced from an early 20th century reprint in *Le Petit Français Illustré*, which differs in certain respects from the 1890 original, presumably having been adapted to fit a slightly different page size. I have not been able to compare it with the original, so I do not know how extensive the alterations were, but I presume that they were trivial. The translation itself presented few problems, although translating humorous texts is always dogged by the problem that puns and other items of wordplay often do not translate. This difficulty was considerably more awkward in respect of *L'horloge des siècles*, from whose text many items of wordplay have unfortunately been lost or lamed in translation. The following version was made from the Grama edition of 1994, but I have compared that text to the London Library's copy of the first edition, and the two seem to be identical.

Brian Stableford

YESTERDAY NOW

I. Terrible projects of an unappreciated scientist.

My friend Célestin Marjolet was a very clever man, a great scientist, but he could not manage to get the public to take him seriously. There were several reasons for that. First of all, he did not wear spectacles, he had all his hair and he was 35 years old.

Now, I ask you, what kind of scientist can a man of 35 be, who is neither myopic nor bald? Then again, he was not even American—and to cap it all, he had published a volume of verse when he was young. In brief, he was a scientist of an impossible and inadmissible kind!

And yet, Célestin Marjolet was a veritable wellspring of science: an extremely deep artesian well, from which surprising and amazing ideas sprang forth. For lack of money, though, Célestin, forsaking experiments that cost too much, had dedicated himself to certain new researches that only required the outlay of considerable mental effort, and the expenditure of magnetic fluid and will-power. Célestin Marjolet launched himself into the supernatural, searching quite simply for a means of making the past reappear, of reawakening the sleeping centuries—in a word, of beginning the world anew.

He aspired to give new life to those primitive animals that had terrified the first inhabitants of the globe, whose fantastic forms had been reconstituted by the scientist Cuvier. He wanted to reanimate the Egyptian mummies, to bring

Roman warriors out of their tombs, along with the Gauls, Visigoths and Saracens swallowed up by our soil over the centuries.

When the Exposition was advertised, he thought that the moment had come to reveal himself with a masterstroke, and asked for the concession of a pavilion on the Champ de Mars. There was talk of reconstructing workshop scenes in exhibitions of the history of Labor, with simple mannequins dressed as characters.... what was the point of that? Personally, the astonishing Marjolet proposed to expose the people of past centuries in the prime of life—Gauls of the time of Vercingetorix, Franks in war attire, veritable knights and actual burgers of the Middle Ages, surrounded by objects and furniture of the period, a few tradesmen acting and working according to the fashions of yesteryear, specially resuscitated for the occasion—to the eyes of the modern public, including a few historical individuals familiar to everyone, whom it would be very interesting and instructive to know in their true aspect. To contemplate Bayard and Duguesclin in the flesh and bone, really to make the acquaintance of King Dagobert and many others... how astonishing for the visitors to the Exposition!

But the requested pavilion was not granted to him. Marjolet and his alleged discoveries were disdained: a complete lack of success. Marjolet would not participate in the great sensation of the Exposition! He became furious—and such was his wrath against the present time that Marjolet swore to play the fine prank of abolishing it!

One fine evening, Célestin revealed his idea of *recommencement* to us, and got violently carried away when we dared to raise objections. "You're telling me that it's impossible because you're donkeys, minds closed to progress!" he cried. "But it's perfectly possible, as you shall see. Just wait a few days."

Needless to say, a loud burst of laughter greeted this declaration.

"Give me my back my lost teeth and my vanished hair," said one of Célestin's uncles, "and I'll call it quits."

But Célestin Marjolet had recovered his scientist's calm of mind. He simply added: "Wait a few days, and you'll be convinced. I'll content myself, by way of a small trial, with going back a century or two, and then I'll start on the great *recommencement*!"

II. In which Célestin Marjolet begins to make good his promise.

One day last June, all of us who had dined with Célestin Marjolet on the day when he made his declaration received the following note:

Go to the Sun King's antechamber at the Palace of Versailles tomorrow morning, and WAITTT!!!!

That cool and reserved man had put three Ts in "wait" and four exclamation marks at the end of his note. It was an indication of great emotion. We were intrigued, and we were all at the rendezvous well before the appointed hour.

At ten o'clock precisely, preceded by the guide, we went into the Palace of Versailles and moved slowly through the ground-floor galleries, astonished not to see our friend.

We arrived in the large halls on the first floor; the guide continued his explanations. "This is the Bull's-Eye Room, where the courtiers waited for the Sun King to get up." [2]

The guide suddenly stopped in amazement. In the Bull's-Eye Room, a man in a strange uniform was barring his way with a leveled halberd.

"What are you doing here, if you please?" exclaimed the guide.

---

[2] Robida includes a footnote to say that the room was so called because of the oval window, known as a bull's-eye (*oeil-de-boeuf*), above the rear door.

"No one may pass!" said the man with the halberd, in a thunderous voice.

"That's a bit rich," complained the guide. "You want to stop me passing—me, the official tourist guide."

The halberd remained leveled. The furious guide was about to raise his voice when the half-open door behind the man with the halberd suddenly gave passage to a newcomer. The latter, dressed in the manner of the 17th century and wearing a large periwig, had a very imposing manner. He demanded silence with a gesture. "What is all this noise, gentlemen," he said, "in His Majesty's antechamber?"

"But…" the guide attempted to say.

Two other people of aristocratic appearance, wearing the costume of lords of the time of Louis XIV had emerged quietly from the royal chamber.

"Who the Devil are these people?" grumbled the bewildered guide, "And how did they get in here when I locked the doors myself yesterday evening?"

Our astonishment was not yet complete. Both panels of the door suddenly opened; the man with the halberd rapped three times on the tiled floor and cried out in a Stentorian voice: "Gentlemen, the King!"

"The *petit lever* is over," one of the bewigged gentlemen said to us, hurriedly. "The King grants audience while the table is being set for breakfast. If you have a petition for His Majesty, you may give it to Monsieur the Lord Chamberlain."[3]

---

[3] Robida inserts two footnotes in this paragraph, the first to explain that the *petit lever* was when the King actually got out of bed, and that that it was a great honor to be admitted to his presence at that time [a *grand lever* followed, when he emerged fully-dressed from his apartments to display himself to the world], the other to explain that the Lord Chamberlain served the King while he dined in his room and introduced those to be admitted. I have omitted those of Robida's subsequent footnotes that are references to previous issues of

Were we hearing things? Were we seeing things? Was it possible? These gentlemen in splendid costumes, all covered in lace and ribbons, those gold-edged sashes, those periwigs, in our own era, in 1889? Mirage, illusion, madness! And yet, when we went slowly and respectfully into the King's bedroom, we were convinced that our ears and eyes were not mistaken.

Everyone knows the room, with its sculpted paneling overloaded with gilt, divided in two by a balustrade. It was full of people of noble and majestic appearance; great lords magnificently dressed, superb and sparkling, surrounding—at a respectful distance—an individual even more superb and sparkling than them. That individual was... the Sun King himself!

It was impossible to doubt it; we were perfectly familiar with his portrait. It was Louis XIV! And among the great lords grouped around him, we vaguely recognized faces that we had seen in paintings or illustrated histories of France. Finally, behind the balustrade, the Bed of State that the guides had shown us on previous visits to the Palace of Versailles was crumpled; valets de chambre were busy remaking it.

"The King's bed unmade!" murmured the guide. "What will Monsieur the Director say? I'll lose my job!"

"Oh!" one of us whispered, pointing to one of the people putting the monarch's bedclothes in order. "There's Molière."

It was, indeed Molière; there was no doubt about it. He resembled his well-known portraits.

"Yes," a gentleman said to us, smoothing back the curls of his wig, "Sieur Poquelin de Molière is in service as valet de chambre. This Poquelin has a certain talent for farce and comedy, and His Majesty does him the honor of amusing himself occasionally at his plays...hum! It's very indulgent of him, for this Molière is hardly respectful!"

---

the magazine in which the story was serialized, and those which labor the obvious.

Meanwhile, His Majesty had sat down with two or three individuals at a sumptuously-laid table in front of the large window. The other members of the audience formed a circle and looked on respectfully as the august monarch gave proof of his royal appetite.

"His Majesty has deigned to dine with Monsieur Colbert, his minister, and the Maréchal de Turenne," said the obliging lord who had just spoken to us about Molière. "His Majesty is demonstrating his satisfaction with the Maréchal's last campaign..."

Colbert! The great Turenne! Now, in fact, we recognized the severe face of the minister and the final martial features of the Maréchal. It was no illusion; the great Turenne, victor of so many battles, was before us in the flesh.

Our aristocratic individual in the periwig made light of our astonishment and continued in a low tone. "I see that you've come to Court for the first time; your costume is unfamiliar to me, and you've doubtless come by coach from some distant province. I'm His Majesty's Chamberlain, and I can give you all the information you desire on the people and customs of Versailles..."

"A thousand thanks," I said to the Chamberlain. "I don't want to put you to too much trouble... I seem to recognize almost all the faces in the illustrious assembly now. That lord with the proud manner is..."

"It's the great Condé!" said the Chamberlain. "He's chatting with the Marquis de Louvois and Monsieur de Vauban, the grand-master of he kingdom's fortifications... To the side, that's Monsieur de Tourville, Amiral of the King's fleet, Monsieur de Vivonne, the Gneral of the galleys and Monsieur Duquesne..."

Jean Bart came to join the group. The Chamberlain had no need to name him; we recognized him by his proud bearing, and his manners—those of a seaman unused to Court etiquette.

We had arrived at the limit of amazement, and were no longer able to say a word while the chamberlain continued to list the great names of the great century.

I looked for Célestin Marjolet; he had not met us but he had to be there. Suddenly, we caught sight of him behind a group at the back of the room. Unlike the others, he had no periwig, no sword, no lace; he was dressed in a modern black suit with a white cravat and an opera hat under his arm—and had a very respectful manner too.

"Isn't that man from your province?" asked the Chamberlain, who had followed our gaze. "His costume bears some resemblance to yours. He's a savant named Marjolet, who asked for an audience in order to talk to His Majesty about some novelties and marvelous inventions, which he described—but His Majesty's apothecary, who is a great expert in all the sciences, told me that it's stuff and nonsense, dangerous to the health..."

Louis XIV had finished his breakfast; he stood up and looked around at the crowd of courtiers with the clear and tranquil gaze of a master. The courtiers bowed, all of them hoping for the favor of a particular word, but Louis seemed to be looking for someone. We hid ourselves as best we could, but Louis' gaze fell upon us nevertheless and manifested an astonishment that His Royal Majesty quickly suppressed.

Colbert made a sign and the brilliant circle of great lords immediately stood aside to let our friend Célestin Marjolet pass. His manner was serious but he was entirely at ease. Without saying a word he came forward and bowed to the King.

"Sire," said Colbert, "Monsieur Marjolet has solicited the honor of entertaining Your Majesty with certain discoveries and new inventions with which other savants following in his footsteps, his colleagues, are destined veritably to change the faced of the world..."

Louis' august eyebrow arched. "Is the world not good enough as it is?" he asked.

"To transform the habits and ameliorate the general conditions of life," said Célestin Marjolet.

"All for the greater progress of the peoples and wealth at Your Majesty's service," Colbert hastened to say. "Monsieur Marjolet has shown me some of these novelties, and I thought that it was my duty to examine the assertions of this man of science with the utmost care."

At a gesture from the King, Célestin began to speak. We could not hear him very clearly; the circle of courtiers had tightened around the royal group, and we humble folk, not daring to mingle our simple jackets with the embroidered doublets of all those illustrious lords, remained discreetly in the back row.

Besides, we were plunged into such amazement that we scarcely had the strength to pinch one another to assure ourselves that we were not dreaming. One of us even pinched so hard that a little squeal was emitted within our group, which made the Lord Chamberlain turn a severe eye upon us. Unconsciously, we edged towards the door, ready to escape if we committed any further breaches of etiquette.

Célestin was still talking, replying to Colbert's questions; we also hear the King's voice, which seemed to be giving orders—but a heavy tread in the antechamber, accompanied by the clink of weapons, caused all heads to turn. Chamberlains rushed to the door, and we went out with them.

"Go on," said Louis' imperious voice to our friend Célestin Marjolet.

III. The Great King's Court in an Omnibus.

What a sight greeted us in the antechamber! Four exceedingly modern young soldiers in red trousers, commanded by a corporal and guided by the château's warden, were involved in an altercation with other soldiers clad in 17th century uniform: the yellow jerkins and blue hose of Louis the Great's personal guards.

Soldiers of the line and guardsmen, each party as astonished as the other, were looking at one another in stupefaction, the gazes of the troopers taking in the guardsmen's swords, their embroidered bandoliers bearing cartridge-cases, powder-horns and *pulvérin*,[4] and their lace cravats and ruffed sleeves, while the guardsmen's eyes were drawn to Lebel rifles, cartridge-boxes and bayonets.

Needless to say, the dashing guardsmen could not help curling their lips expressively at the sight of army boots and coarse cloth tunics. The warden and the Swiss with the halberd, an important person, were exchanging words angrily; it was evident that things are getting heated.

"But what are you doing here in my museum?" demanded the warden. "And when are you going to leave?"

The Swiss rolled his eyes, astounded by the audacity of this man who dared to raise his voice in the King's antechamber. "Scoundrel!" he cried. "Peasant! Bumpkin! You want a taste of the Bastille, it seems! That won't take long! Guardsmen, take this man away, I beg you!"

"Put this man under arrest!" said the warden to the corporal in red trousers, pointing at the Swiss.

What would happen? The soldiers of the line were advancing, and the guardsmen, for their part, were already reaching for the warden's collar—but a number of aristocrats, drawn by the noise, appeared at that moment. Monsieur de Turenne himself was among them, and compelled everyone to fall silent with a single glance.

---

[4] Robida inserts a footnote to define *pulvérin* as an exceptionally fine gunpowder placed in the pans of muskets or flintlocks to communicate the fire to the charge set in the interior of the barrel. [According to Webster's, the English word "pulverin" means something quite different, so I have conserved the French term.]

"Monsieur le Maréchal," said the Swiss, "it's this peasant…"

At the word *Maréchal* the infantrymen immediately formed a line and presented arms. The frightened corporal went as red as his trousers. Meanwhile, Monsieur de Turenne gazed with visible astonishment at the uniforms and weapons that he did not recognize.

"What is this?" he said, turning towards a young gentleman in military uniform who was accompanying him. "Have they changed the troopers' uniform during our campaign?"

"Not so far as I'm aware, Monsieur le Maréchal," the gentleman replied.

"Where are you from, young man?" the Maréchal demanded of the corporal.

"I'm from Noyon, Maréchal," stammered the corporal, executing a military salute.

"A Picard regiment, then? This new uniform lacks elegance somewhat, but it's very military and seems suitable to me. And that musket? Let's see that musket."

"It's not a musket, Maréchal, it's a Lebel…"

Monsieur de Turenne took the rifle and attempted to cock it; his face briefly expressed a profound amazement. "What changes have taken place during our campaign!" he said. "I don't know this mechanism. It must be a trial model…"

"Adopted, Maréchal—a repeater, 15 rounds a minute…"

The Maréchal did not ask anything further; he hurried back towards the royal chamber, doubtless to ask for explanations, while the warden, reverting to his plan, raised his voice again.

"Corporal, carry out my order—arrest this…"

The Maréchal turned round and made a sign to the soldiers.

The corporal put his hand on the warden's collar. "The Maréchal's giving the orders!" cried the soldier. "You're trying to be clever, aren't you? Getting us involved in reckless stupidities, when the Maréchal could have us banged up. It's you I'm arresting. One, two, my good man!" And the poor warden went away crestfallen, flanked by four soldiers, while the guardsmen installed themselves on the benches at the back of the antechamber and the triumphant Swiss proudly took up his halberd.

The chamber door opened wide; we heard the voice of a chamberlain calling for the King's coaches.

Louis XIV came out; we looked at one another. Where were the Sun King's coaches? At the Trianon, or Cluny? Perhaps nowhere. But Célestin Marjolet hastened to speak.

"Sire," he said, "I wonder if Your Majesty would like to take advantage of an entirely new form of locomotion, which will doubtless surprise him, but whose advantages he will appreciate…"

We did not hear everything he went on to say. A slight agitation was manifest; people were arguing. I recognized the voices of Monsieur Colbert and Monsieur de Turenne. Eventually, the King deigned to acquiesce to our friend's suggestion, and it appeared to us that the Court was bound for Paris.

My God! What sort of transport was the audacious Célestin Marjolet about to offer all these noble personages? Was he expecting the Sun King to get into a tram?

We soon found out. Seeing all the courtiers preparing to depart, we ran down the staircase to arrive before them at the bottom step of the Marble Courtyard.

Ranged in front of the colonnade were dozens of tricycles and four of those immense omnibuses that carry English tourists around Paris.

Tricycles! Omnibuses! What would Louis' courtiers say? Might not those august eyebrows frown of their own accord?

Célestin, opera-hat in hand, came down in front of the King. A number of ladies had joined the procession—ladies of the Court of the Sun King before our astounded eyes, princesses and duchesses who seemed to have emerged from the frames of the paintings that ornamented the corridors of the Palace! We immediately recognized Madame de Sévigné, the great letter-writer of the great century, among them.

Meanwhile, the King and his Court were studying the tricycles attentively.

"Must I wait?" said the King, severely. "These carriages are not hitched up."

"You said that everything was ready," Colbert said to Célestin Marjolet. "Where, Monsieur, are the horses?"

"There are no horses," said Marjolet. "It's the traveler who propels the vehicle by moving the pedals... This is the carriage of the future. It makes costly stables unnecessary; its advantages include lightness, speed, economy..."

"Economy?" said Colbert, interestedly.

"Were you able to imagine, Monsieur," declared the King, "that I would get into that carriage, in order to serve as my own coachman and my own horse?"

The courtiers raised a murmur of disapproval, looking at the audacious and disrespectful scientist severely.

"No, Sire," cried Marjolet. "These vehicles are for the members of the Court who wish to try them out; I have carriages for Your Majesty."

As no one seemed inclined to try out such a novel form of locomotion, though, Célestin had to set an example by getting a tricycle moving before a few people decided to imitate him. The Sun King having paused to smile, the smile convinced other courtiers, and a few ladies to join them on the tricycles.

"My God," said Madame de Sévigné, climbing on to the pillion of a noble duke. "This invention seems delightful to me. I must remember to mention it to Madame de Grignan."[5]

Colbert was moved to take Monsieur de Turenne's arm by the sight of an extremely fat lord perched on a tricycle,

---

[5] Madame de Grigan, who was Madame de Sévigné's daughter, was the addressee of the letters on which the latter's posthumous celebrity was founded.

breathing heavily and wearing himself out trying to impress the monarch.

"Look at that, Monsieur le Maréchal," said Colbert. "Could we not mount our cavalry regiments in this manner—our light cavalry, at least? We'd save a lot on fodder!"

The great Turenne burst out laughing. "If that's all your savant has to show us, it seems to me he's wasting the King's time!"

Meanwhile, the King and his entire Court were installing themselves in the omnibuses. They were a trifle cramped. No one dared complain, but the coaches were missed. Only two men took exception right away—the painter Lebrun and the architect Mansard, who were being shown into the last omnibus with a few men of letters and lords of little importance.

"These coaches are very unstylish," moaned Lebrun. "They aren't even gilded."

"It's too much!" said the architect. "Several changes have been carried out to my Palace of Versailles without my being consulted. Am I in disgrace, then?"

The friends of Célestin Marjolet were piling into this last omnibus. Beside us we had Boileau, who was constantly reciting verses; Molière, the great comedian, who was in a rather bad temper that day; Racine; La Fontaine the fabulist, a very distraught fellow who had come to Court to reclaim a position in the superintendency of Champagne, from which he had been retired because he had forgotten to take it up ten years before; and finally, a gentlemen who told us that he was the celebrated Vatel, the Prince de Condé's cook, summoned by his master for the preparation of an official feast in honor of the King.

IV. His Majesty experiences
some astonishment on the Versailles road.

The cortège set off. The tricycles went on ahead and waited for the omnibuses in front of the statue of the King on horseback. Louis had the carriages stop here and questioned Mansard, pointing at the statues. He seemed satisfied with his equestrian effigy—a surprise that someone had obviously prepared for him, by way of delicate flattery—but what did all the other statues distributed around the courtyard signify?

"Bayard, Duguesclin, Sully, very good! You've had yourself put up there too, Colbert… hum! But those: Masséna, Jourdain, Lannes, Mortier? Who the Devil are they?"

Mansard, who had got down from our omnibus, bowed to the royal omnibus without making any response.

"Generals, evidently," Turenne answered, "but I don't know them any more than Your Majesty…"

"You take the liberty," cried the King, turning towards Louvois, "of sending the commander-in-chief of your armies generals that I do not know? Monsieur Mansard, you will prepare me a report on the changes made to my Château de Versailles, and you, Monsieur Louvois, will inform me at this evening's Council of State regarding the services of these generals that I do not know."

The cortège got under way again. As it passed through the château's main gate, trumpets were heard and a platoon of the 8th Cuirassiers, after saluting with their sabers, took up position trotting behind the last omnibus.

Louis XIV had another surprise on seeing these cuirassiers; we saw him lean towards Monsieur de Turenne, who was equally astonished. The arrival of the cuirassiers to escort the Sun King surprised us too, but what had happened was that the warden, having been placed under arrest on the order of Monsieur de Turenne, had been able to alert the château's curator. The curator had only understood one thing in the warden's confused report: that a Maréchal had come to visit the château, with some people of distinction. In response to an instruction sent to the barracks, a guard of honor had come to wait for the Maréchal at the gate.

What astonishments awaited the Sun King on the road! In the beginning, the sensibility of his dignity prevented him from manifesting his continually increasing surprise, except by slight movements of his eyebrows and his wig, but in the end, he could no longer restrain himself and summoned Célestin Marjolet—the only man able to enlighten him regarding the prodigious changes he observed on all sides—to sit beside him. Such an infraction of etiquette almost caused the master of ceremonies to faint; but this great favor raised my friend considerably in the esteem of the courtiers.

The cortège encountered numerous pedestrians, including a military band, two parties of schoolchildren on day trips, four wedding parties and a dozen groups of English tourists on omnibus excursions. Bewildered looks were exchanged on both sides. The ladies of the Court studied the costumes and asked us questions, while the omnibuses moderated their speed slightly, in order to permit the King a better view of various objects of interest.

"Has this transformation been brought about by waving a magic wand?" said Madame de Sévigné. "The world has been turned upside-down since yesterday. The Parisians will take us for people from Monomotapa![6] No more hoop petticoats! No more coiffures *à la* Fontanges! Look at those ladies over there, who are certainly women of quality, but have no pages to carry their trains!"

"What strange constructions," said the King, pointing to some distant factory-chimneys. "What are those slender towers that I've never noticed before? They're like the minarets of mosques—I don't much like that architectural style. And what are those bizarre black things?"

---

[6] Monomotapa was an African country in the region now occupied by Mozambique.

This time, Louis was pointing to some gas-holders in a production factory. When Célestin Marjolet replied, the King did not immediately grasp the meaning of the word "gas" and exclaimed: "You mean they're making light fabrics in those ugly buildings?" [7]

Célestin Marjolet did not have time to explain the misconception. The strident blast of a whistle caused every head to be raised. It was the railway; a train was advancing noisily alongside the road. The jets of steam, the formidable gasping of the machine and the long line of carriages, which made an infernal racket as they rolled along, abruptly plunged the royal cortège into complete disarray. Louis XIV had gone pale; Monsieur Colbert went green; Turenne launched himself forward, tore the horses' reins from the coachman's hands in order to bring the omnibus to a halt, and Jean Bart leapt down to the ground. As for the ladies, they all fainted—and a few gentlemen with them.

"What's that?" cried Louis, when the train had disappeared like a thunderbolt. "What is that demonic apparition? Are there people in those infernal carriages?"

"Might it not be a certain invention of which Monsieur Blaise Pascal spoke a while ago?" stammered a courtier. "A vehicle named, I believe, a wheelbarrow? I've heard it talked about in the most eulogistic terms…"

Célestin replied gravely that what they had just seen was not a wheelbarrow but a railway train. Louis XIV had him repeat the words. In order to be better understood, Célestin pointed out the rails of the road's tramways.

Colbert slapped his forehead. "How simple that is! Why didn't we think of it sooner?" He turned abruptly to a Secretary of State, who happened to be behind him, carrying his portfolio, and rapidly scribbled a few words on a piece of paper:

---

[7] Before the era of gas-lighting the French word *gaz* was only used in a sense equivalent to that of the English word "gauze."

Make a report to the King on the advantages there would be for His Majesty's service and for his subjects in establishing iron rails in all the roads of the Kingdom.

"Rails aren't enough," Célestin went on. "There's another thing—the vapor…"

"What's that? Smoke? Morning mist?"

"No, Sire, the vapor produced by boiling…" Célestin Marjolet was about to launch into an explanation, which would have been rather difficult for unprepared minds to grasp, when, the carriages having reached the heights of Sèvres, Paris suddenly appeared: an immense and formidable agglomeration of houses, traversed by the shining silky ribbon of its river, with its monuments, its bell-towers, and, at one point, an accumulation of domes, spires and pinnacles at the foot of the transparent Eiffel Tower. That sight drew an exclamation from the entire court. Louis sat up straight on his bench, his eyes making a rapid tour of the horizon before fixing on the area of which the Tower formed the center. His eyebrows furrowed.

"It's Paris and it isn't! It's scarcely two months since I last saw my capital. What is the significance of all these changes that have overtaken it is such a short space of time… and without my orders?" He turned to Colbert, who was too surprised to find a reply. "Is this, Monsieur Colbert, where all the money from my treasury goes? When I ask for a few miserable millions, I'm told that the taxes haven't been gathered, that the excise duties produce nothing; people tell me that money is lacking, and construct buildings without my order, including pure monuments, like that Tower…"

"The Eiffel Tower!" said Célestin.

"Like that Eiffel Tower whose immense scaffolding we can see. Have the plans for that construction been submitted to me? Or the plans of all these new monuments for which a host of other edifices have been demolished! Who ordered these changes? Who has permitted himself to touch my capital without orders?"

During the entire journey through the Bois de Boulogne the King did not calm down; he enumerated the well-known monuments whose disappearance he was able to observe. He did not address a word to Colbert, whom he instructed to send orders to the Governor of the Bastille, as soon as they arrived in Paris, to prepare cells for a large number of criminals.

The viaduct of the Pont-du-Jour, glimpsed as they passed by with two trains crossing in different directions, renewed the emotion experienced at Sèvres. Louis softened slightly. "There's something good—but why has no one spoken to me about it, and how have they dared to transform my Kingdom thus without submitting the projects to me in advance?"

In the other carriages, people less constrained by etiquette were releasing cries of amazement at every moment. So many new things! A few people seemed to be prey to sharp anxieties.

Monsieur Boileau considered his village of Auteuil with astonishment—a village no loner, but a town; no more market-gardens, no more vineyards, no more little cottages...

"Where's my hermitage?" he said to Molière, "and my cottage, and the garden where we played skittles so happily?"

V. How Marjolet introduced Louis XIV to the Eiffel Tower.

The director of the Exposition, forewarned by Marjolet of Louis XIV's visit, had thought that it was a joke on the part of the fantasist scientist. The functionary posted at the entrance at the Pont d'Iéna, however, was utterly stupefied by the sight of the strange visitors.

The carriages came to an abrupt halt in front of the entrance, interrupting the lamentations of the anxious courtiers. The Court got down; the tricycles were also arriving, one by one, having suffered a few accidents. Two tricycles had overturned in the roadside ditches, another had crashed into an English velocipedist, who had challenged him to a boxing match. One of the lords was missing; following an altercation at the barrier with the employees in the toll-booth, the town sergeants, threatened by the officer of the watch and the lieutenant of police, had put him under arrest.

Louis XIV passed majestically over the Seine without saying a word. He would have had too much to say. He contented himself with staring and promising himself that he would see everything before demanding a serious explanation from his ministers and accounts for the enormous expenses disbursed without his authorization.

Arriving beneath the Eiffel Tower, the Sun King stopped, and his entire Court arranged itself in a semicircle behind him. The ladies were playing with their fans; the great aristocrats had their plumed hats under their arms, each with one hand on his sword and the other stroking his lace. They waited respectfully for the monarch to speak.

"But after all," cried the King, pointing at the Tower with his cane, "it's still no more than scaffolding. What building are they going to erect for me with that immense framework?"

"It's not scaffolding, Sire," said Célestin, bowing deeply, "it's a monument, quite finished…"

"Finished!" cried Louis XIV. "As a tower or palace, this monument, with its construction open to the sky, is uninhabitable. It's not a palace, it's not a tower…"

While expressing his discontentment, Louis XIV headed towards the entrance of Pillar No. 1, and the entire Court followed. As the news of the Sun King's arrival spread, the crowd of ordinary visitors to the Exposition ran to the tower in dense masses, which the town sergeants had difficulty in containing.

There was a king at the Exposition! But what king? No one knew, exactly. He called himself Louis XIV, but Louis XIV of where? From what distant country did he come? Was it in Europe, Asia or Africa?

"Mama," a child suddenly cried, at the sight of the Sun King, "it's our Louis XIV. I recognize him; I've seen him in my *History of France* book!"

At that moment, the news-hawkers arrived, quite out of breath, with bundles of papers under their arms.

"Get the *Liberté*, the evening paper!"

"The *Intransigeant*, third edition!"

"Get the *Cocarde*! Latest news!"

"Return of Louis XIV to Versailles! Read all about it!"

"This populace is very bold," said Turenne. "We'll have to get a company or two of guardsmen to keep them at bay!"

The King passed through the Tower's turnstile and stopped in front of the elevator.

"Sire, that's the way up," said Célestin Marjolet, pointing to the elevator. He attempted to explain the mechanism and describe the apparatus in every detail; when he thought that everyone must have understood, he opened the door and stood aside respectfully.

"Go on!" said the King, instructing two people to get in: the Marquis de Balantin and the Seigneur de Cabiol, a fully-fledged duke. The two courtiers hurried forward. At a sign from the King, the elevator suddenly moved off and carried them up into the air.

The two courtiers emitted several improvised curses and begged for it to stop—but cries and protests were futile. The King calmly watched them rise up and vanish into the framework of the tower. When Célestin spoke to him about taking the same route in order to go up to the upper platforms, Louis shook his head and declared that he refused to compromise the royal dignity in all these machines.

"The Sun King laments his grandeur, which he left on the bank," murmured Boileau in Molière's ear.[8]

Everyone headed for the pillar reserved for petty staircases; when we arrived there, there was a movement in

---

[8] The quoted phrase is Boileau's most famous reference to Louis XIV.

the crowd. A dozen photographers ran forward, aiming their objective lenses at Louis XIV, who was moving forward with majestic slowness. At the sight of the battery of these unknown instruments arrayed before him, the King stopped; several lords threw themselves forward, striking the poor photographers—who had a great deal of difficulty getting their hands out of the way—with their canes.

"An outrage!" cried Colbert. "Someone take these criminals to the great Châtelet and put them on trial!"

Célestin attempted to explain to the minister that the photographers were not criminals, an that their cameras were not at all dangerous; they were loaded, to be sure, but merely with sensitive plates for making the King's portrait."

Make the King's portrait! Was not the painter Lebrun there? The latter waxed indignant regarding the pretensions of photographers, and talked of having them hanged. To pacify the minister and the painter, the town sergeants advised the delinquents to disappear forthwith.

The King, slightly unsettled by the occurrence, climbed the stairs to the first platform, where a light snack awaited. After so many surprises, the court needed to get its strength back. A few slices of pâté, accompanied by plentiful wines, restored the equilibrium of their unquiet minds.

After another snack and further refreshments on the second platform, the King and the entire Court eventually had a proper meal at the tower's summit. Everyone was rested and restored. They now set about discussing everything they had seen—but they were not done with surprises.

The Duc de Cabiol and the Marquis de Balantin got up from the table, chatting to one another, and went to another table, on which, among other things, there was a little box that appeared to contain nothing but reels of metal thread; they both seized these threads disdainfully. What tremors and what grimaces! The Duc and the Marquis hopped from one leg to the other, dancing and letting out inarticulate cries. The locks of their wigs, standing up on their heads, appeared to be giving off sparks. The box imprudently touched by the two courtiers was an electrical junction-box.

Their neighbors, who had hurried to their aid, were also dancing; the neighbors' neighbors, then Colbert, then the King himself, were subjected to electrical shocks. When they were separated from the dangerous box, they looked at one another in bewilderment, while readjusting their wigs. A few courtiers were talking about throwing Célestin Marjolet off the top of the tower.

VI. The Great King and his Ministers use the telephone to send a few belated orders.

"That's not all, Sire," said Célestin, when the emotional moment had passed, "We have many other silly little things— as Monsieur de Balandin puts it—to show you. Among other interesting devices, here are the telephone and the phonograph."

At this, everyone drew away.

"Don't be afraid, gentlemen—there's no danger!"

Célestin began to demonstrate the two instruments; he was as precise and as clear as possible, but he soon perceived that no one understood him and that everyone remained incredulous. People were smiling. The King was showing signs of impatience.

"The invention of an American scientist?" said one of the lords. "There are no scientists that I know, there are only savages…"

"If he's American," added another, "your Mr. Edison is a savage dressed in a feather skirt, with more feathers in a diadem around his head… He couldn't have studied anything in the wilderness but hunting beaver and buffalo!"

Monsieur Colbert made a gesture to put a stop to this mockery. "Don't waste His Majesty's time," he said to Célestin. "One cannot, except by sorcery—and sorcery is dangerous—imagine any correspondence in words between Paris and Marseilles or Lille…"

By way of reply, Célestin activated the telephone bell and spoke into the receiver. "Hello? Hello? Put me through to Brussels!"

The reply bell soon rang.

"Would you care to listen, Monsieur le Ministre?" he said to Colbert, inviting him to approach the apparatus.

Colbert listened briefly, and swiftly handed back the receiver. "What is that?" he asked, anxiously.

"That little whistling voice is the voice of an employee of the Belgian Telephone Administration; I'll ask him to put me in communication with a person I know in Brussels. I'll talk to that person, that person will answer me and you'll hear his replies. Listen! Hello? Hello? Put me through to Monsieur Van Klack, 66 Place Sainte-Gudule. Hello? Hello? Are you there, Monsieur Van Klack?"

"Yes."

"Good. How are things with you, Monsieur Van Klack?"

Célestin passed the receiver to Colbert. "Would you care to listen, Monsieur le Ministre?"

Colbert put his ear to the receiver. Surprise was immediately painted on his face. He heard a little voice, which said: "Good day, Monsieur Marjolet. We are in good health, except that Madame Van Klack is still suffering from rheumatism—and I would like to recover the 10,000 francs that I lent you 18 months ago, you know. When will you send me the 10,000 francs, Monsieur Marjolet?"

"You're a sorcerer, or a ventriloquist!" cried Colbert.

"Neither one nor the other."

"If your invention is real, then—whether it is yours or another's—His Majesty will reward you by paying the 10,000 francs that you owe Monsieur Van Klack. His Majesty will have the telephone examined by a few savants from his Academy…"

Célestin had to begin his explanations again.

"In that case," said Turenne, "His Majesty can correspond by this means with his provincial governors, the generals of his armies… even give orders to the governors of besieged cities. I'll send an order to an officer in one of my detachments, which is at Birkenstein on the Rhine, to advance a few leagues in order to establish a stronger position. I'll give him my instructions myself…"

"There's no point, Monsieur le Maréchal. Your detachment has left Birkenstein."

"Infantry and cavalry."

"Yes, Monsieur le Maréchal… Two hundred years ago," Célestin added in a whisper.

"Permit me," said Colbert. "Following His Majesty's instructions, the governor of Tournai ought to have sent a company of 500 horse yesterday night to mount a surprise attack on one of the Prince of Orange's positions eight leagues from there, making subsequent operations awkward. Ask the governor if the expedition succeeded. Another thing—order the governor of Hardenberg to hold out in spite of the famine… The King will send him help by sea. While awaiting help, the garrison should eat its horses—and its straw and boots, if necessary."

Célestin was about to respond when, Colbert having been summoned by Louis, other lords approached the telephone.

"A marvelous invention, Monsieur," said one of them, with exquisite politeness. "What progress! Will it permit correspondence with Bordeaux?"

"Yes, Monsieur," answered Célestin.

"Ah!" said another courtier. "This is the governor of Guyenne and Gascony, who has a pressing matter to settle with his government…"

"Yes," said the other. "A very minor matter. I sent an order yesterday, by means of a courier who will not arrive for a week, to release certain individuals retained in the dungeons. I've reconsidered, having slept on it—they're to be hanged!"

"Too late, monsieur," Célestin replied. "They're free."

"Has my secretary sent my orders by telephone? That's annoying—very annoying! I'll give him a severe reprimand this evening. I'm extremely vexed. I'll dock his pay, damn it!"

Célestin, bowing deeply to the King, asked for permission to demonstrate the second invention made by the American savage Edison. He had several of the recently-perfected phonographs there; he asked Monsieur Lulli to sing an aria into one of the machines, Monsieur Molière to improvise a tirade and Monsieur Boileau to recite a few verses...

The phonograph, to everyone's profound amazement, repeated Lulli's *aria*, Molière's tirade and Boileau's verses, in the voice and accent of each man, including interruptions and fragments of conversation unwittingly recorded by the apparatus. The court was greatly interested. The phonograph had an even greater success than the telephone. It was impossible to show incredulity; it had to be admitted that there was no question of fraud and that no ventriloquist would be capable of imitating voices thus. Célestin put several phonograms into the machine, allowing several songs to be heard, and eventually went so far as to let his audacious phonograph sing a couplet of the Marseillaise!

Célestin had not finished; to everyone's great astonishment, the phonograph suddenly emitted the voices of the Duc de Cabiol and the Marquis de Balantin, the two lords made to try out the Tower's elevator by the King. The two courtiers, with no suspicion of their imprudence, had spoken too close to the phonograph while waiting for His Majesty at the top of the Tower, and this was the conversation the instrument reproduced:

"Monsieur le Marquis?"

"Monsieur le Duc?"

"What do you think of His Majesty's demands? Making us come up in that box—it's unprecedented!"

"It's disheartening! I'd leave the Court forthwith if I weren't afraid of losing my privileges and positions..."

"Me too, Marquis! Versailles is becoming impossible! The King is great in everything, even his faults!"

"Especially in his faults! In that respect, Louis the Great is truly immense!"

"Colossal, rather! Everything about His Majesty is colossal: vanity, selfishness, severity…"

"And avarice! Just yesterday he refused me a trifle, a tax of 30,000 livres in cash, to which I happen to have the right…"

"Me too…"

Nothing more was heard; the Marquis de Balantin had hurled himself forward and covered the apparatus with his hat—while Louis XIV ordered the Duc and the Marquis to be taken to the Bastille.

VII. In which His Majesty glimpses many more new things.

In response to Louvois' proposal, the King declared that the Council meeting that had not taken place at Versailles that day would be held immediately, before the continuation of the excursion. That way, they could immediately employ these astonishing inventions, the telephone and the phonograph, for the transmission of orders to the armies and the provinces.

The courtiers, who were not admitted to the Council, crowded the balconies outside or went back down. Madame de Sévigné installed herself before a phonograph in order to talk for the benefit of her daughter, Madame de Grignan:

"My dear Grignan,

"I shall not write to you any more, and you shall not address any more missives to me; you shall remain out there among your olive-trees, and I shall not budge from Versailles, and yet we shall speak, chat and gossip! You shall hear my voice, which will question you as to your health, my dear daughter, and I shall hear your voice, which will reply to me

48

immediately and not after a fortnight! However, there will not be any witchcraft involved, and I'll wager 100, 1000 even, that you will never guess the mechanism of such a marvelous invention—and no more shall I, who am no savant…"

With his elbows on the balustrade, the thoughtful Molière sketched out an idea for a comedy about savants, in which the new inventions furnished material for several amusing scenes. Not far away from him, Vatel, the great Condé's cook, lamented everything he could see.

"It's extraordinary," he said, looking at the crowds swarming in the gardens of the Exposition and the neighboring highways. "The world, the people, the vulgarity! And the food to nourish all of them? I can no longer see anything in the market-places; they must have eaten everything. There will be no fresh fish for Monseigneur's great feast!"

After an hour, the Council meeting was concluded. Colbert and Louvois sent urgent dispatches by telephone or telegraph to the governors of the provinces; prefects and sub-prefects replied. The ministers did not understand any of the replies, declaring that the inventions were worthless and that the system of couriers on horseback was decidedly superior to all these novelties.

The King was discontented when he descended from the Tower, and he spoke to Célestin severely. The latter endured the King's bad temper philosophically, and led the Court to the Central Dome. They did not go quickly; there were many things to see on the way and the cortège stopped frequently, in the midst of a terrible crush of gawkers, who stared at the King very disrespectfully. A veritable caravan of English people with large eyeglasses set themselves obstinately to walk backwards in front of the royal party, scrutinizing it and taking notes from the explanations provided by a guide. Twice the King gave the order to summon the archers of the guard; when the guard did not arrive, the King became extremely angry.

The lords who had spread out through the Exposition during the Council meeting rejoined the cortège, bringing news. While he walked, Monsieur de Louvois read the newspapers that had been brought to him, and could not help starting with astonishment on reading political articles that were veritably incomprehensible. There was mention of a lot of unknown people, who were represented as important statesmen, of entirely new institutions, of subversive deliberations, of elections, and so on. All of these unknowns seemed to be involved in the government, but there was not a word about the King or his actual ministers. It was the same with foreign affairs. Had the governor of Hardenberg received the help he was expecting? It was entirely unreasonable. Louvois promised to send everyone involved to sleep in the Bastille that very evening.

Racine, Boileau and a few lords who were going off to visit the galleries were attracted by the booksellers' exhibits. In leafing through books they were subjected to one surprise after another. Molière could not get over it: 20, 30 editions of his works in magnificent bindings! And that was not the most surprising thing. What was truly extraordinary was that plays that were still at the planning stage in his head were there, complete and finished!

And the histories of France—by various writers, but all equally astonishing—were stupefying! Instead of stopping at the present time—which is to say, at Louis XIV—the authors continued, encroaching upon the future! And these historians, in their appreciations of the Sun King, exhibited a harshness bordering on severity!

One of the King's councilors, scandalized and indignant, seized the books and took them to the ministers. Monsieur Colbert, duly informed, ordered that the historians and their publishers should immediately be put on trial. This affair increased the King's bad humor; he moved through a number of galleries at a rapid pace.

So many subjects to astonish His Majesty! So many new and unknown things! The French had always had a hunger for change, to be sure, but that hunger seemed to have become a fury, to judge by all these objects so new in appearance, all these bizarrely-formed items of furniture and all other these strange things! All that iron, bronze, copper!

The Court went from metallurgy to photography, and then fell out of the noisy gallery of pianos into the clothing section, confronted by the window-displays of tailors and fashion-designers…

The King looked askance at Célestin, interrogating him continually about these novelties. Suddenly, the King stopped; they had arrived in the vast Hall of Machines. All of them were in motion, steam belching, wheels turning, drive-belts purring, pistons, crank-shafts, levers, gears all working, rolling, striking, grinding with a metallic clamor, the rumble of 100,000 thunderclaps—enough to make heads that were less than solid burst asunder.

Louis XIV refused to go in, and the Court recoiled, gripped by fear in confrontation with the infernal racket. "What's that? What are all these engines vomiting smoke, these machines with arms of iron and claws of steel? Is this gallery not the antechamber to Hell?"

The din prevented Louis from hearing Célestin's explanations. The Court made haste to get back to the open air. Only one person had dared to venture a little way into the gallery of machines, and that was the cook Vatel, who subsequently hurried to rejoin the cortège.

"I've worked it out, Monsieur!" he said, breathlessly, to Célestin. "What we just saw are the kitchens; all those devices breathing steam are perfected ovens, aren't they? It takes all that to feed all these people."

"Yes," said Célestin, to get rid of Vatel—but the latter took him by the arm and wanted to know how many oxen and sheep were consumed every day by this Paris overflowing with people.

"I don't have time…"

"Tell me, I beg you…"

"All right, but you'll let me go? Three thousand oxen, 20,000 sheep and 5,000 pigs are thrown living into those machines, transformed instantly into roasts, stews, joints, sausages and sliced meats…"

"What about the hides?"

"The same machines that produce a delicately browned shoulder of mutton or a braised leg of pork, simultaneously produce comfortable shoes, and pairs of boots on which one only has to mount the spurs."

"Many thanks, Monsieur! I prefer my simple ovens! I'll run to the market right away to buy some fresh fish!"

VIII. The horror of war perfected.
The final catastrophe.

Célestin ran to catch up with the Sun King.

Louis XIV no longer wanted to appear to be astonished by anything. He made no objection when Célestin asked him if he would deign to climb into a carriage on the Decauville railway. Because the King said nothing, the Court dared not display its astonishment.

Only Vatel, in the last carriage, declared that he was not at all surprised. "These Parisians have to pull their carriages with mechanical contraptions," he said, "because they've eaten all their horses, damn it!"

On disembarking on the esplanade in front of the Algerian Palace, Louis XIV was greeted by native music; the colonial troops—Algerians, Senegalese, Annamites, Sepoys, Spahis—formed a line. Louis, astonished, passed along it in review.

"Who are these people?" Turenne asked. "Where do these colored people, these black and yellow folk, come from?"

"They're French soldiers, Monsieur le Maréchal."

"Have we stolen the troops of the Turkish Sultan and the Great Mogul?"

"They're new regiments," said Condé, who had just ascertained the fact. "Royal Algerian, Royal Tonkin… Some idea of Monsieur de Louvois…hmm. I prefer the deportment of our musketeers and pikemen!"

New surprises awaited them at the pavilion of the Ministry of War. What were these engines of such unfamiliar appearance, these strange and complicated cannons, all this totally unknown equipment? Célestin Marjolet gave explanations to the King and the generals. Those iron cones were projectiles, shells bursting at the slightest shock and capable of blasting everything to pieces, men and ramparts alike! Those frightful engines were advanced cannons that sent monstrous projectiles over ranges of two, three or four leagues!

Louis, shrugging his shoulders, looked at his ministers severely, accusing them of having diminished his finances in ridiculous trials. Turenne and Condé waxed indignant. To send projectiles two leagues, to combat without seeing at such a distance: that was not war—which is to say, the struggle of brave men, body-to-body, eye-to-eye, matching courage against courage! What would passion, spirit and valor be worth? For what would our cavalry, charging with swords in hand, count against these engines?

"To invent machines permitting random massacres at a distance of leagues of terrain," Turenne declared, forcefully, "is criminal folly, and we propose that the King should have the inventors hanged, beginning with Monsieur Marjolet!"

Louis XIV shared their indignation, and when Célestin Marjolet had led the cortège into the aeronautical exhibition, the King directed a severe stare at the poor savant, demanding to know whether he had the audacity to mock him by trying to make him believe that a man could go up into the sky and travel among the clouds.

"Try to understand, Sire," Célestin attempted to say.

"Enough!" cried the King, in a thunderous voice. "Beware! You seem to me to be responsible for all these singularities that are spoiling my Kingdom. If I cannot put everything back in order very quickly, I shall have a strong desire to have you shut up in the Bastille for the rest of your life!"

"Deign to look, Sire!" Célestin replied, pointing at the tethered balloon that was soaring majestically in the sky above the Champ-de-Mars.

The King, Turenne, Colbert, Louvois and the entire Court released a cry of amazement and looked at one another.

"If that is possible, must everything be possible?" cried the King. "Balantin, if you want me to pardon your recent lack of respect, you'll go up in that."

"The air is the one remaining element that man was not yet able to conquer," Célestin said, triumphantly, "but it is done, Sire—the immensity of the atmosphere is ours! Would you like to see this marvel at closer range, Sire?"

"Yes," said the King, in a somber tone. "Let's go, gentlemen!"

On the way, Marjolet perceived that the captain of the guards and two other gentlemen had set themselves at his sides, their hands on the hilts of their swords. He turned his head and saw Louvois scribbling on a piece of paper, which appeared to be an order for his imprisonment in the Bastille...

The tethered balloon had been brought back to earth when the court arrived in the enclosure. Louis XIV studied the colossal aerostat with astonishment and lent an attentive ear to Célestin's explanations. The Marquis de Balantin persisted in believing that he was the victim of a hallucination, refusing to recognize the reality of the balloon even when he had touched it. He did more than touch it, though; the King ordered him to climb into the basket, and the balloon soon made a restrained ascent just for him.

At the first swaying movement of the rising balloon, the poor Marquis de Balantin threw himself on to the floor of the basket and refused to look at anything. He heard the exclamations of the Court diminishing by degrees, then heard nothing more. He opened one eye then, lifted himself up slightly, and looked out. Horror! He was floating in mid-air, in the domain of the birds! Four hundred meters beneath him, the people of the Court, having become mere units in the seething mass of humanity, could scarcely be distinguished.

He closed his eyes again and did not open them until he heard the exclamations of his friends again. He had come down safe and sound! Whew!

The entire Court precipitated itself into the basket to congratulate him on his voyage and ask him what impressions he had felt.

"You are the first man to have risen so high, Balantin!" said the King.

As soon as everyone was in the basket, the balloon rose a little way into the air and began to oscillate.

"I want to go back down!" cried Balantin

There was no time to say any more; a violent agitation cut his speech short.

Célestin, fearful of what he had done, recoiling from the increasing embarrassment of the return of the past, had just cut the cable retaining the aerostat—and the liberated balloon set off majestically for the clouds.

Horror! In the blink of an eye, the Sun King and his Court disappeared into the sky!

In the emotion of that frightful event, we all hurled ourselves upon the guilty Marjolet...

And I woke up, abruptly!

It was a dream... A very vivid dream that I had had, sitting in a corner while Célestin Marjolet belabored us with an interminable account of his crazy research.

THE END

THE CLOCK OF THE CENTURIES

Prologue.

I. In Anticipation of Delights to Come

The Annual Conference of the I. C.—formerly known as the House Rolling Club and the Ambulant Village Conference of International Chauffeurs [9]—had been exceedingly brilliant and sumptuous for many years, held in hotels in Paris, London, Berlin, Vienna and other capitals.

This evening, however, the physiognomy of the famous congress was truly strange: dimly lit rooms alongside dark and empty ones, a very visible disorder, dusty corners—and, amid the disarray of things, a less visible sadness hanging over the people distributed in little groups, chatting in low voices in the corners, their brows furrowed, their hands clenched about

---

[9] The nuances of the French word *chauffeur* are not readily communicated to its English equivalent. Although its most common literal reference, in 1902, was to the people who operated steam locomotives—drivers and stokers—it had a rich assortment of potential metaphorical overtones, sometimes referring ironically (as it does here) to the entrepreneurs who "drive" and "stoke" market economies. In a similar spirit, the word "house"—which Robida gives in English—seems to be intended to invoke the idea of gambling as well as, or rather than, residence.

newspapers or official telegrams. It was far from the joyful evenings of 12 or 15 years before, the rooms full of beautiful women, the parties bringing together artistic elites, the cheerful companions of every social stratum. This evening, among the twenty or thirty habitués of the Conference, lost in the immensity of splendid but seemingly-abandoned reception-rooms, all the faces wore anxious fixed smiles and all foreheads were frowning; all eyes were staring at the floor or rolling in their sockets, according to temperament, while moustaches bristled.

In the half-silence comprised by murmurous conversations in hushed voices, a slightly louder exclamation caused all heads to turn abruptly.

"If only that were all!"

It came from the middle of a group of people sitting with lowered heads and dangling arms; one man standing up had just spoken, emphasizing his remark with a brusque gesture.

"What do you mean, if only that were all?" several voices murmured. "My dear Laforcade, if you're not exaggerating your situation, you're ruined!"

"My God, yes, my dear Morandes, yes, Monsieur Clémency, yes Cazenal, you've said it: I'm ruined—but I have a few months in hand before I hit rock bottom. Besides, so many other ruined men have had to survive, and will survive in future! There have been so many bankruptcies since the social edifice began to shake and crack beneath our feet and everything began to collapse on our heads! There's nothing to be done; you know that as well as I do. No one will escape; at best, the most fortunate will only be able to delay their personal bankruptcy until the general catastrophe! I find the political industry too repugnant to try to get out of it by enrolling in the communist bands that are seizing power and will soon overthrow the old society that took centuries to build, brutally and legally, thus changing our country—for a while—into something akin to a vast prison-camp. Am I right?"

"Alas, yes!"

"Since it's absolutely inevitable that the world will collapse in that manner, I'm thinking about other things. If I appear today to be virtually indifferent to my own personal collapse and the general misfortune, both of which are certain, complete and inevitable within six months, it is, you see, because I am facing something worse, and just as certain, almost immediately!"

"But what could be more frightful?" said the man that Laforcade had addressed as his dear Morandes, a florid gentleman with a large curled moustache and eyes overshadowed by thick eyebrows.

"What could be more terrible?" murmured Monsieur Clémency, a thin bald man with soft eyes and a silky beard. "For tell us—for we all agree with you regarding the fate that awaits us in the world that is in the making."

"Dead right!" said Cazenal, supportively, lifting his pince-nez to look at Laforcade with an intrigued expression. "Tell us what you mean."

"Quite simply, my good friends, that divorce proceedings were initiated this morning."

Amazement brought Cazenal, Clémency and Morandes to their feet, their chairs abruptly pushed back.

"You're getting divorced?" said Morandes.

"From Madame Laforcade?" exclaimed Clémency.

"From whom to do you expect me to get divorced?" said Laforcade, with a bitter laugh.

"You're getting divorced!"

Laforcade's three friends surrounded him, talking in low voices, while the people in another group, on the far side of the room were unfolding newspapers and telegrams that a Conference servant had just brought in, and reading them through almost feverishly.

"Nothing to be done, nothing at all!" Laforcade replied to various questions. "It's all decided. Life impossible…better to end it! And yet, in the dark times ahead, what strength there might have been in finding, beneath the miserable and broken-down roof that might perhaps remain to us, the consoling affection of a loving and devoted heart…"

"Listen!" said one of those scanning the newspapers. "Riot at Black Well; the anticipated clash has occurred; 30 dead, 168 wounded."

"Strikers?"

"No! Those who wanted to work, along with two engineers and a clerk. The strikers opened fire. The mayor has declared martial law."

"Who is the mayor?"

"The assistant manager of the Social and Libertarian Bar, of course!"

"I think he's really a United Factories man."

"He was, but that's all smashed. I don't think you understand what's happening, you know…"

"Things are getting heated at Le Creusot!" said another. "Shots were also fired at this morning's meeting of the Great Collectivist Syndicate of Mines, Foundries and Factories of Le Creusot. The miners besieged the metalworkers in the factory; two blast-furnaces were destroyed last night… A civic guard patrol has disappeared, and there's a great deal of anxiety as to their fate…"

"Is there no news of Saint-Etienne?"

"Yes! Forty deaths attribute to hunger, despite the 15,000 kilos of bread distributed daily, an entire street burned and a quarter looted…"

"And the Chamber?"

"Nothing. Fists flying in the gallery, the speaker knocked down, arm broken, that's all….ah! Yes, revolver shots in the corridors, a journalist and a deputy…"

"No result?"

"No, an usher stopped one of the bullets, that's all… Debates are continuing."

"Personally, I had business interests in that region of mines and blast furnaces, in the days when business deals were still happening… I know the situation out there. The

United Factories was a company fief, with dukes and princes of finance at its head, as in the North…"

"So what?"

"So what? The ultimate result of excessive industrialism, it must be recognized, is the pauperization of the workers, who become mere serfs of large-scale industry, riveted in chains, mere implements of human flesh crying out in constant hunger and desperation, sometimes rebelling, but only hurting the lower orders by lashing out blindly in the upward direction of the true masters, international and unreachable…"

"The United Factories belong to the Rixheim Company…"

"Belong, you say? Rixheim has sold his shares, a few at a time, accelerating the anticipated crisis and leaving the manager of the Social Studies Bar to serve as his lightning-conductor… Do you understand now?"

Laforcade went to get a paper. He sat down, setting himself as if to bury himself in his reading, then got up abruptly, threw the paper aside and marched back and forth, eventually doing the same thing all over again in another corner, with another newspaper.

"Look at that," said Morandes to Cazenal, in a low voice. "Do you know how hard he's been hit, beneath his habitual mask of indifference and irony."

"No I don't," said Cazenal, "even though we've been his friends for 25 years. I've followed his career from the beginning, since his earliest ventures. It was already brilliant long before he had his big idea, the lakeside factories in the Alps and the Vosges producing energy transmissible over any distance. We were close friends in those days, Madame Laforcade was charming, simple and sweet…"

"Of course! The success, the excessive wealth in the first ten years drew them into a life of ostentation and showing off in high society—fake, exhausting, deadly. Always on the go, at work or in society, with no rest or respite, Laforcade became the irritable and short-tempered man, horribly weary and demoralized, that we know. Madame Laforcade, addicted to society, is desperately holding on to the vestiges of her luxury now that the bad times have come. It all adds up to profound and destructive discord in the home, moral ruination…"

"And complete material ruination, as he just said! How many others have already gone to the wall since the crisis reached its present pitch?"

"Old Europe is famished and ruined. Threatened from every side, and handicapped by all the socialist ring-leaders in its desperate Industrial competition against Asia and America, it's breaking its own arms! We know what it's done to Laforcade—but I think it might be harder still…"

"You're talking about ruination, I suppose," said a new arrival. "Who isn't ruined, nowadays? Not me, as yet!"

"It's a dark time, my friend…"

"All wealth is false and temporary, damn it, while we wait for the final collapse. The universal apathy manifest since the commencement of this crisis of disorganization, and the incredible absence in our era of all spirit of resistance, have rendered it inevitable. Confronted with all these attempts to apply collectivist theories, everyone is retreating into a corner, huddling there and waiting for the violence to break out."

"It's too late for resistance now. The storm's broken, watch out for the ground shaking!"

Another newcomer interrupted. "Are you talking about the disturbing series of earthquakes that have been afflicting the ruins of Japan, the Indies and South America for three months? The non-volcanic countries seem to be entering into the dance too; dispatches from Russia are announcing some kind of collapse in the Urals, hundreds of league in extent."

"Bah, that's a long way off—mere trifles! We were talking about tremors of a different sort."

"My dear chap, it's a case of veritable cosmic perturbation. I have a friend at the Observatory, and it appears that they're extremely anxious. Do you recall those scientists in France, Australia, America and elsewhere who made announcements to the effect that there have been disturbances in the working of the universe for some time, vague breaches of natural law? Well, it's getting worse. You're wrong to laugh, you know. My friend tells me every day about the possibility of catastrophes that he refuses to explain… But today's Russian dispatches seem to justify his fears…"

"Gossip! Let's talk about more serious threats. Have you seen the program of the Central Committee of Vigilance?"

"No, the Central Committee should be meeting in secret session to delay it…"

"It's over—it's in this evening's news. The session was cut short, the program containing the minimum of reforms demanded by the Central Committee was passed by acclamation and will be taken to the Ministry in the morning. The Minister will have to accept it or resign…"

"He'll accept!"

"Of course! We still don't know certain items in the program; the ring-leaders are talking things gradually and keeping surprises up their sleeve. While awaiting further developments they'll press on with the realization of the famous Universal Conscription so beloved of the leaders and imposed in the name of the great principle of Equality: obligatory, integral and equal education for everyone up to the age of 15; professional conscription—we need so many masons, so many carpenters, so many roofers, so many mechanics, each year's contingent to be provided by means of a Selection Committee… Something like the old Military Examination Board. Don't laugh or shrug your shoulders; there are, it seems, a host of carefully-planned accessory measures—for example: the formation of mobile brigades for all state bodies, designed to equip the supplementary workers temporarily assigned to whatever point; the obligation for industrial conscripts to remained at their assigned posts unless authorized to effect an exchange; access in principle of everyone to all the ranks to be established in each profession, but creation of various posts and cadres dependant on the State, etc., etc…

"Wait before you protest; everything is anticipated—it seems that there's a little article at the end, which decrees the closure of the borders to prevent emigration, or rather desertion, and a whole host of measures to suppress resistance in advance. And that's only part of the program; we still don't know the details of the grand project of the Law of Capitalist Liquidation and Collectivist Organization...

"You understand that, confronted with these prospects, one can't get very excited about the cosmic perturbations that generate so much emotion among the brave scientists at the Observatory. I'd even say, my dear chap, that your friend the astronomer is more likely to make our mouths water."

"Personally," said one of the waiters, who was sitting on the billiard-table, to a colleague, "I've had enough of all these exploiters. It's time for the reign of true equality to begin—I've been promised a job as an inspector in the Ministry of Works!"

II. Particular Disasters

Madame Laforcade, negligently sprawled in an armchair, directed her lorgnette at the sheet of stamped paper that was being held out to her by her lawyer, Maître Fardel, a socialist deputy famous since the general strike at Anzin, which he had led so artistically until the strength of the belligerents finally gave out, and from which he had emerged as one of the acknowledged leaders of the party.

Madame Robert Laforcade was a pretty woman, tall and very shapely, extremely elegant, with a flighty attitude. She was very lively, laughing and talking loudly and rapidly, but excessively restless. She seemed to be very young, but also quite worn out. Perhaps a desire for intoxication, or something similar, was distinguishable in the hectic enthusiasm that she habitually manifested. She was 35 years old, but did not look it, save for certain momentary nervous contractions of her lips and certain creases at the corners of her eyes.

"Very well! Very well!" said Madame Laforcade. "I've no need to read the document all the way through. I'll sign…"

"Sign, my dear Madame—then, after a few formalities that I'll try to cut short, and a few boring details that I won't bother you with, your divorce will be concluded…"

"Perfect. See that I don't have to do anything more. How can we poor society wives, whose existence is a perpetual hustle and bustle, possibly find the time for divorce?" Madame Laforcade's laughter rang a little less true than usual. In spite of the laughter and the irony of her exclamation, her expression was not at all cheerful.

"In finding myself the political adversary of the husband of such a charming Parisian lady, I sometimes experience a degree of remorse," said Maître Fardel. "I'm truly grateful to you for having got me out of that difficulty; henceforth, I shall be more at ease…"

"To finish our… strangling him. Your committees, your syndicates, your delegations won't leave him with much, it seems… I don't know much about it, although I've vaguely heard mention of… but that's no longer my concern, do battle at your ease! I no longer want to know anything about my ex-husband's troubles. Besides, life is too short and too full of obligations. I'm going out in my carriage; I have five or six five o'clocks before coming home, then dinner at the Ministry of Public Works. Shall I see you there?"

"Not at dinner. A committee meeting to chair—we have five or six strikes under way. Fortunately, I have secretaries, otherwise, all my time would be taken up—but I'll have the honor of greeting you at the reception…"

"Goodbye—don't forget our little divorce! Let a strike or two be arranged without you, my dear friend, but disarrange our marriage, and quickly!"

Madame Laforcade burst out laughing as she left.

III. An Old Beard and Old Arms

In every family there are branches particularly favored by profitable circumstances, and less fortunate branches that waste away: rich branches and poor branches, to sum up with two of the most important words in any language, ancient or modern. Among the Laforcades, whose roots were in the Angoumois region, there was the rich and happy Robert Laforcade, with whose scarcely enviable present situation we are familiar, and there was poor old Etienne Laforcade, also from the vicinity of Angoulême: an honest, upstanding and courageous man, formerly a journeyman carpenter, but now—broken by old age, worn out by a life of hard work and privation—an insignificant worker in one of the rich Robert Laforcade's factories, earning a wage of four francs a day.

Robert Laforcade had no suspicion that there was one of his cousins humbly exercising what little remained of the vigor of his old arms in his employ, any more than poor Etienne suspected that he was related to an employer he had never seen.

Having come to Paris as a young workman, Etienne had rubbed shoulders with the veterans of '48. In the prime of life he had felt his naïve and honest heart beat faster in response to a host of fine ideas that were floating in the air at the time, candidly accepted as absolute truths: such pretty and clear ideas, which had never been put into action, their beautiful dresses never sullied and tarnished by application to the difficult and sometimes muddy ruts of reality. Etienne had dabbled in politics, as people often do who have only experienced misfortune and do not know how to profit from good opportunities encountered on the staff of a committee or as a result of some petty election. The great political industry requires battalions of these obscure workers, forever destined to remain humble instrumentalists of the ballot paper, or sometimes of the rifle. They are among those who create great fortunes—but the butter, of course, never end up on their bread.

Etienne had lived; he had children. Paris, to which the robust families of the old French countryside come to die out in two or three generations—or sometimes only one—had only left him, for his old age, one sickly daughter and a son who had gone to the bad, an idler and drinking-den orator. Steeped in their youth in pure air and broad daylight, the father and mother had survived many tribulations and, what was worse, much disillusionment; both were approaching their seventieth year. In the old man's dreams, the green meadows and yellowing harvests of their youth passed vaguely before his eyes, without the hope—which had vanished long before—of ever being able to nourish them again with any but flat horizons, foggy skies and the rampart of factory chimneys that enclosed the somber and terrible urban ant-hive.

Their daughter, without any memories to console her, knew even worse poverty. Married to an electrician, Arnoult, nicknamed Tue-le-Ver,[10] she vegetated sadly and fed three children with the produce of dogged labor as a seamstress and the few *sous* that her husband occasionally consented to give her from his pay.

The little document below will suffice to indicate the kind of familial joy that the father of these grandchildren was able to deliver for the relish of the unfortunate Etienne:

"Whereas citizen Etienne Laforcade has called Citizen Arnoult, his son-in-law—an honest worker who had been refreshing himself on absinthe for four hours in the establishment of Citizen Prunet, spirit-merchant of the Amer Collectiviste—a filthy drunkard; and has also spoken sharply and impolitely to the citizens who happened to be in the establishment, and caused a veritable scandal;

---

[10] Literally, Kill-the-Worm; the expression is used metaphorically to refer to individuals who drink hard liquor in the morning, so the nearest English equivalent would probably be Hair-of-the-Dog.

"Whereas he has broadcast, as he continually does, reactionary statements and opinions prejudicial to the dignity and the liberty of citizens worthy of that name;

"Whereas, to the observation made by Citizen Prunet, that everyone has rights that cannot be restricted, even by a father-in-law, he responded with insults—among others, that duties take precedence over rights;

"Whereas, interrogated by us, he was unable to do anything but stammer ridiculous and manifestly reactionary explanations;

"Whereas he is constantly seeking, on an everyday basis, by his hypocritical and retrograde statements, to injure the harmony of the working class and disturb it by anti-libertarian excitations every time he finds an opportunity, in the workplace as elsewhere;

"The Jewelry-Makers section of the Syndicate of Electricians and Mechanics enjoins the managing director of the Laforcade & Co. factory to put Citizen Etienne Laforcade on suspension for a fortnight, as a 'first warning,' under pain of the factory being blacklisted in case of refusal.

"The above decision has been unanimously approved in the Prune Socialiste, the Verte Espérance, retailer of liquor and congress of socialist studies, the Grand Soir, the Jeunesse Collectiviste, the Avenir, the Grand Bar de la Guerre des Classes and all the meetings in which true Progress is slowly sought, discussed and elaborated." [11]

---

[11] The names of the various fictitious establishments listed here are intended to emphasize Robida's sarcastic contention that trades unions and other socialist institutions are firmly rooted in drinking dens—where such organizations tended to hold their meetings in the late 19th century, for want of other venues. Prunet's *Amer Collectiviste* [Bitters Collective, or Collectivist Bitterness] encapsulates the gist of the argument. The others are roughly translatable, respectively, as The Socialist Plum, The Green Hope, The Great Eve, The Youth Collective, The Future and The Great Bar of Class Warfare.

IV. The Former Academician Palluel

In his mansard at the very top of a partly-unoccupied terraced house, Eudoxe Palluel, political journalist, novelist, poet and philosopher, a member of the Academy for 18 years, was bent over his ancient desk, writing. He was rapidly scribbling lines in coarse handwriting on stamped paper, while following a text on a notepad of similarly-stamped paper.

"That's my documents finished, 24 *sous* earned, dinner and cigarettes!" he said, stopping after releasing an oof! of satisfaction. "I can now work for myself...alas! To pile up another stack of manuscript pages for which I'll have trouble finding a publisher among the few brave souls who still persist in printing anything but dispatches. A little morning or afternoon job in one of the offices of the Laforcade company would at least have assured me peace of mind while leaving me time for myself, but Monsieur Laforcade did not seem to understand when I talked to him about it—or, rather, I did not dare to explain myself clearly. My coat is a trifle too threadbare to risk going into Madame Laforcade's drawing-room, as I once did...then again, it appears that all is not well in the household, if what they say can be trusted....bah! Let's get on with it, for as long as the solicitor continues to give me documents to copy, and as long as he and all the other solicitors aren't carried off to Hell along with their clients!"

At 68, Eudoxe Palluel was in dire straits. The Academy had been abolished three years before; all art and all literature, ornament or bread of the mind, honor and finery of societies, had disappeared as occupations, gradually swept aside by a kind of dominant bestiality that had submerged all the delicacies within the coarse and brutal struggle that life had become. In order to subsist while awaiting an improvement for which, in his wild optimism, he still forced himself to hope, Eudoxe Palluel found himself obliged to perform the humblest tasks of the only instrument of labor he had ever known, the pen. The pen, the blade of thought, sometimes the instrument of glory—but also, alas, the first and most terrible agent of social disintegration.

He wrote:

"In these first years of the 20th century, under the frightful cloud of the imminent tempests, it is a son of Old Europe who darts a melancholy glance over the maternal earth, glorious and exhausted, over the meager continent whose sons have held the scepter of the conquered world for such a long time, and governed hosts of peoples in the name of the ideals for which Europe thought, dreamed and stood.

"Like individuals, races, fatherlands and continents also pass through the fundamental phases of life—youth, middle age and senility—that invariable succeed one another in the same order. Gamboling in the foam of oceans, the more-than-adolescent America, young Oceania, daughters of Europe as she was a daughter of venerable Asia, are leaping forward to grab in their turn the scepter that Europe is allowing to escape from her weakening hands. Must the empire and direction of the world, in the era that is about to begin, really pass into the audacious hands that are claiming them? Is the ancient blood of Europe, tainted by many poisons—and poisoned above all else by the alcoholism of ideas—entirely exhausted? Has the time really come for some new and ardent race to take its turn, overturning all the traditions of the Old World, trampling underfoot the memories of thirty centuries, smashing their accumulated works forever, and steering the universe in a new, unknown direction?

"What will the queens of tomorrow, America and Australia, do once they are enthroned? Will the world bubbling in the crucible of the future be able to fill these new continents with splendors comparable to those that the lands of Europe have produced in the vast Past, during the peaceful or violent struggles of greedy civilizations, while its nations influenced and were influenced by one another.

70

"Today, everything seems to be finished. The curtain is falling on our final act. If we turn a dazzled eye upon the past of Old Europe, at hazard, peering through the centuries and the nations to the most distant yesterdays, what magnificent frames for active and thinking beings we can admire from age to age, modifying and transforming themselves while the torrent of ideas and events flows on! The slow accumulation of progress in spite of abrupt setbacks and formidable catastrophes, while the arts are born and develop, wounded by the devastations of barbarous invasions, germinating again in the dust of ruins and flowering in spectacular blooms, and while the sciences emerge gradually from the meditations of thinkers—all leading to a terminal point that is difficult to identify, an invisible and fatal limit that must be surpassed, after which art becomes corruption, science unhealthy and destructive madness, and progress the perfidious and inflexible executioner of life.

"That fatal boundary has, alas, been crossed! The role played by our Old Europe, the enlarged fatherland to which we are bound by every fiber of our being, is concluded! Proudly ordained splendors of great epochs, you shall never be seen again; exquisite flowers of extinct civilizations, your perfumes shall no longer be respired..."

The pen of Academician Palluel came to rest. His forehead furrowed sadly. He consulted a little notebook in which he had noted down his plan and set out a long list of chapter titles:

The Roman City

Celtic and German Forests

Italian Republics and Lordships: Venice; Florence; Genoa; Sienna

Flemish Cities and German Free Towns

The Feudal Rhine

The Swiss Cantons

The Château and the City

Etc. etc.

"Eighteen months of work, at least; two volumes, each of 500 pages, needless to say! Will my solicitor furnish me with documents to copy until then? There's so much competition in these sad times…my old fingers are too awkward to operate a typewriter, alas, or I would have been able to type addresses at two francs a thousand… An appreciable supplement… Enough!"

V. A Few Newspaper Cuttings and Other Documents Found in the Pockets of a Half-Burned Coat, Which Fragments Might Serve As a Rapid Explanation

RECTO

….tories no longer dare deny the possibility
catastrophe. All indications to the contrary
news arriving by the minute confir-
pprehension that the hour has come of
courage and to wait for the fright-
lamities, in seeking the means
ith the energy of which we are
the frightful destiny that menaces us
seeking to calm the terrors

VERSO

The forces of nature unleashed,
these cyclones ripping up the ground in all directions
ravaging and destroying immense
beneath the ruins, entire populations
in any epoch of prehisto-
in human memory, it
no memory of parallel cataclysms
solutely nothing similar to

RECTO

Picking up a few rare dispatches. Telegraphic and telephonic lines all destroyed or out of commission almost everywhere; useless to attempt wireless telegraphy in the midst of this electrical deluge.

All social life has virtually come to a stop; there are only people madly fleeing the devastated countries or populations gone to earth in precarious shelters.

VERSO

Six weeks ago we thought, at the time of the first disturbances and the first cataclysms, that it was a simple matter of local catastrophes, of which the world had seen so many in all sorts of places, and we were already thinking about the usual means of assisting the victims. We opened subscriptions and advocated lotteries. Alas, there is no question of all that, now that the catastrophes are multiplying and becoming general.

VI. Other Morsels

The tidal wave that ravaged Western Europe the day before yesterday, to an extent as yet undetermined, was definitely accompanied by powerful earthquakes, since collapses were also numerous in areas of high ground that the immense wave did not reach. That frightful night lasted thirty-eight hours before its darkness dissipated. The survivors of the disaster are asking questions, interrogating one another. What has become of Paris, France and the world?

Telephonic communication is gradually being restored. Some news is beginning to reach us, of one disaster after another. Northern Europe has had its share too, and it seems that a second wave originating in the Baltic must have joined up with the Western wave. That must be the cold countercurrent observed, it is said, after the first and most furious flood.

A large ship, extensively smashed up, lies embedded in sand near Rennes; not far away, an entire forest of twisted and tangled trees, still dressed in their foliage, has buried two or three villages. Where has it come from? No one knows. Timbers with the remains of signs in English and Swedish, it is believed, are obstructing the valley of the Seine as far upstream as Rouen, of which there is no news. All the ports have been destroyed...

We did not expect, on hearing three days ago of the frightful earthquakes in Greece, Sicily and Italy, to see Western Europe ravaged so rapidly in its turn. The Observatory has been completely destroyed; there is no longer any possibility of reliable observation, and no definite information can come from that source. The few surviving scientists who have been able to come together amid so many ruins are in dire accord in dreading that new disasters will descend upon us very soon.

Nature has granted us a truce, nothing more; the electrical charge in the atmosphere remains the same, the storms burst and intersect as if to complete the world's collapse. We are waiting. This newspaper will appear until the end, every day if possible, so long as a single writer remains standing and a single press in working order.

SHEET OF PAPER: VERSO

May 16 or 17. 8 Boulevard du Sud, Neuilly.

The Word has been pronounced: the Word at which we once laughed, as if at a fairy tale: the End of the World! Is this not the end of the world, the end of our universe, or our Earth, the poor petty ball on which humankind, for thousands of years, has suffered, loved, worked, hoped? The end of everything?

The terrifying cataclysms of which we have been witnesses—or victims—can only make us think so. All the elements are unleashed; we live, if this is still life, amid the

74

fracas and the supernatural flamboyance of millions of thunderbolts, rolling and hurtling down upon terrified populations.

Between the explosions, the sky is black. Is this really night? Will day come again? What time is it? I don't know.

The stars seem to be entering into the universal oscillation; the Moon appears to be falling on the earth; they say that it's drawing closer, that it's passing obliquely through the terrestrial atmosphere.

And I make these notes, while waiting for the house to collapse on my head at any moment. Why make notes? Why, if we are all doomed to perish? To tell the truth, I think it's simply to occupy my fingers, calm my nerves and, in a word, to divert my fear a little.

SHEET OF PAPER: RECTO
ACTION OF DIVORCE
Madame Claire-Berthe Palluel, plaintiff, against Monsieur Robert Laforcade, engineer of Arts and Manufactures, proprietor, her husband.

In virtue of… etc., etc…

Given on the one side the most complete incompatibility and lack of understanding, etc.

And on the other side, etc., etc.

ANOTHER SHEET OF PAPER:
Monstrous collapses have occurred. I don't go out. It would be impossible to go out without risking being squashed flat before taking 100 steps. A sort of turbulent cyclone. Earthquake? Probably. Everything's shaking. There are two feet of water in the boulevard, with violent whirlpools. Where has the water come from? It hasn't rained for at least twelve hours. The entire block of houses on the other side of the street is cracked. If I lean out of the window I can see heaps of debris like enormous barricades to the right and the left. With the interlacing lightning flashes and the explosions of thunder, one could believe that the barricades were under attack and

75

being defended. Alas, we'll see no more of those petty trifles, those silly quarrels between human insects....

Our house is trembling, the ceilings giving way. Where to seek refuge? Is there a refuge to find?

I can see the flames of a great conflagration in the west.

The water-level's increasing downstairs. Squalls of rain now—or, rather, deluges of rain beating down as if a lake were emptying above our heads.

I'm alone since the divorce proceedings were begun. The word "divorce" almost makes me laugh, given the terror we're experiencing—those of us who are still breathing.

ANOTHER SHEET:

An hour ago, I thought that it was all over. With my hands above my head to protect it, I hesitated between two courses of action: to remain in the shaking house or to go out, to die just as certainly, but on the move, running, fleeing...and here is a sudden calm; the storm has ceased its roaring....

Resumption. Lightning has struck the house. Everything in the apartment is upside-down. I've just regained consciousness.

The noise and, it seems to me, the tremors are increasing.

This time, I think this is it!

End of Prologue

CHAPTER I
In Which The World Is Astonished
To Find That It Still Exists

A great calm. A nature weary of turning somersaults, which seems to be catching its breath. After the cyclones and the torments, the breeze that is blowing now is scarcely strong enough to disturb a few leaves at the very tops of the trees.

After the deluges of water, which changed the smallest streams into furious torrents, after the eruptions of lava and mud, and after the terrifying tidal wave, nothing but occasional showers of warm drizzle, sleepy rivers, gently-trickling streams, and clear and limpid pools. After the frightful uproar and the formidable collision of all the forces of incensed nature, the most complete silence everywhere: a silence that the birds, still mute, seem to be afraid to disturb.

Human beings, after the five months of the Great Upheaval, observe in surprise that the universe has not been utterly annihilated by decree of the Supreme Will—a fate to which, with their strength exhausted and their nerves stretched to breaking point, they had fully resigned themselves.

During those five months, when the globe shuddered beneath electrical discharges, people eked out a living in their various hiding-places, in the precarious refuges into which they had fled, trembling, shivering and waiting—as their prehistoric ancestors must doubtless have done during the cataclysms of the world's earliest ages.

Having no news of anywhere else, no society existed any longer among the ruins accumulated by the catastrophes, save for small disconnected groups of humans, vegetating while prey to every possible anguish. The humankind of cities, ultra-civilized humankind, thus lived a prehistoric life in caves, with the sole ambition of escaping the wrath of the unchained elements and of finding meager daily nourishment amid all the dangers…

The calm arrived suddenly and unexpectedly; in the space of a few hours the phenomena became less terrifying; the roar of the immense torment faded to groans that grew duller and duller. Finally, daylight reappeared…

The life-cycle of humankind was, therefore, not complete, as everyone had believed. The stupefied universe observed that it still existed. The Sun was still shining, the sky became blue again; the air that people breathed was no longer charged with sulfur and electricity; people could emerge from their holes, cellars, caves, trenches or partly-collapsed houses without the fear of receiving a mountain upon their heads, a tree across their bodies or a Niagara about their legs.

Robert Laforcade, intoxicated with cheerfulness and befuddled by astonishment, recovered consciousness in a covert in the hills of Burgundy, into which he had been thrown without knowing how, where he had lived in holes, quarries, cellars and caves with other fugitives brought from different directions by the catastrophes. Robert perceived that he had a long beard, clothes reduced to tatters held together by threads, a body covered in cuts and bruises, an atrocious hunger and an immense desire to know, now that it was over, what had happened: to take account of events; to learn as quickly as possible what might remain of the old world—and, if he could, to find his wife, about whom he now thought without anger.

Robert Laforcade stood up, raised his arms to the sky and immediately tried to launch himself forwards. He leapt down rapidly to the foot of the crag he had climbed and took a few paces, but his head swam, a pallor invaded his hollow features, and he fell heavily to the ground. Other people ran towards him: emaciated and ragged individuals dressed in the ill-fitting debris of clothes, who had emerged, as he had, from the shelters in which they had long been trembling. These people, companions in misery and terror, seemed almost mad with joy before the extraordinary and sudden appeasement. They rushed to help him, lifting him up and carrying him into a sort of cave hollowed out in the flank of the hill, in which they had been cringing for a fortnight, like their troglodytic ancestors, under perpetual threat of being struck by lightning, crushed, drowned or starving to death.

After long weeks of overexcitement and terror, a crisis of exhaustion had struck Laforcade down just at the moment when the danger seemed abruptly to have vanished.

CHAPTER II
In Which The Survivors Observe Several New Facts And Some Rather Significant Changes

Robert Laforcade was ill for three months, weak and feverish, suffering—like many others—from nervous exhaustion. He slowly recovered his strength in a large house, which had been discovered open and abandoned near to the refuge. He was cared for by some of his companions—men and women unknown to him before the Great Upheaval, for whom he had once struck down a wild boar with hatchet-blows, at a time when they were suffering greatly from hunger, in the same manner as the ancestors of the world's earliest days, and for whom he had risked his life to go in search of a few meager vegetables in the ravaged fields.

The calm was permanent. Since the day when the immense fracas had been abruptly interrupted, nothing had troubled the gentleness of the appeased elements. There had only been benign winds and benevolent showers of rain, after which rainbows appeared in the field of clouds: the ancient sign of pacification and protection, a symbol of hope greeted by all hearts with the same gratitude as before.

One by one, the refugees had left. The only one who remained with Laforcade in the house whose owners had disappeared was a stout fellow named Houquetot, formerly a petty clerk in the Auxerre registry office, who had run aground there like all the rest, and who had broken a leg in one of the last quakes. Robert Laforcade had been delirious for a long time and then had remained somnolent, oblivious to everything, his head empty and almost devoid of thought. Houquetot had taken a long time to recover the use of his leg, limping from room to room, doing the housekeeping and cooking with the help of a woman from the neighborhood, still bewildered by the prodigious events. He tried to make the convalescent Laforcade rest while he got better, becoming impatient and anxious in the meantime.

"Go? Go?" cried Houquetot. "My dear Monsieur, you were wandering in the head three days ago; you have to be patient, damn it! You and I—but especially you, who were more than three-quarters dead last week—have come too far for a few more days in this house, which is pleasant enough, to be too much of a burden."

"What's the date?" said Laforcade, walking over to the window even though he was still dizzy.

"The 25 or 26… Or perhaps the 30, for…"

"Of what month?"

"December—I'm sure of that."

"Go on!" said Laforcade, dazedly. "I can see greenery, fruits even, and flowers…and yet…"

"As to that, my dear Monsieur, I'd risk breaking my leg again by falling down if I hadn't already got somewhat used to these strange fantasies of the season. It may seem to you to be a literally supernatural excess, but that's the way it is. No, you're not dreaming—and I spend my time mopping my brow, in December!"

"Let's see—it was in early May that the first disturbances…"

"That the Great Upheaval began, just as I was about to draw my salary and be replaced at my desk in the registry office, because…"

"And I remember marking off the days in my pocket-book when I could, while it was still possible to distinguish day from night…"

"Me too!"

"But I had to skip several days."

"So had I!"

"That lasted several months. When it was all finished, we must have been in October."

"As you say—between the 15 and the 22, by my count. Good. Your little accident happened, you fell ill, you spent… hang on… you spent 64 days in bed, so we are now, according to the calculation of Jean Houquetot, ex-clerk at the registry, I have the honor of telling you, between December 25 and 30. Noël, Noël! Merry Christmas! You aren't finished with astonishments...

"While you were lying there at full stretch, dreaming, and I was sprawled in an armchair by the window with my poor injured foot, I looked out and listened to the tales that the others, who had the use of their legs, brought me from outside. For a week, after the end of the Upheaval, we had winter, snow and ice, fallen leaves, streams covered with ice—then, no less abruptly, warm breezes returned. We thought that it was autumn, from which we had emerged prematurely, coming back on the scene, but not at all—it was spring!"

"What?"

"Yes, at least a fortnight of a delightful spring after the terrible tumult—of which, despite everything, my head was still full. The frozen fruits on the trees have fallen, have been replaced by flowers which very quickly became buds, then fruits, as you can see, while the summer and autumn succeeded one another with a haste that neither I nor anyone else can understand... along with many other little things, besides."

"What other things?"

"Almost everything—for instance, the Sun no longer rises on the same side!"

"What?"

"Yes. And the Moon is playing funny games with us. I won't try to explain it, because my knowledge of astronomy is limited to being able to tell the Sun and Moon apart without too much risk of error, except on foggy days... and at night, the stars aren't the same as they were..."

"You're dreaming!"

"I've thought I was dreaming, and told myself that the emotions of recent times must be making me see things, but everyone else saw it too... The thing is verified now, the scientists have taken it up, the newspapers are talking about it..."

"The newspapers have reappeared?"

"Life has begun again in the ruins of the world while we were both here being looked after. Hold on—here's a few that I got in the village. They aren't the latest issues, but they're new to us, anyway. Look."

Houquetot handed Laforcade a few small sheets of printed paper, akin to posters, with large headlines and brief articles, like broadsheets published in times of political crisis. Laforcade unfolded them hastily and scanned them, jumping from article to article, his eyes attracted by the headlines.

OUT OF THE DEPTHS:

It is with tremulous hearts that, as survivors of the terrible cataclysms that have ravaged the globe and threatened its conclusive destruction, we take up the pen again…

The human race has not perished—at least, not entirely. We have emerged from the Great Terror, and have resumed our march along the furrow traced by our ancestors…

Let us not deceive ourselves; it is a new era that is beginning. The old times have gone forever. The Sun has risen on a new world…

IN THE RUINS:

Communications are beginning to be re-established with out nearest neighbors in Central Europe. Under the direction of worthy citizens who have taken the business of government in hand, regiments of workers have taken on the most urgent tasks and are trying to get the principle railways and telegraph lines back in working order. There is no news yet of America, all the cables being broken; the few dispatches sent by wireless telegraphy remain unanswered, but one of the few remaining ships that did not suffer too much damage in the devastated ports is preparing to depart with an elite crew on a voyage of discovery. What news will the new Christopher Columbus bring back?

AMAZING MODIFICATIONS:

It is definitely and routinely in the west that the Sun now rises, as all the world can see. Science is obliged to recognize the extraordinary change that has overtaken the movement of the earth, and the absolutely regular speed at which our globe now turns from east to west, contrariwise to its behavior in past ages. What is the cause of this enormous modification? Is it an effect or a cause? What will its consequences be? Far be it from us to dare audaciously to lean over the vertiginous abyss. Human beings have been punished for their pride, and have perceived that they are but wretched insects, or even less, in the order of nature, which is as incomprehensible as ever and vastly out of range of their intelligence.

THE SILENCE OF THE POLITICIANS:

Hi ho! In the ruins of the flattened world, when efforts to reconstitute society and nations are being made everywhere, here are the debris of our ancient assemblies, the leaders of baneful politics, the supporters and profiteers of the cruel divisions of yesteryear, trying to swim up to the surface of the great shipwreck and seize power again, in order to put things back they way they were before the cataclysm—which many people elect to see as the merited chastisement of the social follies of a civilization gone astray. Stop there! The apocalyptic lightning-bolts of the Great Terror have shown us the abyss...

THE APPEAL TO SCIENCE:

A congress of prominent figures in all the branches of science is being organized as quickly as possible, which will collect and collate all observations of the present situation of the globe: all the new facts, the paradoxical anomalies overturning ancient givens, reversing the certainties of yesteryear.

What happened during the month of the Great Terror? What is the extent of the terrestrial or cosmic perturbations that we have undergone? Has the active period of these perturbations really come to an end? What modifications have they brought? Are they transitory or permanent?

Absurd rumors reach us from every direction, exaggerations or follies caused by the universal disruption; we shall not reproduce them—it is for science to study and to verify…

Robert Laforcade passed over these articles rapidly, hastening over information on the general disasters, the universal devastations of five terrible months of convulsions. Thus, in times of ancient terrestrial revolutions, the first men must have seen their cities or their poor huts smashed up, their first attempts at civilization stifled and destroyed.

According to all these news items, however, it seemed that the destruction was less than might have been supposed, that the human race had weathered the storm. The number of victims within the population of each nation was certainly immense, but the masses huddling in their shelters had survived.

Robert's companion in suffering, the brave Houquetot—who was evidently cheerful by nature, and had already got recovered is aplomb, forgetful of the catastrophes—drew him from his reading.

"Do you want to know the funniest thing that happened to me, in the universal upheaval? Well, my dear Monsieur, I've got two teeth back that I lost at least 25 years ago! Is it the effect of these springtimes that are coming back to us? And it seems to me that certain stabbing pains that I had begun to get over…"

Robert Laforcade looked at the rags in which he was dressed and rummaged in his torn pockets. He found a few items there: a sturdy knife he had picked up somewhere along the way, which had rendered him sterling service; a box that had once contained matches, a precious treasure that he had been obliged to eke out but which had finally been exhausted; and a damaged wallet, torn and partly burnt, containing the fragments of paper reproduced in a previous chapter. That was all; he, who had formerly dealt in millions, no longer possessed a *sou*.

"How am I to get back to Paris—or what remains of Paris?" he murmured. "No money, and clothes in rags."

"Bah!" said Houquetot. "Money hasn't yet recovered all of its former value. Besides, I've got about 50 francs in my pocket, and I'll go with you. As for clothes, mine have almost as many holes and frayed edges as yours, but do you think anyone pays any attention to such things in the present state of affairs? Listen—get some rest, have a good night's sleep, and tomorrow we'll be off! You've got a head that aches, and I've got a leg that shakes, so we'll make our way in small stages."

CHAPTER III
Impressions of Return

Robert Laforcade and Houquetot, limping along and supporting one another, made their way to Paris, assisted and transported from time to time by one of the convoys of carts and carriages carrying provisions, which were occupied in the immense and general task of clearing the ruins and repairing the disasters. Already, with entire populations at work, the greater part of the work was done. Almost everywhere, towns and villages were recovering their former appearance and resuming the normal course of affairs that had been so rudely interrupted.

Everywhere they went, masses of debris or the trees of some fallen forest were being raised up again, broken bridges and land-slipped railway embankments were being re-built, and the ruins of towns burned out or destroyed by earthquakes were disappearing. Everywhere, the entire human ant-hive was at work.

Laforcade, with the practiced eye of a businessman, noticed all these unexpected changes and all the tasks undertaken, marveling at the sight of masses of men working without strife, all with evident good will, their collective efforts perfectly orderly. "How well it's all going!" he cried. "Must men fall victim to great catastrophes for their qualities to gain the upper hand over their faults? One would think that misfortune has brought back calm, reason, wisdom. Has the cataclysm brought back natural man—the good human dough relieved of all evil leavening, the healthy and generous creature?

"The good times are back—provided that it lasts!" Houquetot rejoiced. "For more than a few days, at least—that being the usual maximum span of good things."

It had to be admitted that the benevolence of everyone towards everyone else was plainly visible: no shouting, no vulgarity, no more quarreling, no more harsh and arrogant superiority, no more envious expressions or angry and hateful glances at others. On the contrary, there was a sort of confused fraternity born of universal ruination and perils shared.

They finally arrived at Neuilly. In a fever that made his heart beat as if it were about to burst, Robert Laforcade no longer saw anything, paying no more attention to the immense upheaval. He no longer felt weary, and hastened towards his house, dragging Houquetot—who could not hold him back—along with him.

Did the quarter still exist? Was his house still standing? He dared not hope any longer; he had not been able to learn anything certain while he was en route. Information, details and stories about what had occurred during the five months of the great catastrophe in the countries of Old Europe, devastated throughout, had arrived by the minute—hurried telegrams, complicated, confused and contradictory news items, including news of the other continents with which communication was being restored—but there had not been the slightest revelation of the fate of Neuilly.

Neuilly, however, still existed in large measure. Finally! A few more steps, a few more avenues to cross, and there was the Laforcade town house, still almost intact. Laforcade abandoned Houquetot and hurled himself forward. The gate was open. A rapid glance in the direction of the concierge's lodge—no one there. Blocks of stone and builders' tools on either side of the façade: the house was being repaired, but the masons were not there; it was lunch-time.

Robert ran up the front steps. As he opened the door to the silent vestibule and stopped, intimidated by the silence, Houquetot caught up with him. At the same instant, a door opened at the far end of the hallway, and a woman appeared in the frame of the doorway.

"Berthe!"

"Alive!"

Robert Laforcade and his wife are in one another's arms. They have both obeyed their immediate impulse. Their second movement is to draw back to look at one another briefly.

Neither of them seems very sure of the reality of the event; they look at one another, the wife still elegant in her simple black garments, the husband, of course, in a bad way in his ragged clothing, with his beard and hair unkempt. But the third movement is a reversion to the first; the wife weeps on her husband's shoulder, and it seems that the husband is spilling as many tears as she is.

"Oh well, not too bad for spouses in the middle of a divorce," said Houquetot. "This might call for a reconciliation!"

CHAPTER IV
The Extraordinary, Unexpected And Stupefying Truth Begins To Reveal Itself

The most obvious traces of the great perturbation disappeared some time ago, thanks to the hard work of the multitude. Seasons have succeeded seasons, years have passed. Society is reconstituted. The world can breathe. There seems to be no reason to fear a new offensive of the cosmic phenomena in which the world nearly perished.

The march of the seasons has become regular, and no longer accelerated, as in the interval immediately following the crisis. Since the commencement of the new era, however, unprecedented and extraordinary events have continued to emerge in abundance, with every passing minute of daily life, and it is, so to speak, the accumulated details of the extraordinary—one little fact after another—that emphasizes the difference between the New Era and the time before with every day that passes.

Monsieur and Madame Laforcade, who were suing for divorce before the great event, are not divorced. The solicitors have not seen either spouse again. That does not mean, alas, that everything is settled! After the initial effusiveness, the emotional shock of Monsieur's return, he and Madame have both recalled memories of painful years of sulking and quarreling; a certain coldness has come back, and the household has begun to exist in a local atmosphere somewhere around zero degrees.

Madame, although much less preoccupied than before by social relationships, is still fretful. Robert is very busy; like everyone else in the wake of the great upheaval he has thrown himself wholeheartedly into work, in order to reconstitute his life and recover the means of subsistence. The general catastrophe has saved him from imminent personal catastrophe, but for him, as for everyone else, incessant effort is necessary to the gradual reformulation of the state of affairs. Even while thus embroiled in work and all sorts of personal and general preoccupations, however, he cannot avoid noticing certain things. There is a sort of continuous amelioration in the conjugal relationship; the glacial atmosphere of the early days seems to be warming. He and his wife speak to one another more easily and in less formal tones of voice. Admittedly, they have a great many new impressions to communicate to one another, and so many more-or-less amazing observations to make to one another.

"Berthe has a charming appearance nowadays," Robert thinks, as he looks at his wife. "She was nearing 36 when it all happened. It's three years since then, and 36 plus three is 39, even if the ultra-rapid seasons of the first phase don't count as years, as people claim. I would never have thought she was as old as that; she's rosier and younger-looking than before!"

"Robert astonishes me," Madame Laforcade said to herself, in the meantime. "The years haven't touched him; on the contrary, he looks better every day!"

And it also seemed to both of them that the same excellent appearances were manifest in the faces and bearing of many of the people surrounding them; doubtless there were exceptions, but, in general, public health was good. There must have been a sort of renewal since the terrible events—to the extent that one might have thought that the earth had purged itself in that bath of lightning and sulfur, as in an immense Turkish bath, of all its ancient impurities and evil ferments.

A few days into this interval, however, Madame Laforcade fell seriously ill. She felt ill one morning; her head became dizzy and she felt weak. The following day, a violent fever kept her in bed.

Robert interrupted his business affairs to wait for the doctor, an old family friend, who had been summoned immediately by telephone. This was Doctor Montarcy, whose work on neurasthenia and the exhaustion or perturbation of the nervous system, no less than his studies of microbial diseases,

91

had elevated him to the first rank of modern therapists. Everyone was familiar with his slender and clean-shaven face, his golden pince-nez and his long snow-white hair.

Monsieur Laforcade had not seen him for a long time, and found him changed—older and a trifle worn out, which was not at all astonishing. After the preliminary explanations, the doctor sank into an armchair next to the invalid and studied her silently, with an anxious attitude that alarmed Robert and the sick woman noticed herself.

"Well, doctor, what are we dealing with?" said Robert. "It's nothing, isn't it?"

"Nothing?" exclaimed the doctor, leaping to his feat so abruptly that his pince-nez fell off. "Nothing, as you put it— but it's immense, it's amazing!"

"I beg your pardon?" said Robert taking him by the sleeve. "Ahem! You're dreaming, my old friend."

"I'm dreaming! When I explain it to you, you'll see whether or not I'm dreaming! You must have some suspicion, though, having noticed…" He took a notebook from his pocket and consulted it, making an occasional note while playing with his pencil-holder. "As observers and analysts, society people really don't shine; they only have eyes, it seems, in order to take delight in their foolishness. So you haven't noticed…but let's get on with it; you'll understand soon enough. You can judge the enormity of the phenomenon and its consequences for yourself—which are, I assure you, extraordinary, unexpected and fantastic. What asses, all the same, what idle talkers—I don't mean you, I mean my intellectual colleagues who are quibbling, still discussing it between themselves, in low voices, so that it doesn't get out too quickly…"

Robert and Berthe, who had become very pale, looked at one another anxiously.

"It's necessary to finish up by recognizing it for what it is. Madame's illness, for whose effects I grieve, will serve as my immediate demonstration."

Berthe was on the point of fainting.

"I've never seen you like this, doctor," cried Robert, furiously. "Are you in your right mind today? Can't you see that you're scaring your patient? It's nothing very serious, though—I'm sure of it!"

"Nothing very serious—on the contrary, as you shall see! If you recall, I've already treated Madame for this…wasn't it about nine years ago?"

"Yes, indeed, nine years ago, Berthe was rather ill—a nervous illness, primarily, but not very serious."

"That's exactly it… This will be more benign, don't worry…"

"But you said…"

"I said that nothing in the world was more serious, in terms of consequences more than phenomenal, almost extravagant, of which I hesitate even to give you a glimpse. Formidable consequences, which…but you…you cannot, however, have failed to notice some of the strange things that constitute, not merely veritable breaches of ancient natural laws but inversions of them—their complete reversal, my dear Robert!"

"Certainly," said Robert, impatiently. "Numerous bizarre things, reversals of the seasons—but that's not the point. Let's get back to my wife's illness."

"But I already got to it, when I told you that it's the illness she had nine years ago…"

"Yes, but…"

"But it's the same, my friend, the same! But beginning at the end, of course, for Madame Laforcade is presently suffering the last ill-effects of her convalescence. They will become exaggerated, and then…"

Robert and his wife looked at one another.

"He's wandering in the head," thought Robert.

"He's mad," Berthe told herself, somewhat reassured. "I like that better."

"No, I'm not mad!" exclaimed the doctor, who had understood the significance of that exchanged glance. "Not at all! Listen to me. When I tell you that it's the illness you

93

suffered nine years ago that has come back, I mean that it's you who have returned to that epoch of your life, in the course of the general reversal to which we are all subject—you, me, the neighbors, and every other human being on Earth, and perhaps our entire Solar System! Have you got it yet? Do you understand? Have you grasped it? I'm giving you the key to the strange events and improbable phenomena, in the midst of which science is arguing against itself, trying to hypothesize, to comprehend, to co-ordinate…

"I'm not the only one to have understood, of course; scientists everywhere studying their particular specialties, assembling the facts, have arrived at the same conclusions, and the truth has become obvious! Many of them, of course, are still struggling and don't want to yield to the sovereign evidence of the facts, but the last resistance will collapse when this year's International Congress, which opened three weeks ago, hears the report of the committee appointed last year…"

Madame Laforcade, very pale as she lay on her pillow, said nothing, her eyes questioning her husband, who was thinking hard, with his head in his hand.

"Yes, my friend, life is going backwards—that's the absolute truth! The universal upheaval, in the course of which the human race thought it had reached its end, was more complete than anyone thought in the early days that followed the Great Terror, when the first strange and bizarre things were observed. One cannot say that the world has ended, since it continues in its course, but it is continuing in the reverse direction! After the great breakdown, when one might have believed that time was in revolt, the clock of the centuries started working again—but it's working in reverse. The world, in short, is going backwards!"

Berthe could not help smiling.

"Oh, you can laugh!" said Doctor Montarcy. "Don't hold back—plenty of others have laughed through their noses at me and all the others who were among the first to solve the great mystery. But let's get back to you—how old were you nine years ago, when you fell ill? About 30, weren't you? Well,

94

you're 30 once again—you're reaching that milestone for the second time, but from the opposite direction. Come on, my dear Laforcade, look at your wife—haven't you noticed that she's getting younger every day? She thinks she's 39, but she's only 30, my friend, and next year she'll be no more than 29! There you are! There's nothing in that to cause you grief. And you, my friend, are nine years younger too, as am I and everyone else in the world…it's quite simple. Hold on, look at me for a moment: honestly, don't you think that I've been growing younger for some time?"

"My word, doctor," said Robert, laughing, "since you're appealing to my honesty, I'm forced to confess that it doesn't appear so."

"Truly?"

"Yes, I think you've aged. Your hair's white…"

"White! But I have to wear a wig nowadays, my hair having fallen out…"

"That doesn't seem to me to be a sign of rejuvenation, you know…"

"On the contrary! My hair has fallen out—my white hairs—but others are growing, black ones…look!"

With a rapid gesture, the doctor flung away his respectable crown of white hair. Underneath it, his head had a close-shaven appearance, and was almost completely black.

"Extraordinary!" said Robert.

The doctor picked up his wig and brandished it, his pince-nez dancing a frantic sarabande. "And I feel, my friend, the youth that's coming back to me. I was in the winter of my life, but here I am in the middle of autumn! Tomorrow will be summer, the glorious summer of valor and strength! The day after will be spring, with all its promises. Oh no, let's say no more about promises… spring no longer promises anything…"

Berthe let her head fall back, and closed her eyes.

"But we're tiring you out, Madame," said the doctor, putting his wig back on and letting his enthusiasm fade away. Her convalescence is passing now and she's definitely a little worse; you'll have to wait for the fever to die down, but it won't be anything much… Let's leave her to rest; I'll give you a prescription…"

Robert took the doctor to his study and sat him down at the desk. He heard people talking in the drawing-room and opened the door, having recognized the voices. There were two people there he knew: the old and celebrated writer Palluel, and the worthy Houquetot. They had come in search of news of Madame Laforcade, having learned that she was ill.

"It's nothing," Robert relied to their first question, "or almost nothing."

"On the contrary, it's all very serious!" exclaimed the doctor, while scribbling his prescription.

Palluel and Houquetot looked at Robert. "I'm talking about the illness, doctor," said the latter.

"Ah! Good, the convalescence is over; here comes the worst of the fever!"

"Eh? What's he saying? Funny doctor!" murmured Houquetot.

"I'll explain it to you shortly," said Robert.

"Don't explain anything—don't abuse my confidence. When I've revealed the matter to the Congress, and all the world will know—your friends can wait until then!"

Palluel and Houquetot sat down, looking at one another curiously. Palluel had been visiting the Laforcades frequently for some time, Madame Laforcade having suddenly recovered her sympathy for the venerable but scarcely worldly and elegant historian. As for Houquetot, who had made Robert's acquaintance in such terrible circumstances, he had become a friend of the family, and Robert had found him a job that completely realized his most ambitious aspirations: easy work and modest duties.

The doctor had finished scribbling; his pen had cracked audibly as he underlined his signature with a flourish. He was now making notes in his pocket-book, while his pince-nez continued performing acrobatics.

"There you are," he said, getting up. "I'll come back tomorrow. Not a word until this evening—this afternoon I'm reading a summary of my observations to the Congress of Investigation and I'll reveal everything. Ah, Monsieur Palluel. Delighted to see you, my dear colleague! Are you keeping well? Look at me—you seem a little peaky?"

"Not at all, not at all!" exclaimed Palluel, getting up excitedly.

"Yes, yes, you can't hide anything from me—I've got it. I still have a physician's eye for deciphering the slightest untoward symptom in the most unreadable physiognomy. You're not looking well, my friend—take care of yourself!"

"Doctor," said Robert, laughing, "you're terrible this morning. You see illness everywhere. Monsieur Palluel is holding up very well. Personally, I think he looks superb—flourishing."

"Well, I can discern an anxiety in his expression. Come on, my dear colleague, you're a studious man, admit that you feel a certain anxiety about... Let's see, I can't explain myself too clearly... About all these phenomena that your observant mind cannot have failed to perceive, and for which you're seeking an explanation..."

"Well yes, that!" Palluel admitted. "I'm worried about the general state of affairs, and particularly on my own account. There's something that's bothering me personally—I've gone back to writing poetry!"

"What? But that's excellent. You have every reason to go back to writing poetry!"

"Yes, yes, I've gone back to it—except that I dread that I'm returning to childhood and, not to put too fine a point on it, going senile, because, all the verses that I write, I discover subsequently that I've written them before!"

"Very good! Very good! Oh, how delighted I am that you've told me that! Let me make a little note. And these verses that are coming back to you—when did you write them?"

"Thirty-five years ago!"

97

"Perfect! I anticipated as much... Irregularity in the phenomena, some proceeding more quickly, others more slowly... You've corroborated it, my friend. Thank you!"

"What do you think, then?"

"You're returning to childhood, as you said. Me too! Come with me to the Congress and you'll understand!"

"I beg your pardon, doctor," Houquetot put in. "Since you're here, spare a second consultation for me, for I also have things to tell you..."

"Verses are coming back to you too?"

"Oh no, not that—with me, it's teeth. This is the 12th one that's come through again! I'm dying of starvation—my gums are permanently swollen!"

"How old are you?"

"I've jumped the six."

"What?"

"I'm over 60."

"Well, you've jumped the six again, and the five, and perhaps the four. Don't worry—you'll understand this evening. To the Congress, my dear Monsieur Palluel!"

CHAPTER V
Time Going Backwards:
The Astonishment of the Investigative Congress

For several weeks, the Grand International Congress of Investigation, meeting for the fourth time in the New Era, had been holding sessions in the great amphitheater of the Sorbonne, which was too small for the occasion. Delegations of scientists from all over the world, representing almost all the civilized nations, had been compiling reports, detailing their studies of the new phenomena, opening inquiries, assembling and collating masses of evidence gathered from various places or reported by special commissions.

The hall was definitely too small, filled up and overflowing into the corridors or smaller annexes, opened in haste by knocking down partition walls. All the most illustrious men of science were there, together with numerous less famous savants, the courageous workers and obscure pick-wielders digging in established furrows, not to mention many literary men and the serried battalions of reporters sent by the entire world's press.

It was literally stifling, and the work would have been rather difficult without the organization of the Congress into sections and study committees operating in various offices and not communicating with the plenary assembly until they had obtained their final results.

Today, as he had said, the illustrious Montarcy, the president of the Congress's central committee, was to read in public his general report summarizing his own research and personal discoveries, of which there had been loud rumor, and the entire works of his colleagues from every country. Although the illustrious Montarcy had balked at every interview and any indiscretion, refusing to give the slightest indication of his findings, many things were suspected and everyone was expecting a session of the greatest and most exciting interest. In the hubbub of voices, comprising disputes and animated conversations in every language in the world, the name of Montarcy was incessantly repeated, and everyone was waiting impatiently for the session to open.

Monsieur Montarcy had brought Robert and Monsieur Palluel with him, but he did not let them out of his sight for a minute, thus prohibiting any conversation with anyone, so as to avoid the risk of a casual word putting them on the right track and spoiling the great effect that he was expecting.

When he appeared at the rostrum, the most complete silence instantly fell, extinguishing the tumult. All conversations ceased, all documents were replaced in brief-cases, and all heads turned to the front of the room, while Montarcy, with the coquetry of an orator who knows how to wait, slowly arranged his sheaves of notes and mountains of documents in front of him.

The entire first part of his report was a summary of various generally observed phenomena: a rapid list of all the changes manifest, so to speak, on the surface of the human habitat.

Monsieur Montarcy paused briefly. His peroration had made him hot; with a mechanical movement, he lifted his wig slightly in order to mop his brow. It was very rapid, but some members of the audience were amazed to glimpse the black crew-cut beneath his white wig. The illustrious Montarcy hastened to start speaking again, beginning a new chapter.

"Everywhere, gentlemen, the same observations have been made regarding the perturbations in the cycle of the seasons. After the great upheaval, nature, it seems, has been ill for a while, and during that convalescence, the order of the universe, profoundly disturbed, has presented the strangest anomalies: seasons altered or succeeding one another—take note—with a remarkable velocity, winter mingling with summer, spring following autumn, a complete confusion in which we are lost; abrupt changes of temperature, abnormal and ultra-rapid vegetation, plants sprouting and blooming exceptionally, then the withering and dying of innumerable vegetables in week-long seasons…

"Well, gentlemen, these strange perturbations in the formerly-regular course of life, this exceptional blooming and withering, have also been experienced by human beings—and it is to this point that I ask you to devote your complete attention…"

"Silence! Silence! Listen! Listen!"

"These strange upheavals and these maladies of simple vegetable species in the great crisis of nature, have applied equally to human beings, without them yet paying overmuch attention to the fact during the period of feverish labor that has followed the Great Terror. But physicians, as all my colleagues can testify, have had numerous causes for amazement in the meantime. Medical science, the fruit of the experience and reflection of centuries has become a vain jumble of false notions, across the board. The usual development of diseases seemed changed, the order of their phases inverted—in a word, reversed, like our seasons…"

"Yes, yes! Exactly!"

"Quiet, please, gentlemen! Let the Master speak."

"Yes—that was the moment at least to try my method… the meth…."

"Silence!"

"To continue, we have seen people beginning their illnesses at the end; we have seen it again and again, and we shall see it for a long time to come…" Montarcy turned to Robert. "…commencing with the end, I say, finding, so to speak, the cause of death at the beginning and then seeing the illness terminate in a mild indisposition, with the initial symptoms at the end! The doctors did not understand immediately. I hasten to say that it is only after a large number of observations, gentlemen, that the fulgurant light of truth was suddenly ignited within our eyes! Doctors, have we not all had to care for people who, scarcely ill, seemed suddenly to age rapidly…very rapidly…like our seasons?"

"Yes! Indeed! That's true! Go on!"

"That's not all," cried a voice from one of the benches at the very back of the hall. "My observation No. 108, the sick man who…"

"It's certainly not all!" exclaimed another. "My observations 85 and 318, especially, the rejuvenation…"

"I'm getting there," Montarcy went on. "Be patient; all your remarkable observations will figure in my report—no, that certainly isn't all. Our invalids, I said, seemed to grow old suddenly—but immediately afterwards showed unequivocal signs of an extraordinary rejuvenation! At how many of our medical meetings in the Academy of Sciences have we discussed it? You know it, gentlemen, and the medical journals are there to testify to it… But all of us, as we were then, when we sought to determine the causes and desired to calculate the consequences, were swimming in a sea of errors! Errors as to the causes, errors as to the effects! Errors everywhere!"

"Well, what of it?" Palluel put in, getting up and taking Montarcy by the sleeve. "You're simply demonstrating the bankruptcy of the science for which so much was once claimed. In my capacity as a poet, permit me to say that I am delighted to see you recognize the fact."

A storm of protests and vociferations broke out in the hall. Everyone stood up; quarrels broke out and angry remarks were exchanged. The president and his assistants rang their hand-bells desperately or rapped the desk with their rulers.

"No, Monsieur," cried Montarcy, when the tumult had calmed down somewhat "not the bankruptcy, but, on the contrary, a concordat, which I claim for the Supreme Mastery of Cause and Effect! The concordat of Science with eyes from which the scales have fallen! Science, gentlemen, does not know and will never know more than a percentage of the great Hidden Truths—a percentage that we may increase, but which will still only be a percentage."

"Pay it to us immediately!"

"Here is one new and absolute truth: the general rejuvenation that so many observers have recorded, and which we have been able to observe in ourselves, is not merely a local or temporary phenomenon; no, gentlemen, science today, after several yeas of study and these innumerable observations coming from every part of the word, can loudly and solemnly affirm that it has become…the new rule of Life!"

Another hubbub broke out in the assembly. Profound sensation, recorded the stenographers.

"Explain yourself! Listen! What? Silence!"

"Yes, what was believed to be phenomenal and merely transitory, has become the rules, and constitutes, according to all indications, a new and definitive way of life. An immense change and profound upset. Since the great upheaval, humankind, nature, time, everything, has been borne away by a vast and regular backward movement. There is no longer any question of ancient natural laws; they no longer exist; there is an entirely new set now! The world that almost perished is still working, but it is working backwards! It is no longer the limitless Future that extends before us. In the Course of Time, the Future had a limit, and that limit has been reached. Today…"

The stenographers forgot to write. They were listening, as pale with emotion as all the rest. How, in any case, could they record the dull murmur that was running in ripples around the room: a rumor made up as much by the halting respiration of the audience as by stifled exclamations?

Monsieur Montarcy, his arms in the air, brandishing papers, seemed to have grown much larger. His eyes were gleaming. Without being aware of it, he had taken off his white wig, and his pince-nez lay broken beneath the feet of the audience.

"Today, gentlemen," Monsieur Montarcy said, solemnly, "it is the Past that we have before us, the Past that is unfolding and offering itself to us for review, the immense, almost infinite Past that we are also going to relive!"

A cheer went up from the assembly, a formidable cry springing forth from every throat. Everyone precipitated himself towards the desk, knocking it over and jostling one another to get to the Master, who had slumped voiceless into a chair. Everyone was shouting acclamations and enthusiastic interjections at the top of his voice, among which a few protestations and timid objections were immediately drowned out and annihilated.

Yes, they felt it; it was, indeed, the truth, divined and anticipated by some, which Montarcy, with the incontestable authority of his immense knowledge, had finally extracted and formulated.

That session of the International Congress of Investigation could not continue with the calm regularity of other seasons. That was now impossible, given the disturbed condition of the audience. Monsieur Montarcy continued talking, no longer at the podium but standing on the desk in the middle of a packed circle of listeners, pushing and shoving one another, climbing on chairs or tables—for, in response to the rumors that had immediately spread outside, the Sorbonne was overflowing, invaded by hordes of new arrivals: students, journalists, passers-by…

"Yes, yes!" said Monsieur Montarcy. "It's the Past that we shall relive, and I feel a vertigo take possession of my mind when I think of everything that will follow from this new order of things, of all the consequences of this reversal of the ancient laws of nature! Think about these consequences, in your turn, from the viewpoint, firstly, of the individual, secondly, of the family, and thirdly, of the race! We have already…you have certainly become familiar with certain strange, incomprehensible cases."

"My observations 138 and 192!" cried a nearby doctor.

"People who were known to be definitely dead, people who disappeared ten years ago, recently reappeared in the light of the Sun! I have there, in a report that I cannot read in its entirety, more than 600 authentically established cases; my report has gone to press… They are my proofs… My colleagues and I have been working in silenced, resolved not to bring the truth into the light of day until we were able to say: one would have to be blind not to see it! We are all, therefore, eight or ten years younger today than we imagine. Next year, we shall be a year younger, then two, then three...

"The constitution of the family will change utterly. You will see each human group return slowly to its origins. I shall not waste time in philosophical considerations; some will ascend, others will descend, now as before there will be a game of see-saw, but this time, seemingly, in accordance with a law of fate! That is the way it will be for the family in the utmost detail, and that is the way it will be for the larger group, for the nation, or the race."

He could do no more. In his effort to dominate the tumult, so long victorious, he had finished up shouting at the top of his voice. Now his raw throat refused to let anything pass but whispered phrases. It was necessary to carry on talking regardless, to respond to all the challenges, the enthusiastic questions, the bewildered exclamations, the demands for clarification, the timid objections and the protests of a few—for there are always St. Thomases everywhere, who dispute and quibble.

Monsieur Palluel embraced Montarcy. He made no objection himself, he was almost weeping with joy. He also embraced Robert and the members of the committee; for a little while, the dignity of the Academician, beneath which the ardent poet of yesteryear had been revealed, had responded to the objections of some protesters with blows of the fist. "Montarcy! This morning I behaved like a blockhead. You're a great man; permit me to address you as *tu*, illustrious Master! No more Monsieur so far as you're concerned! I adore you! Long live Montarcy! Shout 'Long live Montarcy,' the rest of you!"

"Long live Montarcy!"

"And long live the New Era! You down there, the fat red-faced chap—shout it out, if you please! Ah, you're not happy are you? You'd rather hold on to your soot-colored epoch, to your civilization in shades of black, to your false Progress, to your lugubrious Future...with all its threats, with its universal leveling, its definitive crushing of the beautiful, the good, and the healthy! What luck, my friends, what luck! What incredible and unexpected good fortune! We shall avoid it, that future, we shall turn back! For each of us individually, for all of us, there's already the joy of reliving the sequence of spring-times in the spring-times of our lives, and for society there's the return of the most beautiful things of the past…"

"There've been plenty of difficult moments too, damn it!" someone shouted.

"Who knows? Perhaps all that can be rearranged!"

"Enlightened by experience!" croaked Montarcy.

"He said it—enlightened by experience!" cried Palluel. "We'll surely find ways to render those difficult moments less harsh! With history in our hands, we'll have the power to it better second time around. You down there, the little student, let yourself go—show a little enthusiasm! What's the matter with the youth of today?"

"I beg your pardon," replied the student, climbing up on the shoulders of a few comrades, "but if all this is serious, I'm doomed. My past isn't very long, and will soon be used up."

"That's true, though," said the Academician, turning to Montarcy. "He's right—he's doomed. Poor youth!"

"What do you expect?" said Montarcy. "We have to accept it. Humankind is nothing in the breakdown of the Clock of the Centuries; we must accept the decree of the Supreme Clockmaker and try to adjust to it! If I'm to be charged with optimism, I accept the charge, but I have an intuition that this enormous change, this absolute reversal, will only result for humankind in a sum of advantage much superior to a few foreseeable petty inconveniences…"

"Once again, I ask leave to speak," Palluel resumed, "and I propose that the assembly should close this memorable session, in which the extraordinary event has been revealed to us, with three hearty cheers in honor of the New Era!"

"Hurrah! Vivat! Hoch! Long live Montarcy! Long live the New Era!"

"No! No! Non! Nein!"

"Oui! Si! Yes! Hurrah!"

"No!"

A small opposition group formed in a corner of the room, composed primarily of English delegates, which was joined by the young student protester and some of his friends.

"But then, by your count, what year is it?" shouted one member of the opposing group, making a megaphone with his hands.

"I don't know exactly! You've observed, as we have, the ultra-rapid succession of the seasons in the early days of the New Era. How can you figure it out, exactly?"

"If I've understood your system correctly," said another, "at a certain moment the world began to live—I mean to work—backwards. From evening it returns to morning?"

"Doubtless—and what we take for the setting of the Sun is actually, in truth, the dawn that is extinguished. Our hours are radically overturned, like our seasons! You remember what a time of crisis that was for the trees and all vegetable species...they ended up adapting themselves to the permutation of the seasons, and we shall adapt to it as well, as to everything else, after a more-or-less long and difficult time of crisis."

"No! No! Absurd!"

"If you wish!"

"A word?" said a congress delegate. "Among these returns of people known to have disappeared from the world and legally counted as dead, among all these people contradicted by old acts of the Civil Estate, emerging everywhere in increasing numbers, I see in the observations communicated to the Congress that these people returned from the great beyond, did not all depart on the same dates, and that there are notable age-differences..."

"That, gentlemen, has preoccupied my colleagues on the central committee and myself for some time. There is indeed a complication...but after mature reflection—and I think that my colleague are of the same opinion as me—I see nothing in that but the result of perfectly comprehensible difficulties in getting the new system of the world under way: difficulties previously observed, I repeat, in the vegetable world. Besides, gentlemen, if a clear-sighted man equipped with scientific notions had been able to witness the first phases of the world's formation, can we believe that he would not have had occasion to observe even greater difficulties?

"Yes! Oui! Ja! Si! No! Si! Yes! No!"

"Then should we not number our years in reverse from now on?"

"No, gentlemen. I've just told you that we don't know exactly which year we might be in. I propose that the assembly votes on a special numbering system for the New Era, based on the supposition that today is in year X. That would be safest...we might do better, if you want to, to nominate an international calendrical committee to study the question and to negotiate an agreement with the various governments." [12]

"Yes! Oui! Very good! Perfect!"

Exclamations of approval in various languages intermingled; all the hands were raised, the opposition finding itself veritably drowned out by the enthusiastic and near-universal agreement. The opposition had to content itself with sniggering and muttering quibbles. In the corner where the young students had taken refuge, an anxious and despairing silence had fallen.

---

[12] It is as well to remember that Robida was writing at the end of an era in which the measurement of time had been gradually globalized and standardized by a series of committees and conferences, beginning with the International Geographical Conference in Brussels in 1876. The necessities of railway timetabling had killed off the old customs of local time, and the International Meridian Conference in Washington, D.C. in 1884 introduced the modern system of time-zones. The practicalities of the new system were still problematic in 1902; it was not until 1910 that the Eiffel Tower was used to transmit a wireless signal that allowed all the clocks in France to be readily calibrated to Paris time.

"Let's go," said Houquetot. "But that's not all, and you see me distressed on my own account… I came back to your house for another reason. I got…can you guess?"

"What?"

"A telegram from my own father! He's disembarked at Auxerre…"

"When?" demanded Montarcy.

"Arrived yesterday, it seems."

"No, when did he depart?"

"Oh, depart? Twenty-five years ago."

"You see," said Montarcy. "Notable differences in dates… Returns confused… Crisis…"

"And he's asking me for money for coach-fare," Houquetot added.

CHAPTER VI
The New Era: Official and Other Documents

REPUBLIQUE FRANÇAISE

To the Minister of the Interior,

Given that it is now proven by the multiple observations of science that the mechanism of the terrestrial universe has recently been subject to a complete and absolute change in its general operation, and that modifications no less radical have appeared in the former order of the succession of time, beyond and above all possible explanation;

Given that there is certain and absolute evidence that a truly new era has commenced with the change, establishing the backward march of time and the world officially recognized by the Grand International Congress of Investigation, with the sanction of all the governments;

Given that the numeration of years following the former Gregorian, Russian, Mohammedan calendars and other previously employed, is now discordant with the reality of things;

It is decreed that:

From today, the sequential numeration of years following those of the elapsed era is abolished.

To avoid errors of calculation, the years elapsed since the great change will not be counted, by reason of the recognized fact that the clock of the centuries, having broken down, operated during the critical period of the crisis with irregular velocity and possibly expended many years in a matter of weeks.

The Government and the Academies have reached an agreement only to commence the numeration of years of the new era from the date of the official establishment of the backward return.

In consequence, the present year will be number 1 in all official and unofficial acts.

Paris, September 17, Year 1

Despite what was said in the preamble to the decree, the unanimity of nations on the matter of the change of era had not been acquired. England persisted in not accepting absolutely the affirmations of the Congress and in denying the backward march. Let us say immediately that this prejudiced opposition lasted several years, and only yielded in the face of complete evidence. It became impossible to deny the rejuvenation when a prince who was supposedly an octogenarian[13] was seen compromising the royal dignity at the feet of a music-hall actress famed for her beauty, and that one of two famous statesmen of a similar age contested the football championship while the other rowed with the Oxford crew in the annual university boat race on the Thames.

A considerable event completed the rout of the former opposition. The deceased Queen Victoria and the Grand Old Man Mr. Gladstone appeared almost at the same time. The existing ministry collapsed. The following day, the new era was officially recognized.

JOURNAL DES ECONOMISTES

October 1, Year 1

It is time!

Now that no doubt is any longer possible regarding the astonishing and providential reversal of the former progression

---

[13] In fairness to the British royal family, it ought to be pointed out that the oldest of Queen Victoria's sons, who succeeded to the throne in January 1901 as Edward VII, although no stranger to affairs with actresses, had been born in 1841; there could not, therefore, have been any English prince who might have been supposed to be an octogenarian at the time when the story is set.

of things, it is up to us to explain in a few words the reasons for which humankind, on the threshold of new times, ought greatly to rejoice in the immense event!

It is time! The overpopulated world glimpsed the imminent moment when space to accommodate human beings would run out, the fatal and ineluctable moment when the Earth, exhausted by ceaseless and relentless overproduction, would find itself powerless to nourish the swarm incessantly accrued by the flow of generations, by the multiplying hordes whose legitimate appetites could only become more and more difficult to satisfy. The law of the struggle for life[14] has always been imposed on humankind, but how the sorrows and difficulties of the harsh combat have increased in the 19th century! Previously, human beings had latitude, continents to discover and exploit; now, the last unknown deserts and continents of the Earth have yielded their secrets and resources and humans, too numerous at the feast, find nothing more before them; the Earth will no longer be anything but a vast raft prey to distress and famine.

It is time! Our Old Europe, of 80 million inhabitants in 1800, has passed 350 million, crowded and heaped up in our poor little corner. Had the increase continued at the same rate, its population at the end of the 20th century would have been the fabulous figure of 1500 millions, fatally destined to attack one another and to devour one another to obtain their daily bread! All other questions and political struggles would have become insoluble once absorbed into the sole concern of the

---

[14] Robida renders this phrase in English; it would not be appropriate to substituted the more familiar "struggle for existence" here because the passage is parodying Malthusian economic theory rather than Spencerian evolutionary theory, with which the latter phrase is primarily associated. Robida does, however, use the English phrase again in Chapter XXI, and there adds an explanatory French translation which employs the French word "*existence,*" which I have transposed directly, thus giving both forms of the phrase.

preponderance of people or races, and no civilization or social order would have been able to hold up under the terrible pressure of hunger. With America overflowing in its turn, and new or forgotten nations created in the former desert lands or reformed in the depths of exhausted continents....

It is time! This backward return is salvation; it is the abrupt and total end put by Providence to the frightful multiplication!

It is time!

CHAPTER VII
The New Progression of Life Imports a Few Problems To the Former Constitution of the Family

The most surprising of all the changes associated with the unexpected reversal of former natural laws, and perhaps the most considerable in its consequences, was that fathers now arrived in life after their sons. Who, in the old world, could ever have supposed that the constitution of the family might be so radically modified?

Feminist ideologists and socialists, in their amiable proposals of societies governed by the rules of central houses, and anarchists of a more brutal stripe, had been able to dream of changes, but even in their craziest conceptions and most audacious inversions of the whole of social life—to employ their gentle terminology—they had never dreamed of the formidable familial revolution that nature suddenly accomplished.

Despite the solemn declarations of the International Congress, the indisputable observations of the scientists and the official sanction of all the academies, several months went by before the truth was accepted by everyone and all nations had consented to admit that the Earth and time had turned backwards. In order for everyone to be fully convinced, and the final doubts cleared away, it was necessary for the orderly rejuvenation to become visibly and undeniably part of everyone's personal experience.

Many people protested for a long time; obstinate scientists raised every conceivable quibble before yielding to the understanding that Nature, inexhaustible in her incredible variety with regard to forms of life, was able to import the same diversity into her means. Unity, diversity, fecundity! What had once been could be again After all, Nature is as phenomenal as rebirth, if not more so.

This return to life, the re-entry of ancestors upon the scene, brought astonishing modifications to families, as we have said, and transformed their ancient organization from top to bottom. If it caused profound stupefaction among sons, how much greater was the burden of astonishment and trouble for fathers! What transports of joy they felt, at first, on returning to the old world and finding their families again! Moments of indescribable delight! Nothing was finished; everything was beginning again, in the reverse direction. But what emotions and reflections followed, when they had finished clasping the families that had believed to be lost forever in their arms, and began to relive their former days?

Ah, what inversions of the soul, what powerful salutary motives and profound reflections, and what abysms of reminiscence, often bitter and painful!

How many aspects of their former existence might have been modified, doubtless for the better, if they had been able to foresee these second meetings of fathers and sons, in absolutely reversed conditions! Many of these new passengers embarked upon a second voyage through life arrived, however, with brains that had become almost new in repose, and from which old impressions seemed to have been somewhat effaced. They only retained confused ideas and memories of their former adventures. The sponge had passed over the slate. Almost everything had become new to them again. They came back open to all astonishment, as to all hope.

Everything having begun again in this manner, the Earth would see all its children again, generation after generation. That was the preoccupation of everyone in the world, simple people as well as thinkers and scientists; it was the concern of politics and statesmen, of those people who had the pretension of guiding the destinies of nations—the only kind of work that too often adulterates and poisons one's true aspirations. It generated hope for those vanquished races which had known better days in the past, and was the subject of interminable dissertations from the various academies, which found ample material therein for intensely interesting studies of every sort.

Everything began again—but, just as human beings had previously lived in ignorance of their end, now that the wheels and hands of the clock of the centuries were turning backwards, humankind was moving towards its beginning, of which it was largely ignorant—a fortunate uncertainty that let life retain all its interest and all its savor.

It goes without saying that there were discussions everywhere, endless and exhaustive, on the question of whether the new course of life presented more advantages to individuals and society or whether the former mode of life as preferable; increasingly, though, people were obliged to perceive that the new progression of things was incomparably superior to the former order in every way, and presented immense advantages from every viewpoint, individual or social.

How often, formerly—O blasphemy!—had people, faced with certain triumphs, doubted eternal justice? They had been in too much of a hurry. To wait patiently would have been sufficient.

Certainly, at present, all this immense change is not proceeding without a few petty inconveniences, general and particular. The new life brings everyone new anxieties, trivial or serious, reveals difficulties of every order, innumerable and unforeseen. The abrupt backward shift inconveniences certain ostentatious and pretentious rich individuals whose carefully-concealed origins have now been exposed by the reappearance of ancestors who are hardly resplendent: frauds, or even bawds!

As it is human nature to worry about the future, even when that future is the past in the process of re-emerging, people have became acquainted with a new kind of torment: "I know that I had a father besotted with such and such ideas, or a grandfather who once did this or that," the anxious head of a family says to himself; "what spanners will these ancestors throw into the works of my plans when they come back?"

Montarcy had slumped into an armchair and was mopping his brow, in the middle of a tightly-knit group of congress delegates of all nationalities, who were desirous of debating the great question with the illustrious savant, elucidating, so far as was possible, a few obscure points, and resolving or explaining certain half-glimpsed difficulties. Of obscure points, difficulties and problems, there remained many—indeed yes!—for whose explanation neither Monsieur Montarcy nor any one else could take immediate responsibility. That was the way it was because that was the way it was; for the moment, it was necessary to accept things as they presented themselves.

At that moment, a man who was trying to force a way through to the desk, in the midst of a sort of furrow of complaints and groans, attracted Robert Laforcade's attention. The man was signaling to him by waving his arms, imperiling a few skulls and a few pairs of spectacles plunged into deep discussion.

Robert recognized Houquetot. He was seized by anxiety and attempted to force a way through the groups surrounding him.

"What's up?" he shouted.

"Come quickly!" cried Houquetot. "As fast as you can!"

"Is my wife's illness getting worse?"

"Yes, I suppose so! But there's something even more extraordinary."

"What! Tell me, quickly!"

"It's…difficult to say! There's an old gentleman…it's your father…"

"My father? The father I lost 15 years ago?"

"Yes, that's what he told Madame Laforcade, who's terrified… At any rate, your father's there…"

Montarcy, who had overheard the conversation, leapt up from his chair. "My dear Laforcade!" he cried. "It's very simple, and it'll serve admirable to clear away the last doubts! Your father's birth has just been announced! Let's run quickly! I knew him personally—I was his doctor once."

On the other hand, what of the prodigal fathers who consumed all their families' fortunes, reducing them to penury, or those who departed having done their legitimate heirs the bad turn of disinheriting them? How will they be received?

Another consequence of the new state of things is the changing of tastes and ideas, which was easy to observe after a certain passage of time. It happened slowly, but it is understandable that the returning generation brought back its ancient preferences, and that it was found to be disposed to criticize those of the generation that succeeded it, taking issue with the greater number of its ideas. That was a delicate issue.

Robert Laforcade and his wife no longer had the definitively broken home, culminating in separation, whose misery and desperation we saw at the beginning of this story. The great upheaval had swept away their divorce proceedings, and since then, every passing season and year had brought about a sensible amelioration in their conjugal relations. They were now asking themselves how they had ever been able to reach the point of wanting to put 50,000 leagues between them, and by what aberration their two minds had coldly settled one day upon the urgent necessity of a divorce.

Following the same unfortunate course in a reverse direction, the desire to divorce had faded into a simple coldness, then to petty annoyances over points of susceptibility; stage by stage, they had now arrived, quite simply, at perfect tranquility and mutual understanding—thus providing striking proof that, in this humble world, everything sorts itself out in the end. People used to say that before, but how much more certain it is now!

Robert Laforcade is no longer the wealthy businessman he was before. His business it must be admitted, is going quite slowly. Industry suffered a violent crisis, and everyone is feeling its consequences. Quite naturally, the inclination of the Laforcade household is now modest. This mediocrity has at least had the effect of moderating Berthe's appetite for social life, and Robert is glad of it.

Oh, we must not forget to mention that Robert is no more than 35 and Berthe scarcely 28 or 29. Thus the world proceeds, getting younger every day. This evening, after the family dinner, Robert is chatting about the day's trivial events with his father and grandfather, installed in armchairs facing one another on either side of the heath in the drawing-room. Yes, his father and his grandfather! His father, you will recall, was born, or reborn, on the evening when the illustrious Doctor Montarcy announced the reversal of time at the Investigative Congress, and his grandfather returned 18 months later—considerably in advance of the time at which he might have been expected—one of those numerous abnormal cases whose frequency was causing Montarcy and the entire scientific world particular concern.

"Well," said Monsieur Laforcade the father, "what's new? Anything much?"

"No," Robert replied. "The question of the advance is still filling the newspapers. Everyone's wasting their breath squabbling over the question of whether it's 30 or 40 years. Monsieur Montarcy is proposing the establishment of another big commission of inquiry..."

"What for?"

"He thinks that it's not a matter of a regular advance of 30 or 40 years, but a residue of troubles caused by setting the new situation of the world in motion. I've read his article in the *Revue* on 'Temporal Flux and Reflux.' He explains it quite well and declares, moreover, that everything will gradually sort itself out. According to him, there's no cause for anxiety. Everything indicates that we'll no longer see excessively pressurized generations arriving prematurely, all at the same time, bumping into one another, as timorous and alarmist scientists are trying to make us fear... Each one will have its turn, and that's all to the good!"

"You're not saying that because of me, are you?" said the grandfather, in a piqued tone.

"Of course not, grandfather—how could you think such a thing?" cried Madame Laforcade.

"It's because we've had a little discussion," said father Laforcade. "Your grandfather seems to be convinced that we weren't looking forward to his arrival and have been sighing every since he came back on the scene."

"Certainly," said the grandfather. "I need to remake the family fortune, which isn't brilliant, you must admit! Here's Robert, a pleasant fellow and a fine engineer, I grant you, but nor practical, too wrapped up in follies, utopias, dreams... All his stories of electricity, his ridiculous locomotive machines, frightful glorified saucepans shuddering and making an infernal racket, which will end up smashing people into pieces, whether they're inside or underneath! I've seen them! They'll never work! They'll all end up in the scrap-yard!"

"But I assure you that they work quite well, grandfather! Tastes have changed. People were horror-stricken..."

"Exactly!" said father Laforcade. "I think it's as abominable and as impractical as those other machines that you tried to explain to me—that unbearable telephone, which tortures people with its perpetual *drin drin*s and makes people ill, costing far more time in migraines and fits of exasperation than it claims to save! You'd do well to let go of that stupidity, good at best for amusing children—like that other bizarre plaything that you made me listen to, the phonograph!"

"You're exaggerating, I assure you. I don't want to defend those inventions, but I can recall once having been very enthusiastic about them myself. It's curious how tastes change; my enthusiasm has dissipated, but it's necessary nevertheless not to exaggerate the inconveniences. One no longer hears talk of that nowadays; a truly extraordinary modification has been produced in ideas and tastes... I can't imagine what has caused it."

"It's our return, of course—a sane and reasonable generation," said father Laforcade.

"One moment," said the grandfather, with a gesture of protest. "The sane and reasonable generation is mine. Serious consideration necessitates the conclusion is that it was on our departure that the stupidities began."

"I beg your pardon, father, but you're exaggerating again. I venture to say that our generation does not deserve your blame; we marched reasonably along the road of Progress. While you were a little difficult to set in motion, we marched steadily, but not precipitately, without racing madly and impetuously ahead like those who succeeded us. It's not our fault that they brought haste, fever, enervation and mortal overwork into the world…"

"Let's not argue about it. It's quite natural that we should prefer our sane ideas and calmer habits to your absurd audacity and all your machinery, electrical or otherwise, which is complicated, pretentious, troublesome and murderous, and in which we can see no value!"

"I'll settle the dispute," said a new voice.

Everyone turned round. It was the Academician Palluel who had come into the room, followed by a boy 13 or 14 years old, of rather bizarre appearance, short and fat, wearing clothes that were too large for him.

"Sit down there," said Palluel, placing the young man in a corner. "Stay calm, and don't speak unless someone asks you a question."

"Yes, uncle."

"Good evening, dear Madame, how are you doing? Admirably, that's evident. One can no longer say to ladies every time one sees the that they're looking younger and fresher than ever; it's no longer a compliment but a banal truth! I recommend, however, that you do not do what I am doing; don't be too hasty in rejuvenation—for I honestly fear that I am proceeding too briskly!"

It is true that the old writer had changed a great deal, not only since the already distant day when we saw him, at the end of the old era, despairing in his cold and lugubrious mansard, but also since the day when Montarcy had announced the great news at the Investigative Congress. Now, the outmoded poet and former academician seemed to be 50 at most; his white hair was in the process of taking on a reddish tint, irrepressible and rebellious, and his beard was spreading magnificently over a flower-patterned waistcoat.

"Now then, you three generations of Laforcades are busy quarreling with one another? If I understood rightly as I came in, it seems to me that it's a matter of establishing which of the three epochs that you represent was the furthest developed in mental alienation, the absurdity of high pretensions and unhealthy hullabaloo. The answer is not in doubt; it's the last! It had the means of going even further, to the extent that the Supreme Technician, to borrow a phrase from the illustrious Montarcy, renounced it and decided to make the machine run backwards. We are all in agreement as to that, as the youngest Laforcade will acknowledge."

CHAPTER VIII
Backwards: The Journal of True Progress

Grandfather Laforcade smiled and clapped the poet on the shoulder. "This young man, at least, has the measure of his epoch!" he said. "Since my return, my dear sir, you're the only person I've met with reasonable ideas. Perhaps you can give me some advice. Tell me, are you in industry, or commerce? My son introduced us the other day, but my memory is still a little vague…"

"I am a jeweler of sonorous epithets," Palluel declared. "An enameller in partitioned stanzas enriched with brilliant rhymes!"

"I beg your pardon?"

"A poet. Let it be said simply, without wishing to humiliate you."

"See, grandfather—that was perfectly obvious," said Robert, laughing.

"And what can I do for you, my dear sir, by way of advice?" Palluel went on, seriously.

"I don't know if I should take the risk. Well, on the off chance, can you advise me about sugar and oil?"

"Sugar? Oil?" said Palluel, slightly taken aback. "Is it for coffee or salad?"

"Am I mistaken? Are you no more serious that the others? I'm talking about oil, sugar, cotton, leather, iron… Where's the best place to make money? Flour, perhaps?"

"Why ask me?"

"My dear sir, you're a member of the family. Aren't you the son of my second cousin Palluel, my comrade of 1825? I can talk frankly in front of you, then. Well, I have an urgent need to get back into business, as soon as possible—its very urgent! Here's my grandson Robert, whose financial situation isn't brilliant, you know. I can see that it's getting worse every day, with their stupid electrical devices and their frightful steam engines, without taking into account the fact that he'll be an adolescent before long, and the responsibility of his parents…and children are expensive! Now here's my son Edouard, who wasn't outstandingly successful in his time; he gives me cause for anxiety too. He has a little manufacturing business that's not very brilliant…."

"I beg your pardon, father," said Edouard Laforcade, "it's me who put the family back in its feet, remember—I did everything I could when you were ruined!"

"Your crinoline factory? That's nothing remarkable. Didn't that collapse too."

"What do you expect? Changes in fashion…"

"Anyway, I'd like to find something; I'm twiddling my thumbs here, idly, when I feel that it would be no bad thing to get back to active life as soon as possible! Business, that's the thing! Myself, I was a post-master,[15] you know, but there'll be nothing to do in that regard for years and years."

"It's too soon," said Palluel, smiling irreverently.

"So you understand why I have to find something else. Oil? Sugar? Leather? Iron?"

"That's the one thing about which I don't have an opinion!" exclaimed Palluel. "I have to admit that you're barking up the wrong tree. I have fixed opinions on many things, and I'd advise you not to contradict me on some of them, but on leather and oil my brain is an infertile desert! Would you like some advice anyway? You were a post-master—well, be patient until stage-coaches come back, and on that day you'll be rich; you'll overwhelm us with your magnificence."

"Will that take long?"

"Who knows? We're going so rapidly! Tastes and preferences are being modified with an unexpected rapidity;

---

[15] Grandfather Laforcade was not, of course, the sort of post-master who organized the distribution of postage stamps but an owner and supervisor of scheduled stage-coaches— *diligences*—transmitting passengers and parcels.

with every day that passes you can observe new aspirations. Look at all the changes that have taken place since the New Era—the great New Era!—began, and all those that are in preparation. The day will come, as others used to say, for the worst of motives! The day will come, and it will all go very well, in accordance with the march of progress—of true progress! Besides, I'm working to accelerate it even further, that march of Progress. I'm founding a journal—don't worry, this isn't an appeal for funds, I have sleeping partners in the big banks—I'm founding a great political, literary and social journal, and here's a mock-up of the first issue, with our program, which is that of all today's young folk!"

Palluel took a sheaf of printed proofs from his pocket, among which a large poster stood out, bearing a legend in large letters:

BACKWARDS
The Journal of True Progress
Organ of the Retrograde Committee for
Politics, Literature, Industry and Commerce

"Listen to this," said Palluel. "Since the immense highway previously traveled by our ancestors has been suddenly reopened before tremulous humankind, the most desiccated hearts, devastated by bleak despair, have suddenly begun to beat again, etc., etc…a dawn of hope has broken over the surprised world, etc., etc…flux and reflux, etc., etc…

"They are coming back, the ancestors, reappearing by degrees, as astonished as we are! Young or old, whether they were formerly happy or unhappy, good or evil, they are all re-emerging at the age when they quite the Earth for the first time. It is the re-entrance on to the stage, with others expected, of a generation whose first experience, it is necessary to believe, must undoubtedly have enlightened them and made them wise, and which will not be inclined to fall into the same traps…"

"Very good!" said grandfather Laforcade. "That's enough—I'll take out a subscription…"

"I'll go on: 'The mounting tide of old generations returned, will increasingly transport and bring into our present the tastes and ideas of the past, which experience must certainly have ripened, and wisdom weighed and tested, but which will still be transitory and destined to be replaced in their turn. You can see them already, these ancestors, with their particular conception of progress, seeking out, rediscovering or reinventing the things of their own time…

" 'Let us enter resolutely into that process; instead of raising obstacles to Progress, let us throw ourselves Backwards!

" 'LET US PERFECT THE PAST!

" 'Despairing thinkers of the last days of the Old Era, trembling at the spectacle of its lamentable follies, you have fully understood that the true Progress is backwards! It was in the past that the world knew its happiest days, the epochs of beauty, when glorious and various civilizations—too soon disturbed, alas, always crumbling rapidly—bloomed in the splendor of the arts. We who once counseled mistrust in confrontation with an excessively dark future now cry: Trust the unfolding past!

" 'Since the past must be reborn, let it be reborn ameliorated and perfected! Let us take measures to avoid the recognized faults, let us carefully set aside the injurious errors, etc., etc…' "

"Better and better," said the grandfather. "I've already said that I'll subscribe—that's for a year…"

"Listen to my political program: 'Let us not seek to hide that veritable difficulties will emerge, numerous difficulties of every sort. In politics, history is not, as one might think, experience; history, alas, is inevitably falsified by both sides, so that it becomes impossible to discern the truth of any event, large or small. We can only be certain of one thing, which is that the truth is displaced from history, always displaced. Let us accept history for what it is—the most spiteful of romances—and let us proclaim that nothing is inevitable, that everything is modifiable, and that the worst situations and difficult passages that we must anticipate, duly warned by the information gifted to us in the form of an inventory, can be negotiated better than they were the first time around!

" 'In the same way that any individual, profiting from acquired experience, can correct the mistakes of his first existence, making up for what it lacked and attempting to realize his dreams without falling into recognized errors, so we should act in political terms, and not be content with straightforward recommencements.

" 'The New Era must be one of true progress, always aiming higher, towards perfectibility! Backwards, ever backwards, champions of true progress!

" 'And we are not only concerned with France and Europe in discerning within the past, and in aiming a little higher, to pierce or oversee the thick layers of fog of every color that historians have accumulated through the epochs.

" 'Closest to us, in the 19th century, there was a formidable eruption of Volcano France, followed, as you know, by terrible collapses, then new upsurges and a final lapse into apathy, into political grumbling, interested or otherwise, social indiscipline and anarchy. Previously, there was the 18th century, perfumed decadence; the 17th, the apogee of grandeur turning to an imprudent distension; the 16th, sparkling and terrible, etc., etc...let us pass on...

" 'Let us first hypothesize a principle, that in going back, one finds in every century, almost routinely, a superiority over the one that succeeded it, a life more beautiful, conditions more favorable, facilities more considerable for the natural development of man and society—and let us, in consequence, recognize that, very probably, it was the tribes of the Stone Age who existed in the best conditions, with their naïve and simplistic ambition to establish a society as perfect as possible in its simplicity, and for the access of the greatest number of its citizens to all the advantages that virtually constitute the essence of the happy medium...' "

"You might be going a bit far," said Robert, laughing.

"Yes, certainly, too far," said his father and grandfather, in unison.

"That's the reaction that will immediately raise its head," said Palluel, with an indignant gesture, "but we shall pulverize it! You're not worthy of my accepting your subscription. Here are the eternal enemies of all progress, so satisfied with what they have, and so besotted with their petty ideas, that they can't see beyond their narrow horizon. Tomorrow, gentlemen—the tomorrow that is yesterday—will take the responsibility for providing your answer!"

The father and grandfather nodded their heads anxiously.

"This damned politics sometimes leads us into terrible trouble," said the father, "with changes of regime, epochs of revolutionary upheaval..."

"You haven't grasped my point—I tell you once again that everything will sort itself out, and that the past can be ameliorated! That must be the work of thinking men; the journal *Backwards* will advocate the formation of a large party of wise men dedicated to cushioning the difficulties, greasing the springs of the chariot of State as it approaches sections of the way that are too deeply rutted! Grave political obstacles seem to be foreseeable at short notice as certain fateful dates approach, for indispensable changes and the return of governments formerly overthrown with some brutality—but you must have noticed the ease with which people have already got used to the idea of reacquiring certain forsaken habits. I may be alone, but I am convinced that it will happen quite smoothly, and that these 'revolutions'—there's no other word for them—these reversed revolutions will seem to respond to almost unanimous aspirations.

"And I terminate my program: 'Trust! Let us trust and support with all our hearts the evolutionary movement that is drawing the world in quest of improvement! Backwards, always backwards!' "

"I'll definitely subscribe, all the same," said the grandfather.

"Are you abandoning literature, then?" asked Robert Laforcade.

"Not at all, except that, my former studies having led me to the conclusions that I revealed to you just now, I want to defend my ideas and try to lend some aid to the general movement of the world, which is currently heading in the right direction."

"Let's wait for Monsieur Thiers then," said Robert Laforcade.[16]

"No, Monsieur Guizot!" declared his father.

"Monsieur de Villèle!" murmured the grandfather, in a low falsetto voice that seemed to come from very far away.

"To secure your agreement, Laforcade senior, intermediary and junior," cried Palluel, "I would like to be able to offer you Monsieur de Sully! But I cannot get as far ahead of events as I would like; the great Sully will be the delight of our successors in a couple of centuries' time. In the meantime, let us attempt to arrange things as if he were already here! But I have so scarcely abandoned literature that I am preparing to make my visits to the Academy…"

"What—but you're already a member!"

---

[16] The sequence of names begun here is an ironic retrograde procession through some of the great survivors of French political history. Adolphe Thiers (1797-1877) eventually became president of the Republic in 1871, after the disastrous Franco-Prussian war. His perennial rival, François Guizot (1787-1874), had first served as a minister under Louis-Philippe, after the 1830 Revolution, and came badly unstuck during the revolution of 1848. Joseph, Comte de Villèle (1775-1854), was the chief of the ultra-royalists during the Restoration, prior to the 1830 Revolution, which his policies helped to precipitate. Maximilian de Béthune, Duc de Sully (1559-1641), belonged to a much earlier and more settled era, being a close friend and key advisor of King Henri IV, who cemented the power of the French monarchy and secured its fortunes as a nation state.

"I still am, but our backward progression has almost reached the moment of my election. My predecessor has already returned, one of the numerous advanced cases that Montarcy explains by the difficulties of getting the New Era started, when years were rushing by at five or six a season. I must, therefore, make my visits again, and I shan't hide from you that I shall take advantage of that to tell some of the gentlemen of the Forty what I really think of them... I've no need to hold back, like a candidate desirous of entry, have I?—since I'm a candidate making his exit. Thus, the gentle Palluel that you have known, having become once again Palluel the Romantic, the vibrant voice of Young France, will roar and bite! I've told you that I have advanced too, that the verses and my frenetic ardor of my prime have already come back to me.... As soon as I have taken the time to enter my son Gustave, who has been sleeping over there in his corner while we were arguing, in the Lycée de Bordeaux, I shall begin my visits..."

Everyone had forgotten the young man that Palluel had brought with him. Engrossed in the study of the charades and riddles in a collection of illustrated magazines, he had not said a word, contenting himself with occasionally darting a surreptitious glance at Madame Laforcade, who was doing her embroidery by lamplight beside him.

"That boy is your nephew?" said Robert, in amazement. "I didn't recognize him... I thought he was much older."

"He is my nephew, though," said Palluel. "Isn't that so, Gustave?"

"Yes, uncle," said the strange young man with the wrinkled and bald forehead, extracting himself with difficulty from a riddle.

"I thought he was in the civil service?"

"He was—an agent of the Treasury, deputy head of a Tax Office and decadent poet, or symbolist, or something like that... But here he is; having returned to extreme youth, he's left the Tax Office and I'm sending him off right away to hand in his degree and go back to college."

"Alas," sighed the young man. "Down with college—boo!"

"Ah! There's one who isn't content with the new order of life... What do you expect, my child? We'll all be going back there! You can take it for granted that I won't see much of him, or anything at all, in fact. I wasn't a rich uncle before, but a shabby relation, a wretched old uncle with neither a town house not a place in the Sun, disdained as a relative. Don't contradict me, Gustave... As a poet I was an object of shame and vilification to this joker. Don't contradict me, not again, you little guttersnipe, or I'll write to your headmaster and tell him to put you back..."

Gustave muttered a confused sentence through clenched teeth, in which it was only possible to make out the words "get" and "stuffed."

"I don't know what he was worth as a deputy head in the Tax Office, but as a poet, what must you think, O sad and pitiful Muses, of the manner in which he scraped the lyre? Gustave, do you have your four volumes of verse about you?"

Gustave's pout became more emphatic; he pulled a rather nasty face and started pulling volumes from his pocket. They were bound in various colors: mauve, blood red and bright green.

"Enough, enough," said Palluel. "One volume will suffice; your complete works are tiresomely repetitious! Let's look at the first one."

Palluel opened a volume and held it out to Berthe Laforcade. "Read a passage at random, Madame. It doesn't matter which—there are only masterpieces in there, as one young contemporary critic declared!"

Berthe read aloud, trying vainly to lend some emphasis to the verses:

THE BELOVED WHO PASSES TOO SOON
...On the path, arduous and fluid and fleeting, in her unexpectedly incommensurable flagrancy

The hack which, suave, fragranced with flowering shadow and trembling,

Goes ric rac, trip trap.

And plaintive,

The beauty lies her dying head upon the plaited mane....

Howl, dogs, whoo! whoo! Moon, put on your mask of clouds!

"That's too sad—another, if you please?"

Berthe Laforcade turned a few pages.

WAITING

Oh! Waiting with tense heart, eyebrow furrowed— anguished, ticket in hand, for the omnibus

Always besuited

With cantankerous ladies, on the imperial or the platform

Where the heavy, long, slow trams....

"Don't go any further, dear lady," said Palluel, "you've happened upon the only work in the volume that's fairly clear, but the first remains obscure to me. We're lucky—the author will explain it to us."

Gustave plunged his head back into his illustrated magazine.

"You can't? Little monster, you've ceased to be able to understand your own verses! I knew that—I discovered you this morning in the process of racking your brains, trying to recast them in honest alexandrines and rhyming them properly, and you couldn't! Little guttersnipe, little fraud, as you might say. Do your homework! Tomorrow I'll enter you in college, but before then, I'll force you to translate your lucubrations, or you'll go to bed without supper!"

CHAPTER IX
The Tribulations of a Son

Palluel was interrupted in his wrath by the arrival of Houquetot. He too was looking younger, by at least 20 years, than on the day when Robert Laforcade had been fortunate enough to meet him amid the cataclysms. This was no longer the slightly plump fellow with the cheerful appearance, whose placidity had scarcely been eroded by the worst catastrophes; he was thinner and his face was less jovial. One might even have thought that there were worry-lines on his forehead that had not been visible there in the worst days of yesteryear. Houquetot evidently had his troubles.

"Isn't my father here?" he said, after the customary exchange of polite greetings.

"No," said Robert.

"That's odd—we ere supposed to meet at your house." He drew Robert into a corner and spoke to him in a low voice.

"Hmm!" grandfather Laforcade whispered into his son's ear. "Houquetot the son seems like a fine young chap, but I can't place the father. From the first day I saw that pretentious popinjay, I've felt a certain animosity towards him. Why? I don't know, exactly—but I've seen him before. I'm trying to recall... I have a vague impression that we quarreled. But why? Why?"

"Yes," said Houquetot to Robert, "my father has put me in a difficult position. It's caused me a great deal of anxiety, as I've already told you, and while I'm marking time it can only get worse. So I wanted to bring him here this evening, to keep hold of him for at least one night—he's too careful to have dinner with me. Where is he? I don't know."

"So," said Palluel, who was aware of Houquetot's troubles, "the terrible papa is up to his old tricks again."

"As before, my God yes! The Devil of it is that I still have a court order—500 francs! I can get out of it, I hope, but after... I don't want to be continually borrowing from you, Robert."

"So he still has debts, the terrible Monsieur Houquetot de Mont-Héricourt, Marquis de Chastelandry?"

"Still! He's certainly a Chastelandry, while I, as I've admitted and as you've been able to see, am no more than a simple Houquetot, an orderly, peaceful and tranquil person produced, by some joke of Providence, at the very end of a brilliant, noisy, active and combative family. I was a simple clerk for a long time, a bureaucrat in the registry office at Auxerre; now I'm an accountant at a salary of 300 francs, thanks to my friend Robert Laforcade—but the Chastelandrys, Monsieur Palluel! A château with farms and vineyards in Burgundy, and old Renaissance town house in Dijon, the still-respectable remains of vaster estates eroded under Louis XIV, in the army or at court—all that opulent debris entirely squandered in two or three generations! My father completed a task well begun! I've already given you the details. You only see him know in his old age—which he wears well, doesn't he?—but that's nothing; just wait and see!"

"He's a very fine man," said Palluel. "A superb representative of a strong family. How old is he now?"

"Still in his 70s."

"With all his hair and teeth!"

"Oh yes, all his teeth! More than his fair share, anyhow. As an officer of the royal guard under Charles X, he was, it appears, famous for his terrible escapades. He still had a position and responsibilities then! After 1830, having handed in his resignation to sulk on his estates and no longer having anything to do, he almost turned Dijon upside down with his dueling, brawling and follies of every sort. I only know all that vaguely, although he's dying to tell me all about it. In 1840, three-quarters ruined and perhaps a trifle tired, he married a reasonable dowry and expectations. Nothing was left of the dowry or the inheritance after five years but the Dijon house—mortgaged to the hilt, alas. I feel as if I've been surrounded by money-lenders and bailiffs ever since I was weaned! At 20, I was alone in life, having inherited numerous debts, and I was glad, in order to earn a crust, to find a job scratching paper in an office—the only thing I was good for. There are families that rise and others that decline. Mine was one of those that fall headlong!"

"There's a pork-butcher in my neighborhood called Ronsard," said Palluel, "who might be a descendant of the great poet. I never pass his shop without sighing."

"Personally, I've been as philosophical as possible," Houquetot went on, "arranging my life as simple Houquetot, without a de and without the least marquisate. When I go fishing after office hours, I think about my noble ancestors, looking down on me disdainfully from on high, from the aristocratic corner in which I imagine them enthroned..."

"My poor Houquetot," said Robert, nudging the brave fellow, "business is mediocre, as you know, but all the same, I can put 500 francs at your disposal to settle this court order without inconveniencing myself..."

"Thanks, I can get myself out of it this time. Don't mention that in front of my father—he'd take advantage!"

"This is a very special case," said Palluel. "This prodigal old marquis interests me, and I'll put my petty purse at your disposition, poor victim. Don't stand on ceremony; as a poet I make 70 francs a year, but as a playwright I sometimes get serious royalties. I repeat, the case interests me—you're a true victim of the New Era."

"A poor victim weighed down by innumerable troubles," Houquetot declared, lowering his head piteously, "and I don't expect them to improve, considering that my father is seriously deranged. I can no longer keep him in the house; he's been seized by an ardent frenzy, a burning desire for all sorts of escapades—his old life, in a word, which he's yearning to lead all over again. Until now I've managed to keep going, but how can I continue? I'll soon be buried by the avalanche of legal documents and other nasty things that will rain down on my feeble back and crush me."

"On reflection, though," said Palluel, "I shall stop feeling pity for you! Your family fortune has collapsed, as you say—in that case, it will rise again! You will rise yourself! You will scale the summits again and, in a century or two, there will once again be Houquetots de Mont-Héricourt de Chastelandry—field-marshals in the King's armies, gentlemen of his Chamber, or counselors in his Privy Councils—in the Château de Chestlandry, which will be restored, like the family, to perfect condition. So rejoice, damn it, rejoice!"

"A superb vision, I don't deny—but while waiting, I shall have to fight against squadrons of bailiffs and hordes of creditors. Damn! I remember now—as well as the present ones, there are old creditors—the last ones, who couldn't collect a *sou* of their bad debts after 1850. They'll be reborn too, and will fall upon us! I rejoiced in the new order of things, to be sure, but, by the Devil's horns—to use one of the oaths of my noble ancestors!—I've found nothing in it but torments and disappointments"

"It will all sort itself out, my friend, in two or three generations—which is but a minute in the life of a family, a very short minute!"

At that moment the sound of a bell interrupted Houquetot's lamentations, and he pulled himself together. He recognized the voice of the newcomer in the antechamber and sprang to his feet. "There he is, at last... A thousand excuses, he's arriving just as it's time to go!"

The terrible father of poor Houquetot came into the drawing-room, quite at ease, already offering a polite greeting to Berthe Laforcade, whose hand he kissed gallantly. He was a fine old man, very upright, solidly built and broad-shouldered, squeezed into shape by a corset, wearing a frock-coat cut in an old style with a white carnation in his buttonhole. His entire physiognomy—the hard, bright eyes; the nose like an eagle's beak; the great moustache a trifle too black for his age—declared him to be a fine specimen of a strong family, with the highly-colored complexion of a true Burgundian.

"Well, I'll wager that my son has been telling you that his poor father deserves worse than hanging," he said, laughing, "and I hope that you at least, dear Madame, didn't believe a word of it! He's grumbling still, isn't he? The lad was my despair as a father; he has certain qualities that I recognize, but combined with the ideas of a petty bourgeois exaggerated to excess! No way to educate him! I see that I didn't pay enough attention to him in his youth, and I've been well punished!"

"I was just about to go," said Houquetot. "I was no longer expecting you..."

"It's not yet 11! I ran into an old friend and I was caught up in talking about the good times that are going to return, for which we are waiting impatiently!"

"I think I know his old friend," Houquetot said to Palluel in a low voice. "I was presented with a jeweler's invoice the other day and a bill for flowers sent to the Délassements-Comiques,[17] where the old friend is currently appearing in the chorus..."

"My grandfather is like you. Monsieur de Chastelandry," said Robert Laforcade. "Time isn't going quickly enough for him."

"Ah!" exclaimed the marquis. "That's because we're both men of the *belle époque*; we're bound to be in sympathy!"

"Hmm! Hmm!" said the grandfather, shaking his head as if he were choking.

"Good times, the *belle époque*!" Chastelandry went on, warming to his subject. "None of your inventions, each more far-fetched than the next! I see that your politics are as ridiculous as your ideas, doubtless made by machine! I saw that as soon as I came back, and I don't want anything to do with your steam, your lightning in iron wires, your great

---

[17] The name of this fictitious theater—modeled on the name of the actual Ambigu-Comique—is approximately translatable as "Comic Relief."

ministries, of which there are 12 every three months, your electorate that is made to shout 'Long live the Emperor! Long live the King! Long live the Republic! Long live the Prefect!' simply by pressing a button. I don't want anything to do with your hideous factories, which will soon require the Heavens to be cleaned out. I can't wait for all that to be over and done with! What about you, Monsieur Laforcade?"

"Where the Devil have I seen that fellow before?" murmured the grandfather, without answering.

"Here," Robert told him. "Monsieur de Chastelandry has been here before, as you well know."

"No, not here—before."

"It's quite possible that we've met before," said the marquis, as he turned to draw the astonished Palluel aside. "My dear sir, I have a great favor to ask of you. Are you in finance?"

"On the contrary, Monsieur le Marquis, on the contrary!" Palluel replied, laughing. "I'm in literature…but tell me, all the same."

"In literature—I congratulate you and I congratulate our contemporaries. I thought you were…no matter! You're probably familiar with these money men: bankers, financiers, tax-gatherers—whose trade is doing business at the expense of others, such as we men of the sword…or the pen: an instrument that I honor, sir when it I not wielded by one of those infamous caricaturists who are multiplying like flies! You're not one of those, are you? Yours is the pen of a poet, not that of a political pamphleteer…"

"Which I brandish!" cried Palluel. "The pen of a poet, Monsieur, but also that of a political journalist…"

"Politics is diabolical!"

"That depends on the party, Monsieur!"

"Returned to Earth at a bad time, I have only seen bad ones."

"We shall change all that. Mine will be good, and you can only approve of it! It might be sufficient to quote you my motto, presently that of all progressive men, which is: *Backwards, society, backwards!*"

"You've hit the nail on the head, sir! That's the first sensible thing I've heard since I returned to the mundane world! I shall, therefore, open myself up to you. We seem to have come back, not to our sheep but to those who have sheared them—do you, perchance, know of some worthy and honest money-lender who might have funds available at some percentage or other? You see that I'm quite ready to make him a good offer at my expense—a matter of gold. When France, having gone astray, finds herself back at the crossroads of the great and beautiful highway that she followed for centuries, before hurling herself into the ruts and ditches in which we are presently floundering, when we have recovered all our tranquility, our security, etc., etc…"

"Monsieur, that's the very idea of the article on which I'm currently working—do go on!"

"Well, personally, I expect to recover my family's wealth: my Château de Chastelandry, slightly dilapidated, like all the rest; my town house; my farms, my houses… I'll give you a taste of the excellent wine that I produce on my hills. Do you catch get my meaning? All of that will come back to me in the good time of which we were just speaking, but it's necessary to wait, alas, for the fortunate moment, and I need, while waiting, to meet a brave and honest money-lender who will give me, on any terms he wishes, a serious advance, secured against my property! In case you don't know, I'm seriously embarrassed for the moment—seriously embarrassed, I admit—and it annoys me not to be able to maintain my status, and, most of all, that of my son, who has fallen far too low!"

"I shall do my best, Monsieur le Marquis, to find you one, but it's very difficult—these money men are harsh and hard; they sense that their reign is coming to an end, and even—note this consequence of the new march of time— foresee that a host of businesses, long since liquidated by these same financiers, will re-emerge into light of day, with their dispossessed victims demanding payment and reparation!"

"All the more reason to do a little sure business..."

The marquis was interrupted by grandfather Laforcade, who had just looked him up and down. "We've definitely met before," he said.

"The pleasure must have been entirely mine, Monsieur," the marquis replied, graciously, while whispering in Palluel's ear: "This old man is beginning to bore me..."

"Yes. I can't quite remember, because you've changed."

"Not as much as you," replied the marquis, standing up straight.

"Wait—it's coming back to me. No, a vague memory, rapid as a lightning-flash...but..."

"Indeed," said the marquis, "looking at you closely, it also seems to me..."

"Try to remember yourself... It's coming back to me... There's a connection between us, I felt it immediately....in the Jardin Turc, under Charles X... An old quarrel, I think!"

"Wait," said the marquis. "The Jardin Turc, a quarrel...I remember too...no, it's gone...an altercation..."

"Some insolence..."

"It's quite possible—but be more precise if you please!"

"I can't. It's all vague and confused; I only know one thing, and that's that we were enemies. How? Why? I don't know—but it will come back to me...yes, it will come back to me..."

Houquetot and Robert interposed themselves in order to calm the grandfather, who was becoming agitated, rolling his frenzied eyes and striking his forehead as if that might make the memory he sought emerge more easily. Chastelandry drew Palluel aside, bringing him back to the question of the desired loan. Then, as it was getting late, Houquetot talked about leaving and went in search of his father's cloak.

"Will we still find a coach for hire?" asked the marquis.

"We'll content ourselves with an omnibus," said his son, modestly. "We have to economize."

CHAPTER X
First And Very Serious Financial
And Industrial Disruptions

For months the Bourse had been plunged into an extraordinary state of unease, into a sort of torpor worse than any that the dealers could remember. Passers-by in the Rue Vivienne, during the afternoon hours, sometimes stopped in bewilderment in front of the terrible monument—whose columns, by virtue of what they sheltered, had incited an excessive hatred of columns, of Roman architecture and even of the old Romans themselves (who had, after all merited that hated for a thousand other reasons). There were as many people there as in the old days of booming business: the same black formicary seething in the temple, its members jostling one another beneath the peristyle and overflowing from the colonnade on to the steps, all the way to the gate.

There was the same swarm and the same chaos as before, but without gestures and—which was much more extraordinary—without vociferations: no shouting, no offers, no barbaric questions in unfamiliar languages, no Caribbean roars; without, in short, the usual immense and savage, which communicated such a strong impression of the solidity of the monument's roof. There was the same swarm, but it was slow, bleak and silent. The black multitude stirred as its members circulated and ran back and forth with a distracted air, scarcely sustaining a constant hum of muted whispers, which added away into a mere mysterious murmur behind the columns or on the stairways.

Important things were happening. The Place de Paris was suffering a crisis whose like had never been seen before, even in the heyday of speculation and the times of famous crashes. Never in the history of brokerage, had such a malaise made itself felt in the world of finance; never had such a glacial squall blown over the summits of the great bank, setting the richest houses and the most massive fortunes trembling, and making the faces of certain millionaires white and miserable.

The crisis had been preceded by long months of vague uncertainty, of anxiety building gradually into a state of feverish obsession. The progression of things since the commencement of the New Era, as is expectable, had given rise to certain inversions of habit in the Bourse, like everywhere else. The index was depressed; the lugubrious brokers were all but silent; the big financiers, whose florid faces—like those of ogres who have dined well—had formerly worn triumphant smiles, now wandered around beneath the colonnade with bleak eyes and long faces.

And here, suddenly reappearing among them, were the dispossessed: former boursiers expelled after large-scale disasters without having made their fortunes, who had found themselves among the wrecked rather than the wreckers—and these frisky individuals, rubbing their hands, were the only excited and cheerful people at the funeral celebration that the Bourse had become.

To enlighten ourselves as to the reasons for this extraordinary change in the general appearance of the important gentlemen wandering like lost souls in the edifice in question, it is sufficient to listen to a few conversations and to read a few of the posters stuck to the columns. Yes, times have changed; the people of the former era never had occasion to read such things.

BANQUE MOBILIÈRE
Meeting of former shareholders and bond-holders notice

All persons having formerly owned shares or bonds in the company founded in the name of Banque Mobilière, with a capital of 450 millions, are requested to present themselves at the General Meeting to be held on the 15th of this month, following the verification of their entitlement to a pro rata *share in its restored activity.*

RECONVERSION OF FORMER STATE FUNDS
2½, 3, and 4½ to 5%

Enough of conversions onerous for stockholders, operations which are more like extortion! This time, the bearers of bonds may present themselves at the cashiers' offices without fear. 5% bonds will be repaid immediately. No deductions.

SUMMONS TO THE CASH-DESKS

Shareholders in the General Company of South-Western Steelworks are informed that a restitution of two-thirds of their stock investment will be made to them from the 15 to the 25 of next month, with the remaining third to follow.

CALL FOR BEARERS OF DEPRECIATED STOCKS

The Official Receiver asks the bearers to register their entitlements with the least possible delay. This is not an appeal for funds—quite the reverse.

GENERAL MEETING

Of the former shareholders of United Oil, Central Forges and Glassworks, Metallurgical Bank, High-Life Soaps, Electrical Tramways of Gadhamés, Boileries and Distillers, Giganticorama, Starchworks, etc., etc.
15th inst., at the Bank:
Inspection of old issues, verification of capital and distribution to title-holders.

DIMINUTION OF CAPITAL

The Mining Agency is diminishing its capital. The shareholders are invited to present themselves to withdraw their funds.

143

GOLDSTEIN & CO. BANK

Report on the affairs of the Bank, once subject to disastrous liquidation, for the former shareholders and bondholders. Recall of funds. 345 millions to be distributed. Distribution to everyone possessing entitlements, without formality. Restitution to provincial shareholders by mail.

At the foot of the statue to the right of the staircase, the wide-eyed Laforcade father and grandfather were reading this extraordinary advice over the heads of a group of people who were taking notes.

"Incredible! Incredible!" said a gentleman, shrugging his shoulders as he read each poster.

"Deplorable," murmured another, in a low voice.

"It's scandalous! No one would ever have thought of such things in the good times. The Bourse is doomed!"

"I beg your pardon, Monsieur, but you're preventing me from reading," said father Laforcade, irritated by the movements of a neighbor who was so excited that he had almost put an elbow in his eye.

"I beg your pardon—it's indignation! It's all too much for me! Sad, Monsieur, very sad. No more business! There's nothing now but failed enterprises coming back... Sad, very sad!"

"Sad? On the contrary!" cried father Laforcade. "I see nothing but the re-depositing of funds thought lost, unexpected returns of capital for people once ruined by these failed businesses..."

"That depends on the viewpoint from which you're looking at things..."

"From the right side, of course! I'm putting myself in the shoes of the poor former shareholders..."

"Toodle-de-toot! I see things differently, Monsieur! Business is no longer possible, with these new ways of doing things. It's the final crash, this time—the supreme crash, the

144

crash of crashes! Open any of the financial newspapers, read through it and assess the situation. Oh, that's pretty. Here's a bulletin: Increased withdrawal! Market anemic, collapsed; affairs suspended; reactionary movement; falling rents... It's too violent, this reactionary movement, this going backwards!"

"*Backwards*?" murmured grandfather Laforcade, "An excellent avant-garde journal."

"Don't give me that—an evil rag, dangerous utopias... Look at my *Gazette de la Bourse et de la Banque*. Not one new advertisement, not the smallest issue. On the contra— look here, on the contrary! 'General Meeting of the Immovable Stocks and Bank of Bare Proprietors: Account of the results of the last 35 exercises...' Frauds, Embezzlements, etc. And as regards industry, see here: 'Industrial review: All the reports of industrial societies and all our correspondents are in agreement in observing that results for the last quarter will fully realize, if they do not actually surpass, the most pessimistic forecasts.' What do you think of that? Hang on... 'There is no need to search hard for the causes of this industrial crisis...' You see, industrial crisis, financial crisis, commercial crisis—all the crises at the same time! 'In addition to an exaggerated overproduction that was not in accord with the economic conditions of our time, we also see industry equipped on such a colossal scale, in so complicated a manner, that the efficient functioning of enormous agglomerations of factories is becoming impossible. Too much large and delicate machinery. Reason dictates the abandonment of this peril-fraught system. We have seen the various systems for the mechanical utilization of electricity fall gradually into disuse, and their patents abandoned, following more or less complete ruinations...' "

"Very good," said father Laforcade.

"Hmm! Hmm!" said the gentleman, as he continued his reading... Steam already has its detractors..."

"Excellent! Excellent!" cried the grandfather. "I'm one of them!"

"The employment of steam may have it advantages," said a neighbor, "but it won't last—we'll find something better, you'll see."

"What do you think of stage-coaches, my dear Monsieur?"

"Despite my appearance," said the gentleman—who did indeed seem very young—"I became acquainted, when I was old, with automobiles—a horror, an unbelievably horror, and a folly! Always hurling themselves about at meteoric speeds—there was nothing faster except cannonballs!—as if they had St. Vitus's Dance, with a noise like clattering saucepans and an odor of petrol... and the crashes!"

"Ah!" said father Laforcade, who was still reading the posters. "This is what I was looking for! Finally, I'll get a few funds back, and I won't be sorry..."

"What's that?" said the grandfather, adjusting his spectacles.

"There!"

GRÜNBERG BANK—LIQUIDATION

Meeting of holders of...Credit...Loans...Account, etc... Macedonian loans, Central Bank.

Money will be paid out in Paris, Rue.... and in all the subsidiary branches in the provinces, from the 18th of next month, at 10 a.m.

"How many Central Bank bonds have you got?" the grandfather asked, excitedly.

"Only six, unfortunately, subscribed at 450, if I remember rightly. They were worth 22.50 18 months afterwards.

"And in Macedonians?"

"Fifteen thousand."

"Perfect, my son, perfect!"

The grandfather was interrupted in these congratulations by a slight scuffle; the gentleman who had been moaning about the industrial crisis a short while before had just been grabbed by the collar by a newcomer.

"If I'm not mistaken, you're Corbier, the broker who disappeared with 50,000 francs of mine and tidy sums from many others."

"I'm Monsieur Corbier, but that's no reason to harass me."

"No reason? Swindler! Thief! You'll be tried and sent to prison!"

In less than a minute, a crowd attracted by the raised vices had surrounded the little group gathered under the notices. The Bourse had finally heard a little of the racket of its golden days!

"No fuss, gentlemen, no fuss!" said a fat man, trying to calm the complainant, who had clung so bitterly to the memory of his loss. "Come on—so much noise for such a little thing! Fifty thousand! A pittance! It can be sorted out, I'm sure. Everything is getting sorted out today, as you know full well!"

"That's why I came," moaned the gentleman, whose adversary was still holding him brutally by the cravat.

"No fuss—Monsieur Corbier has the money, that I know. I'm sure of it. No need to get the police involved in such a petty settlement... There'd be statements and formalities. I'm dead set against statements and formalities, myself..."

Two peace officers, draw out of their somnolence by the noise of the altercation, were indeed making their way through the crowd.

"If he has the money..." said the complainant, somewhat mollified.

"Certainly—I'll give you your 50,000 francs, there's nothing more to be said..."

"Evidently, evidently," said a few members of the audience, nodding their heads approvingly. "It's a belated settlement of an old difference, but it's a settlement. On sees such things all the time nowadays..."

"Good, good—that's understood, then..."

The two officers had arrived in the middle of the group.

"What's going on? Come on, gentlemen—what's going on?"

"Nothing at all. Two friends that have met up again, a little effusively, such as one sees all the time nowadays, that's all! Move on! Come on, my dear Corbier, settle up with the gentleman, since, I presume, that's what you've come for..."

"Thank you, Monsieur Grünberg, I did come back for that, as you said. Such an old matter..." The stockbroker sighed.

"Don't moan—there are others in the same situation, and worse, my friend, and worse! Myself included... Am I on a bed of roses?"

"That's true—you too?"

"Me—that's another thing entirely. You know that old story—concluded, settled, exhausted, I presumed. I retired from business to my little estate in Seine-et-Marne, after the settlement..."

"I know, I know... Six months, wasn't it?"

"Yes, six months at Poissy for a few slight irregularities. It was Poissy in those days... Well, my friend, do you know...?"

"Well?"

"Well, here I am in the new era... Machine going backwards, rejuvenating us, eh? But really too... You've come back from Brussels yourself, you can liquidate and be free, with me it's a different matter, and much worse!"

"How so?"

"I've liquidated too, cracked, crumbled, gone under. I'm ruined, they've ruined me, cut my throat! I've been disemboweled, my friend! General liquidation, all my lovely businesses one after another. I've liquidated everything, more than everything. I've liquidated my estate in Seine-et-Marne and I'm going back into Poissy! I have to serve my six months again, my friend, my six months! I'm paying twice over. That's why I told you that you were wrong to complain, and that your fate is enviable by comparison with mine. O youth, you've cost me dear! Everything has begun again, and here I am back where I was then! Ruined, and six months in Poissy on top! And when I'm out again, to attempt to launch a Central Bank! Get away with you!"

"But that's it," said father Laforcade, interrupting the stream of lamentations. "The Central Bank—is that you, Monsieur Grünberg!"

"It's me," said Grünberg, piteously. "A pretty scheme— one of my best ideas... A great success! You remember! I had lots of other afterwards, and the experience allowed me to avoid the little pitfalls..."

"Yes, yes," said Corbier. "It was cleverly managed!"

"If it hadn't been for the envious, everything would have gone smoothly, even better results and no six months, but the envious are always there..."

"Then it's real," father Laforcade said. "Everyone will get their money back?"

"From 10 a.m. tomorrow," Grünberg groaned, "I'll be reduced to beggary."

"Nice!" said grandfather Laforcade, with a ferocious expression. "A great pleasure, gentlemen... Let's get going, to the Grünberg bank!"

CHAPTER XI
Following the Crisis: The Opposite of an Issue

The father and son left the group of stockbrokers, where the discussion continued, some continuing their lamentations over the crisis, others, by contrast, rejoicing in the unexpected consequences of the new march of time. The Grünberg Bank's offices filled a superb building, luxuriously furnished in an eye-catchingly gaudy fashion, in a street just off the boulevard. The entire façade, was plastered with pink posters from top to bottom, around the large door and the windows, which bore the words:

MONEY GIVEN OUT

in enormous letters, above a long list of businesses whose names alone recalled the days of a continuous stream of share issues, the launching of Companies and Societies of all kinds for the construction, mining, cornering, organization and exploitation of everything possible of every kind, from the most improbable in their enormity to the most baroque: the days when funds were raised for the excavation of a tunnel through the Moon, building tramway lines to the Marquesas, founding a company to display advertisements on the pyramids of Egypt, or building an Opera House on the shore of Newfoundland. Facing it, moreover, was another house similarly plastered with posters of the same sort. Those were primarily concerned with railways of local—or, rather, electoral—interest, virtually abandoned, and businesses that had collapsed in consequence of unexpected modifications in industrial practices. Those too were back at their point of departure.

Under the peristyle of the Grünberg Bank, the Laforcades found a queue of shareholders waiting impatiently for their turn to go to the cash-desk. As in the old days of share issues, there were representatives of all the social classes there, with a particular prominence of small landlords and

150

modest tradesmen—stout fellows who had toiled all their lives, prudently setting aside the greatest possible proportion of the rewards of their labor in order to support, no less prudently, innumerable brilliant business proposals outlined so temptingly in their prospectuses...

It was thus that vast lordly estates were built, with historic châteaux bought from the ruined descendants of expropriated aristocratic families, with princely hunting-grounds in jealously-guarded forests. It was thus that sumptuous town houses in fine quarters were acquired, and magnificent villas with carefully tended grounds in suburban holiday resorts, and installations on elegant beaches streaming with wealth and social advantages extracted from Holy Thrift—the thrift of others, at any rate. But all that was ancient history now, and the New Era saw the counterparts of all these things. After the flux of wealth came the reflux. Now that everyone, by courtesy of the providential decree of the Supreme Clockmaker, as Montarcy put it, was going backwards with the entire mechanism of the universe and returning to his beginning, the ingenious inventors of all these marvelous and productive businesses were heading back to the days of their innocent youth, as starving clerks or needy menial workers in one industry or another.

The good shareholders, in returning to the old trap, experienced no sympathy for the fate of these gentlemen. All joyful, laughing and joking, they crowded against the barriers, pushing forward to arrive more quickly before the white-faced cashiers—who, instead of majestically gathering in stacks of gold coins and bundles of banknotes with delicate gestures of their fingertips, as before, were dolorously occupied in extracting gold and notes from open safes reminiscent of gaping and screaming mouths.

As each one passed before the cash-desk, he naturally filled in a certain number of petty forms at each of the windows—everything has to be done in an orderly manner—received the indicated sums, carefully counted and recounted—they had all become very suspicious—and did not leave until they had argued over and claimed the interest to which they were entitled.

"What will Grünberg do now?" a cashier was indiscreetly asked by a gentleman who remained at the window after withdrawing rather large sums—10,000 francs for a mining business, 800 francs for some trading agency, 20,000 francs in Macedonian Treasury Bonds, etc., etc.

"He's holding his last big hunt tomorrow," the cashier replied, "sending back his last medals, crosses, plaques and ribbons the day after."

"And then?"

"The six months he got for his first business—the Central Bank, you know. After that, he'll have to scrape by as he did before, with petty commissions and little deals. It will be very hard, very hard!"

Laforcade the father received a number at one window, signed a piece of paper at another, had it stamped at a third, handed it in, signed something else, and finally had only to wait for his name to be called at the cash-desk.

"Monsieur Laforcade?" a junior cashier eventually called.

"Here!"

"Present!"

Two voices had replied. As well as Monsieur Laforcade, a man in a smock and velvet trousers, holding a little boy by the hand, approached the window.

"Here!"

"Monsieur Laforcade!"

"Present!"

"Are there two of you? Wait…"

The cashier riffled through the receipts that had been handed to him. "Very well, there is Monsieur Charles Laforcade and Monsieur Etienne Laforcade. Shall we begin with Monsieur Charles Laforcade? How much?

"Six Central Bank at 450 each and 15,000 in Macedonian."

"17,000.[18] There! Monsieur Etienne Laforcade, how much?"

"One Central Bank bond," replied the worker. "Just a little one."

"450. There! Next!"

The Laforcades pocketed their money.

"It's not as much as yours," said Etienne, but it's a great pleasure to receive it all the same. We put our entire life savings into that, and were cleaned out, ruined... A disaster for us! It was always impossible for us to make it up, you see, with the children and being out of work. Finally, here it is!"

"So you're named Laforcade, like us?" said the grandfather, looking at the workman. "Where are you from?"

"Angoulême."

"Like us! Hang on! Etienne? Was your father Etienne Laforcade, a gardener?"

"Yes, Monsieur."

"I knew your father and your grandfather—we were distant cousins, I believe."

The man with the small bond was the worthy Etienne that we met at the beginning of this story, before the New Era: a poor old laborer worn out by poverty, troubles and disasters, employed as a manual worker in one of Robert Laforcade's factories and, to complete his misfortune, struggling with a degenerate son, a drunkard son-in-law and citizen Prunet, spirit-merchant of the Amer Collectiviste and other poisoners of the body and soul.

The Laforcades chatted. Etienne told them about his strokes of bad luck, his hard life in terrible Paris, and his gradual disillusionment. They discovered that in his old age, worn out by his labor, he had been the humble employee of a distant and unknown cousin. The grandfather wanted to take

---

[18] This arithmetical mistake is presumably intended to emphasize that, no matter what else might have been inverted in the New Era, cashiers have continued to err in their own favor rather than that of their clients.

him to dinner at the house, and urged him to come, but Etienne refused, only promising to pay his rich cousins a visit after work some day in the near future.

"You'll understand, Monsieur, that my wife is waiting impatiently for my return, with news of our recovered savings… I don't want to make her wait too soon, so I'll take the boy home. Who would have believed that this little lad would give us so much trouble when he grew up, and cause the wife and me so much grief! Since the great day, he's gone back gradually to what he was, leaving behind the absinthe merchants and all the exploiters that empty your head of all healthy ideas in order to fill it with their vitriolic lies. I know what it is—I've had a taste. Now there's only rosy cheeks— he's a well-behaved lad that his mother can spoil without any danger, thanks to the new system! And his sister, who had so much unhappiness, so many bad days to pass before, is also rid of it—she's a brave and bonny lass again, without a care in the world, who spends all the holy day singing and gossiping. With our own young days coming back, there's the consolation, Monsieur Laforcade, there it is! See you soon!"

As they were leaving the Bank, the Laforcades caught sight of the fat Grünberg, who made a brief appearance in the office of the head cashier.

"Well, where are we with the Central Bank?"

"46,000 shares, in round numbers," the cashier replied. "I've added it up, Monsieur le Baron."

"In two days! A fine issue!" said Grünberg, rubbing his hands.

"No, not subscriptions—reimbursements, Monsieur le Baron, reimbursements!"

"Am I stupid? I'm confused, losing my mind! Oh, my hounds, my carriages! And the Macedonian Loan? Same thing, isn't it? Don't call me Monsieur le Baron any longer— I'm no longer a Baron. O bitterness!—I'm no longer even a prince of finance. My former sons-in-law, the Marquis and the Comte, are no longer speaking to me, and I've been expelled from the Jockey Club! Catastrophe of catastrophes!"

"When shall we ever recover? What times, Monsieur le Baron, what times!"

"And I've got my six months to serve again, to cap it all!"

CHAPTER XII
The New Era Encounters a Few Malcontents and Detractors

Backwards, the journal founded by ex-Academician Palluel, had immediately found favor with the public. It expressed so clearly, in its title, an idea and a program that was in everyone's mind! Its editorial content echoed the sentiment of many men who, enlightened by hardship and long and repetitive experience, took account of the earlier era's mistakes in the breathless course of false progress, in the dogged forward pursuit of the deceptive chimera of a Golden or Silver Age that was long since past!

Backwards was a success. It was already the most widely-read of all the great organs of opinion, with a bigger circulation than the *Presse*, which Emile Girardin had re-launched, or the *Constitutionnel*. People expected to see the *Quotidienne* again imminently, which would doubtless promulgate very nearly the same ideas, but Palluel's journal had got in ahead, and its long-term fashionability was assured.

Palluel was in his cluttered office, in which mountains of newspapers and pieces of paper were heaped up in every corner and on all the furniture, seats as well as tables. Younger than ever, brisk and lively, with his blond mane in disorder, he was weaving between the heaps of papers, chatting nervously with Montarcy, who was seated at the table. The famous savant was also radiant with recovered youth, his eyes as bright and piercing as blades, his forehead—the forge of thought, of which the eyes seemed to be the fire—still vast beneath a dense shock of black hair.

"Everyone seems to be in agreement on the matter, my dear Montarcy," Palluel said. "Yes, you were right; life was badly designed before, in its old form. It was doubtless just a trial, an experiment, and the true form is today's. Yes, far too often, and to too great an extent, life proceeded from one sorrow to another, finally to end in despair. While the new life…. What advantages there are for everyone in the new life, what general benefits! In spite of a few petty inconveniences, it's impossible to deny the superiority of the advantages and benefits. Isn't it much better, as nowadays, to begin everything with its end result?"

"Peace of mind."

"And modifications of every sort, rendered possible by experience."

"Let us ameliorate the past! That should be the motto of every thinking man!"

"Yes, so many benefits. One chooses the true friends, formerly so often misunderstood, the sincere hearts that one spurned, alas, through ignorance or disdain, and one casts aside the false and fragile friendships that ring hollow, the affected sentiments. One disposes of harmful ambitions."

"One disdains futile concerns, as one discards activity without serious purpose; one distinguishes the true joys and pleasures more easily…"

"And the beloved individuals who are reborn! Invalids to begin with, they gradually return to a state of health before the delighted eyes of their nearest and dearest—that is the true convalescence!"

"For the old vanquished by life, my dear Palluel, what revenge! For the poor creatures laid low by storms, who languish wounded and disabled, lamentable wrecks on the sharp rocks, it's a return to initial hopefulness, to beautiful illusions that send their sufferings to sleep."

"Everything is definitely better—all is well!"

"All is certainly well," said a gentleman who had put his head around the half-open door, "but would you care, Monsieur Palluel, to give a hearing to someone I have here."

"Come in," said Palluel. "My dear Montarcy, do you know Monsieur Dorigny, the secretary of the editorial board? A former politician, municipal councilor, deputy, revolutionary, convict, ambassador and God knows what else."

157

"Former anything and everything," said Dorigny, "but now returned to his first love, journalism! God, how bored I sometimes was in my high offices, and how I annoyed my fellows! O ambition, what stupid things you make us do! But this isn't about me—there are people here who are not content. You must take it upon yourself to prove to them that everything is for the best now, in the best of ameliorated worlds."

"We shall try!" Palluel lowered his voice. "Dorigny was a good fellow, you see, not short of a *sou* or two, a man of letters, thrust by a freak of chance into politics, for which he wasn't suited. He was forced to become swell-headed to maintain the role he'd taken on. He had 30 years of restlessness, disillusionments galore, fastidious speeches to write and deliver, shady deeds to carry out, over which he had to fight duels and commit other violent acts, acquiring high situations from whose summits he often found himself rapidly precipitated because he could not hang on to them securely enough, years in prison, etc., etc. He's beginning to catch his breath since being reborn and returning to his point of departure."

"Still plagued by all the pebbles on the road," said Dorigny, coming back into Palluel's office with a thin, bony man who came forward with his head bowed, wearing an anxious expression, twiddling his long grey beard.

"Monsieur Crozel," said the editorial secretary. "The famous Crozel—the painter who had so much talent."

"So much talent!" said Crozel, bitterly. "I'm delighted to hear you say it, but I've only just learned of it, and it was noticed a trifle belatedly…"

"Have you returned recently, Monsieur Crozel?" asked Montarcy.

"Scarcely a week ago, and you see me still dazed by the event, and by everything that I've learned. At first, I thought it was a joke, when I was told about the incredible fortune of my works."

"Ever modest, Monsieur Crozel—that did you no good before…"

"Don't put the blame on me! Anyway, imagine how flabbergasted I was when I was shown volumes of articles of art criticism—gentlemen building chapels or temples, burning buckets of incense in my honor, when they or their predecessors previously did not deign to look at my poor canvases! And when I saw the prices they were fetching! Eh? What? How Much? 80,000… 100,000… *sous*? Centimes? No! Well, it's too much."

"What, you aren't happy?" cried Dorigny.

"I certainly am not happy! Why, they nearly let me die of starvation in my little garret! For year after year I dragged all the devils in hell by their tails, quite happy to trade one of those paintings occasionally for a slice of bread, which are now selling for their weight in banknotes! Monsieur, I would have painted signs if anyone had cared to commission me to do it! Why, there are gallery owners who gave me 150 francs for my canvases, almost out of charity, when there was no food in the house or when my things were seized—because the bailiffs knew my address very well—who are now selling them on for a cool 500,000! And I should be happy?"

"Personally, I think so," said Dorigny. "Another thing— did you know that you're in the Louvre?"

"And they flung me out of the door of Salons, or put me in the corners!"

"And they've sold a million copies of your mast…"

"Don't say another word! They refused to give me 500 francs for it, the Pactolus glimpsed in my most venturesome dreams! And then, on top of that, I have to begin my life of hardship, torment and bailiffs all over again? I have to start dying of starvation again? What won't I have to do? All the pleasure that I might have had in rediscovering my brushes, my canvases, my illusions, my artistic joy, my old hopes— always dashed but always reborn—all that happiness is spoiled for me by what I've learned! You speak to me of masterpieces, but it appears that people are going back, as

159

regards painting, to the ideas that people had in my time, and that my reputation will decline, my masterpieces becoming mere trifles once again. And I should be happy? To be hoisted so high by fashion or speculation in art on the Bourse, only to be squashed al over again! To climb to 100,000 francs only to return to 25,50 francs!"

"But we'll support you!" cried Palluel. "Rely on our journal, founded for the study, and also for the amelioration of the past, with the aim of preserving us from all the errors into which it previously fell!"

Crozel shook his head sadly. "And do you know," he whispered into Palluel's ear as the latter showed him out, "among all the paintings that I've seen with my name in golden letters on the frame and my signature, there are many that I don't recognize…"

"Here's our art critic now," said Palluel. "I'll introduce you to him, don't worry… Monsieur Crozel, dear friend, the great painter; Monsieur Brignol, who vigorously defends the principles of true art in our journal *Backwards*."

"Monsieur Crozel?" said the critic, with the air of a man to whom that name did not mean very much.

"Ah!" said Palluel. "Yes, our friend Brignol is a little ahead of his time; he's from the *grande époque*, a little before you, Monsieur Crozel…"

"Ah! Very good. Yes, it's coming back to me now!" said the critic, striking his forehead. "Laudable, certainly, your work, but I can distinguish dangerous tendencies therein… Beware of what follows! That which is excellent engenders that which is less good, you know, and that engenders that which, etc., etc… Delighted to offer you my compliments, however. Actually, art is on a better path; it is reversing unfortunate tendencies. As I was saying to this gentleman, who is a very important collector…"

The painter Crozel looked anxiously at the important collector: a middle-aged gentleman with bleak eyes and pursed lips slumped in an armchair.

"Ex-collector!" sighed the gentleman.

"You have no Crozels in your gallery?"

"I had no Crozels in it; I came along afterwards. I said, or rather, someone said to me: art, always moving, never stationary, proceeds in stages… It's necessary to look forwards!"

"Shh!" said Palluel. "Don't pronounce that word here— it's been making us do stupid things for 5000 or 6000 years."

"Stupid is the right word! It's necessary to look forwards, I said to myself; already the modernists…"

"Another dirty word…"

"All right! I'll go on… Already the modernists, realists, plenarists and others are no longer in the movement; art has entered a new stage. I therefore devoted myself to subtle pointillists, luminists, stainers, splashers, smearers and other impressionists."

"Pardon?" said the critic. "You mean that you let in the people who make landscapes in confetti, or who serve up color with a trowel, like roughcast plaster, whose works nevertheless imitate true paintings seen from a distance of thirty-five meters…"

"What do you expect? So much was said to me about it. Extreme sensibility, acuity of vision, spectral analysis, prismatic…fluidity…ambiance—oh, ambiance! And the decomposition of light, the vibration of light, the orchestration of light, the waltz of atoms in light, etc., etc… It seemed that there was all of that in their canvases, it was clearly visible art the time—but the time has passed, and nothing is visible there today but dancing landscapes, trees that are little brooms, viscous waters like dissolved sealing-wax, decomposing faces turning green or purple, zigzags of color, gashes of more-or-less ill-judged shades, palette-splashes on slack and indecisive lines… And I've laid out for that, Monsieur, thus far, 800,000 francs! Today, with the change… Oh, don't tell me how much it would fetch at auction! Don't you find my fate deplorable?"

"Profoundly deplorable! I pity you, Monsieur, we all pity you, but without excusing you, for no one threw you into it by a criminal act—you did it all by yourself…"

"And the worst thing, Monsieur, the very worst, is that in forcing myself to do it, I never succeeded in finding the slightest pleasure in looking at those masterpieces, which cost me my eyes and my head! I racked my brains, I recited passages from books and articles every morning, decreeing that before Messieurs X, Y and Z there had never been any but vulgar daubers and sculptors incapable of cutting up a simple horse-chestnut properly—but nothing worked; in my inmost depths I remained so cold that I castigated myself furiously and almost despised myself! Imagine my state of mind now the decline has come! What can be done? It's necessary to put an end to it all, though, and I've come to ask you to put the following advertisement in your estimable journal:

"HURRY—GREAT OPPORTUNITY—Seek to exchange a collection of ultra-modern paintings—including tachists, sensationists, confettists, vibrists, etc., twelve dozen canvases in total, as new condition, cost 800,000 francs plus—for three landscapes by Bidauld and three by Valenciennes.

"I need to look at works by the most Bidauldian of Bidaulds and Valenciennes, in the fine style."[19]

"Of course!" cried the art critic. "But what of expiation, sir? Twelve dozen... The hair is standing up on my head! At whatever risk—malady, contagion, melancholy or delirium— you must keep your twelve dozen!"

---

[19] The reference is to two of the leading members of the "neo-classical" school of landscape painting, Jean-Joseph-Xavier Bidauld (1758-1846) and Pierre-Henri de Valenciennes (1750-1819). The former is referred to as "the most Bidauldian of Bidaulds" because his elder brother was also a notable landscape painter, of a slightly different stripe, and his father had also achieved a certain celebrity. Robida spells the name Bidault, which is an acceptable alternative, but I have substituted the spelling used in contemporary reference books for the sake of clarity.

"Have pity! I think I might place them with the father of a family... Values are bound to go up, and go up continually, since they've been seen at 4,50 francs a meter..."

"Keep your twelve dozen!"

"Not in perpetuity, Monsieur, not in perpetuity! If I don't find a kind soul to make the exchange, I'll hang all the canvases in the rooms of our maidservants..."

"Have you a grudge against your maidservants?" asked Palluel, angrily.

The unfortunate collector released a long sigh and got to his feet wearily. Crozel shook his head and headed for the door. They were heard moaning in chorus as they went through the editorial offices, beginning to describe their troubles to one another.

The critic had begun chatting with another editor; his mind boggled at the mere thought of twelve dozen vibrist paintings; he shivered in terror and then became indignant. Only a few snatches of sentences were audible: "We of the *bonne époque*... We are certainly not academicians... Rather man the pumps, Monsieur... No, never! And Delacroix, did he not vibrate light? In every work of art, I ask to see artistry... Realism? Modernism? Indifference to motif? Never! I've heard mention of a little modern invention, photography... Much better than them... They're rogues! Nature seen with sincerity in impressionist painting, come on!"

The other editor attempted to speak; he tried continually to insert a few words between Brignol's sentences, but the latter was not listening and maintained the upper hand: "Géricault... Delacroix... Descamps... But then, if those people were in the right, it would be necessary to run off and set fire to the Louvre, Monsieur, and all the museums.... Holland, Italy, Germany, my friend..."

"Yes! Yes!" said the dear friend. "Perfectly... Quite right... Of course! It's like their literature... Hold on..."

"That's the editor in charge of literary criticism," whispered Palluel to Montarcy. "Another one from the *bonne époque*!"

"Of course!" the man from the *bonne époque* eventually said, profiting from a moment when his friend paused to drawn breath. "Do you think that literature hasn't had its maladies too? You can observe the present taste for the excessively sweet, for the insipid, for pure Berquinades.[20] Necessity of convalescence, my good friend! There is nothing unctuous enough for our palace, ravaged and corroded by the naturalist and ordurist malady born of social decomposition. The malady has run its full course, and it has left us with weak stomachs and a bitter taste in the mouth. We are reverting to Monsieur Berquin and the tales of Canon Schmid! And modernism! The endless repetition of the same uninteresting adventure! Turn it around! The little gentleman in tall hats write like that; the beautiful ladies do likewise—and always the same! Are we supposed to follow a story for 400 pages that wouldn't hold our interest for five minutes in real life?

"Modern life? We live it—don't talk to us about it unless you have something particular to say, something that might be the study and the expression of a class, a county, a profession! Yes, you're right... There's a man named Balzac at present— may that one, at least, live long! Of course—let me speak!— Laplanderism... The vogue for foggy and glacial writers, natives of the vicinity of the pole, is another disease of these sick times! They're all the same, these Icelandic or Siberian writers, and so gloomy! These Northern men of genius always have the attitude of grumpy old men! When some genial Laplander sets out to recycle all the old ideas that we've been recycling ourselves for 3000 years, on the imperfection of life, the impacts of destiny, the imperfection of everything and

---

[20] Arnaud Berquin (1747-1791) was an egregiously condescending writer for children; this derivative of his name became a pejorative byword for offensively dreary prose. Jean-Christophe Schmid (1768-1854), nicknamed the Canon, whose name is coupled with Berquin's a few lines further on, continued that insipid tradition of children's fiction in his native Bavaria.

164

anything newly discovered, they're served up as great novelties, with meditations, inductions and deductions on top, around and on the side—especially on the side—cut into four and 14, all the color of the winter sky, and with the most perfect ill humor...

"Am I boring you with my literary maladies? I've listened patiently to your maladies of the palette. We have our epidemics too... Oh, pity the poor readers of this literary period! What a sad festival the unfortunates have had, as the artistic religion has erected the cult of the ugly, the dirty and the mournful! Endlessly repeating the same banalities, exhaustively detailing ignominies and perversities, gorging on the same base deeds, saturated with the same miseries carefully collected by modernists and realists, sadists and naturalists! Naturalism, eh? Under the pretext of sincere study, all classes of society, all communities shown in the same and most complete state of moral putrescence, all vices generalized, every class with its uniquely distinctive and violent stink...brrr! What effect must such intellectual nourishment have on the social organism? Its literary stomach ulcerated, its brain permanently contaminated! I need to start a new regime, my friend, in order to see with a critical consciousness... I can only recover by reading *The Three Musketeers*—which will soon be coming out—14 times over."

Montarcy was pressed for time, but he stayed to hear the complaints of a young man to whom the secretary to the editorial board had just handed back an unacceptable manuscript. The young man protested vigorously, seemingly furious.

"That little chap," whispered Palluel, "is an old celebrity, the most prolific propagator of these literary maladies—debilitating colds or fully-fledged fevers—of which our critic was speaking: 60 naturalist novels, 60 volumes of social pathology! Anyone who absorbed them all in one go wouldn't be cured by reading *The Three Musketeers* 2000 times over! Today, having returned, like everyone else, to his beginnings, the ex-naturalist submits sentimental verses to the *Journal des*

Demoiselles and sickly-sweet novelettes in which, entirely involuntarily, he occasionally slips in reminiscences of his old works, which would cause a veteran of the African wars to blush, among all the prettiness and insipidity."

CHAPTER XIII
A Few Returns, Happy and Unhappy

While all this was going on, the worthy and placid Houquetot had called, as had become his habit, to bring his friend Robert up to date with the uninterrupted series of embarrassments and annoyances he was suffering because of his terrible father. He found Robert rather anxious too, very happy on the one hand on account of some good news he had recently received, but very irritated on the other by certain less satisfying events.

"Has something have happened here, then?" Houquetot asked, interrupting his confidences, having observed Robert's preoccupation.

"A great deal! But tell me, how are things with you?"

"Nothing new—nothing fundamentally out of the ordinary..."

"Tell me anyway."

"Well, my father is getting younger every day—younger than ever!"

"Naturally—so are we!"

"Much more than us! We're growing younger normally, but he's truly getting ahead of himself! He's more passionate, more dandified, more the officer in the Restoration's black musketeers than ever! And that's not without its inconveniences. He gets indignant at being obliged to be stingy, and swears that he's going to sow blood and fire among the bankers who involved him in certain financial operations in 1840 or thereabouts, fruitful for some, disastrous for others. He frequents fashionable fencing schools and the Café Anglais... which means that we have to eat dry bread 20 days a month... ."

"Damnable!"

"He dreams of acquiring a cabriolet by the month, and a tiger, and searches high and low for liberal money-lenders..."

"Diabolical!"

"That's not all! In his heyday, it seems, around 1828, he had an adventure that caused a huge scandal in Dijon— something extremely serious! A lady of the best society, the wife of a councilor at the Royal Court was horribly compromised by him. Did I say compromised? He abducted her!"

"What of it? 1828 is still a long way off."

"I repeat that he's racing ahead in a disastrous fashion. This adventure, the scandal of 1828, is running through his head. He's absolutely determined to return to Dijon to cut off the councilor's ears, and those of a number of other people mixed up in the affair, and to abduct the councilor's wife all over again!"

"Is the poor woman in this world?"

"So I'm informed, yes; once again she is the edification of the faithful swains of her parish—a different one, of course, from that of 1828—and she's 60 years old! When I told my father that, he had a blue fit and strictly forbade me to meddle in things that don't concern me. I dread that he might set out for Dijon at any moment. And now, what's new with you?"

"This: finally my grandfather will no longer be alone in life!"

"You mean he's getting married?"

"He's no longer a widower, at least. He's received a letter from my grandmother, returned to the home of other grandchildren in the distant provinces, near Laval, and I'm going to fetch her…"

"Very good. I'm delighted—my compliments."

"We're all very happy, me especially. I never knew her, the nice grandmother of whom I heard so much talk in my childhood. As for my grandfather, he's almost dancing with joy, and is trying to remember the songs sung at his wedding in 1826. I leave tomorrow morning; the railway no longer goes as far as Laval, so I'll have to take the coach the rest of the way."

"The railway no longer goes that far?"

"No, the main line stops well short, and the smaller lines have long been abandoned. Steam no longer appeals: it exposes us to so many inconveniences, not to speak of the dangers, just to save a little time. But that's not all—there's some news that's not so pleasant."

"What's that?"

"Complications! Old relatives, cousins or something, have arrived…"

"From the provinces?" Houquetot asked.

"And from further away, my dear friend—much further away! The new life sometimes throws us into singular family complications, I must say! On the one hand, my grandmother returns to another family, and on the other, totally forgotten cousins fall into our arms… You'll see them soon; I'll introduce you to them…"

The Laforcades were just finishing dinner; they were still in the dining-room. Berthe, the father and the grandfather were there, Palluel and three gentlemen, the inconvenient cousins, all three of whom answered to the name of Jollyvat: François Jollyvat; Jollyvat from Paris; and Jollyvat from Tours—one short, thin and quite young; one short and flabby, by virtue of lost obesity; and the third short, fat and ruddy-faced. They were in the process of elucidating the question of parentage in order to calculate the exact degree of their relationship. It was rather complicated; while sorting it out, the newcomers were calling everyone 'cousin,' including Palluel, who might have had some vague entitlement to it, and—as soon as they caught sight of him—Houquetot.

"But yes," said Jollyvat from Paris, "the wife of Monsieur Laforcade the grandfather was, I believe, the aunt of my uncle, who is therefore the nephew of Monsieur Laforcade grandfather, and, in consequence, the first cousin…"

"I beg your pardon," said grandfather Laforcade, "my wife, I think, was the aunt in the Breton fashion, which is to say, merely a cousin…"

"You're making an error of one degree…"

"Permit me—you'll see…"

"So, my dear cousins," said Jollyvat from Tours to Robert and Houquetot, in a low voice, "you don't know your cousin François Jollyvat?"

"Not at all! Not even by name!"

"Alas, I knew him too well at one time: an old egotist, an arid heart, and an old rogue to boot! How does he strike you now? What do you make of him?"

"He seems rather pitiful... His doleful expression..."

"Merely crestfallen, and with good reason! I'll tell you why he has such a lamentable air about him! He was a selfish old fellow who, all his life, went to great lengths to care for his plump, rubicund person, and have others care for it! I've followed his career—I know him! Fleeing responsibilities, anything that might inconvenience or hold him back, he was very wary of founding a family. Marry—no way! A confirmed bachelor, François Jollyvat. He preferred to lead a long and merry boy's life. Up with joy! We're not the sort to court melancholy, are we? No cares, no children whose health might give us anxieties and would have to be brought up, directed towards a career, found a place, established...no worries, all our resources applied to the satisfaction of our appetites or our whims. That's my estimable cousin François Jollyvat. Yes, but now he's paying for all that!"

"That's true," said Robert. "Today, he's alone."

"If it were only that! There's something else. At 50, the despicable old fellow appeared to discover a lively interest in the family. He had nephews, and long-neglected cousins. All of a sudden, he became the most affectionate uncle in the world, and nephews, nieces, cousins, happy with the change, after having been long disdained, competed in pampering him, so the second part of his life, which had threatened to be rather somber, as is usual for aged bachelors, was, on the contrary, as rosy as he could have wished. The rascal! He knew how to talk up his fortune, passing for a miser who had amassed a fortune, dangling his glittering inheritance before his nephews' eyes. The nephews fought one another with little favors and flatteries, cosseting him for more than 25 years, until the last minute—but then…"

"Then?"

"Bang! Catastrophe! It was tidy, the inheritance so hard earned. The succession was opened up; the fat inheritance arrived—and there was Monsieur the notary! Collapse! In his fifties, the good uncle had nearly run through all his wealth, and had invested the little that remained in an annuity. He had obtained all the caresses, the favors, the attention, the consideration and the pampering by fraud!"

"And now?"

"Now, imagine how inconvenient the backward progression of the New Era must be for him! Here he is, back among the nephews of whom he made such fools! You can imagine the welcome he received—the worthy uncle, the nice old gentleman uncle with the inheritance, the excellent old relative, was welcomed more than coldly; the entire family is now in revolt against the old fraud. He's only looking to begin again, to be pampered as before, but by others! Come on, dear Uncle Parasite, do us the honor of making fools of us all over again! Mind your health, you horrible old skinflint! Pray take this armchair, these little cushions, go on, let yourself be coddled, industrious uncle! Old lunatic! In brief, a horrible existence. Expiation! He complains, he moans, but what good does it do? He fell into my arms to ask me for help and advice; I told him to be patient and I beg you to talk to him in the same fashion. He must resign himself to it, after all, and it's only twenty five years of annoyance and wear—then he'll be 50 again, as before…"

While Jollyvat from Tours was slipping these confidences softly into Robert's ear, François Jollyvat, the old bachelor newly emerged into the New Era, now a victim, disabled and disoriented, was telling the tale of his woes to father Laforcade in his own fashion, railing against everyone, ornamenting it with a few revelations regarding Jollyvat from Paris.

"Oh, Monsieur, nephews who were, in sum, rather vulgar, scarcely elevated in situation or mind, in whom a man of good education like myself, having seen the world, was generous enough to take an interest—dastards whom I attempted to raise up to my own level! Scoundrels with no hearts and no shame! And I was naïve enough to think their affection disinterested, for I believed that, Monsieur, I was naïve enough to believe it! But what do you think of cousin Jollyvat from Paris? I thought he was in a very different position! I was very surprised..."

"When I knew him, in 1865 or 66," said father Laforcade, "he was a rich merchant, a stout gentleman, very successful, very solid, and rather disdainful of his relatives..."

"It's said that he was a skillful player, whose enrichment was due much more to knowing how to exploit profitable relationships to the full and take advantage of circumstances than to his own intrinsic worth, which is—take it from me, I knew him!—nothing. He was a vain man, puffed up with his own importance and the merit he attributed to himself, because everything he did then was successful—but there's one who'll gain nothing from the New Era! See how annoyed he is as he goes backwards, retracing the route he followed before, utterly humiliated by his decline and deflation, returning modestly to the petty origins he concealed so well: to the humble shop where he once served two ounces of pepper and half a dozen candles—for he's back in the little shop now, although he hasn't admitted it to you..."

"Bah! I'll give him my custom—it's the least I can do!"

"Ah, the new life! There are some of us who find it rather bitter."

"Yes," said the third Jollyvat, the thin Jollyvat from Tours, who had heard these last words and who drew closer. "Who are you talking about? I'm undergoing a cruel experience at present!"

"You're complaining about growing younger," said Palluel, "and reliving your best years?"

"I'm certainly not complaining about growing younger—I've welcomed the backward progression just like everyone else, but there are delicate circumstances and difficult phases…"

"What do you expect? For so many advantages, it's well worth enduring a few petty inconveniences!"

"It's precisely to get away from one of those unpleasantnesses that you see me so far from my house in Tours, accompanying cousin François Jollyvat, while my business might be in jeopardy. The fact is, I've been married twice!"

"That's better than not at all," said father Laforcade. "Look at cousin François."

"And my first wife recently returned!"

"What about the second?"

"Oh, the second, naturally, returned to her family. But what an unfortunate event—happy, I mean to say, but happy and deplorable at the same time, to see my first wife return…"

"Did she make you unhappy?"

"Not at all—she was charming! She adored me and I idolized her."

"Then I don't understand your distress."

"It's just that I swore to her that I'd never remarry, to live alone with her memory, forever remaining an inconsolable widow for whom the Earth no longer had any Sun, or roses, or joy, or… And I returned to the foot of altar after three…"

"After three years?"

"No, after three months! My first wife was charming, as I said, but a trifle excitable—and very jealous. Horribly jealous! The scenes have already started, but she doesn't know everything yet, and when she finds out who my second wife was—one of her friends, alas, whom she is astonished not to have seen as yet—there's bound to be attacks of nerves, fainting fits, rages, fingernails splayed…

"It's in the hope that the explanations might be made during my absence that I ran away like a coward; I don't want to go back until she's had time to calm down…"

"Bah! Gather your courage in both hands and weather the scene. You'll be tranquil afterwards."

Jollyvat from Tours shook his head sadly. "I've had months to think it over, Monsieur. We adore one another, but I'll never have another quiet meal. We'll recover our former happiness, but punctuated by reproaches and fits of anger! The storm will break over every meal; I'm inevitably bound for a life of indigestion and stomach-ache!"

In the meantime, father and grandfather Laforcade were trying to make Jollyvat the old rogue understand that there was nothing for him to do but resign himself to the situation and try, along with Jollyvat from Paris, to hurry back as rapidly as possible to his sad hearth.

François Jollyvat raised painful objections in a tearful voice; he was in no hurry to go home, and attempted with all possible reticence to obtain information regarding his relations and their marriages. There were it seemed, in this degenerate world, no more worthy nephews and cousins disposed to heap attention and tenderness upon him? Alas, alas, what a sad return to life!

"Come on, come on!" said Palluel, trying to make a joke of it in order to come to the aid of the Laforcades. "Accept it as a penance, and a penance thoroughly deserved; admit, worthy François Jollyvat, that you were a little too fond of your comforts before, and the various advantages of the bachelor life! We joyful celibates have to resign ourselves to inconveniences in our old age! Each to his own: you have to go back to your peevish nephews; Monsieur Jollyvat from Tours has to go back to have his eyes scratched out by the first Madame Jolllyvat. Everyone must pay for his little mistakes— in this transformed world you see, everything sorts itself out in a very just and moral fashion!"

"Boo hoo!" moaned the joyful celibate.

"Heu heu!" spluttered Jollyvat from Tours.

"And what an agreeable transformation!" Palluel went on. "Old, ugly, morose—I'm talking about myself, Monsieur François Jollyvat—old, ugly and morose, as I say, peevish, bad-tempered and disagreeable, I shall gradually and gently become passable, bearable and almost amiable and finally charming! And you will do the same! Isn't poor Monsieur Jollyvat from Tours only a few fingernail-scratches away from being a happy man? He will be adored again! I know other husbands less likely to rejoice in recovering that 'past felicity, which can never return again' in the new life."

Jollyvat from Paris sighed dolorously.

"You too?" said Palluel. "Well despite your lamentations and your sighs, marriage in the new form still seems to me to have advantages over all the different forms attempted in the old life, since the earliest civilizations in the remotest depths of antiquity. It's necessary to recognize, gentlemen, that the institution has now arrived at its most perfect form: the most appropriate to realize all the benefits that one is entitled to expect from it and to give the spouses every guarantee of happiness! Think of all the torments that our ancestors endured on reaching marriageable age, of the family turmoil, of the understandable anxieties of mothers, of the preoccupations of fathers, of all the serious questions that had then to be asked! Marriage was a lottery! How would he and she fare within it? Would he be favored by fortune? Would she, under the protection of the gods, draw a lucky number or a merely passable one in that terrible game of chance?

"Well, today the preoccupations are suppressed, the turmoil and the torment abolished, since the people who are born—or reborn—re-enter into marriage, as into life, at the end! He recovers a beloved spouse…"

Jollyvat from Paris groaned and Jollyvat from Tours sighed, while the horrible old bachelor François Jollyvat released a lugubrious moan.

"….She reconquers a spouse once loved! In every case, there can be no surprises; the spouses know one another: no more lottery, no more hazards, no more disappointments, no more errors, no more unexpected disasters or sudden catastrophes! And if things go badly regardless, as was sometimes seen in the old life—if there was open warfare, quarreling, even divorce—will not time, now far better than before, not set everything in order and inevitably bring back the happy days of the honeymoon?" Palluel darted a sideways glance at Robert and Berthe Laforcade, who were sitting side by side. "And permit me to tell you that I have known spouses whom the feverish and uncertain former existence, so different from the calm and tranquil times we are now fortunate enough to relive, had precipitated into irritation, misunderstanding and open disagreement, which were bound to end in separation and divorce. Look at them now, these unhappy spouses of yesteryear: by virtue of fortunate modifications and agreeable changes, to the great delight of their friends, they have returned to honeymoon bliss, to the tender and rosy days of the commencement of their union..."

Berthe Laforcade blushed and, with a graceful movement, hid her face behind Robert's shoulder, whose ear the smiling grandfather pinched gently. Some time before, Berthe had told him, in confidence, about the sad previous years, the conjugal misunderstandings that had almost finished so badly, and whose very memory was, fortunately, gradually being effaced.

"...There is nothing more edifying than the sight of today's households, their happiness expended, being repairing themselves of their own accord and being re-established by the force of events: the households most tragically upset by storms and tempests, existences shattered into little pieces, all coming back together and healing themselves! The gravest resentments forgotten, even hatreds eased away; nothing is any longer irreparable! Don't we have extraordinary examples set before our eyes every day? For instance, I dined with friends the other day seated beside a charming woman whose name suddenly reminded me of an old scandal—yes, a crime, a very melodramatic crime! My charming neighbor, a gentle and exquisite creature, had once caused her husband—a jolly fellow seated opposite—to drink poison. Well, there was no longer any trace of it as the criminal wife and the victim husband exchanged tender looks across the table; ferocious hatred had turned back into gentle harmony, and my people would have struck you as a delightful little household. All hail the new time, for correcting the errors of the old world!"

With his eternal everything will sort itself out, Palluel, a confirmed and reinforced optimist, returned to the Jollyvats, preaching the gospel of resignation and temporary but inevitable annoyances. By virtually admonishing François Jollyvat, forcing him to restrain his moans, and joking with Jollyvat from Tours and Jollyvat from Paris, he persuaded them to view their situations a little more calmly. And Jollyvat from Paris, as happy as the Laforcades to be rid of the old bachelor, was able that same evening to send François Jollyvat and Jollyvat from Tours back to their respective destinies.

CHAPTER XIV
Monsieur de Chastelandry's Reminiscences

While Robert gladly made his way the environs of Laval in search of his grandmother, awaited with great excitement by grandfather Laforcade, the latter, in order to take the edge off his understandable impatience, was obliged to endure a few unpleasant moments by courtesy of Houquetot's terrible father, the rather difficult Lord Houquetot de Mont-Héricourt, Marquis de Chastelandry.

You will recall that father Houquetot and grandfather Laforcade had already recovered vague memories of an old quarrel—that both of them, while staring at one another, had almost quarreled without knowing why, purely motivated by confused feelings of anger that they could not explain.

Where had they seen one another before? When? They did not know. But they had seen one another before, and must have been animated then by sentiments with regard to one another that were less than amicable. That evening, the grandfather had been genuinely upset; he was at a loss to say exactly why he had been carried away so violently, but carried away he had been. He had suddenly remembered that the old quarrel has taken place in the Jardin Turc, under the Restoration, but the memory had been imprecise and he had lost its thread immediately.

Since then, the old Marquis, wrinkled but more and more solid in his powerful build, and more spruced-up too, with his moustache curled and his buttonhole blooming, had returned to the Laforcades' house several times. The two old men had looked at one another coldly, hardly speaking to one another, but the old quarrel remained dormant. The grandfather continued to search for the reason for the very marked antipathy that he felt towards the marquis. What had happened between them during their earlier meeting in the Jardin Turc under the Restoration?

It was Chastelandry who suddenly remembered one day. Poor Houquetot's father always had one bee in his bonnet, if not several. He had recently tormented his son unmercifully with regard to a lady he had seriously compromised towards the end of his first youth, during the reign of Louis-Philippe, and it was only with great difficulty that he had been prevented from setting off on a journey in search of her. He had only decided to refrain because he was trying to persuade money-lenders, whom he stunned by his loquacity, to lend money at interest to the son of a ruined family—but the money-lenders were still standing on ceremony and drawing the matter out. Extremely annoyed, with his pockets empty, tormented by all his appetites and desires, the old beau wandered sadly along the boulevards, swagger-stick in hand and a luxuriant, but unlit, cigar between his lips. With all his concentration, this man ahead of his time yearned for the good times of his long youth, which was taking far too long to return—the time when, finally, his patrimony would come back bit by bit and he would recover all the advantages and pleasures of the high life.

One day when he was beating the pavement in this manner, in an even worse humor than usual because of certain debts that an ill-bred creditor was refusing to suffer any longer, Chastelandry—who was walking, contrary to his habit, with his head bowed and his brows furrowed—bumped rather violently into a pink umbrella, which was turned inside out.

"I beg your pardon, Madame—a thousand apologies," said the Marquis, raising his hat to the pink umbrella. "I mean, a hundred thousand apologies!"

The umbrella unmasked a lovely lady, very blonde, who displayed pretty teeth and a mischievous—but no less pretty—dimple at the corner of her mouth, smiling at the old man's insistent apologies.

"Malvina!" cried Chastelandry.

"You're mistaken, Monsieur," replied the lady with the mischievous dimple. "I don't know you."

"I'm not mistaken, Malvina. There was a time when you deceived me, but let's not dwell on old errors… Malvina, oh my dear Malvina, how happy I am to see you again! Please accept this freshly-plucked rose!"

Chastelandry had snatched the rose from his buttonhole and was offering it gallantly.

"But once again, I'm not Malvina!"

"Impossible! You're Malvina from the Théâtre Montansier! I recognized you at first glance, you little tease! See here, Malvina, I repeat that I'm prepared to forget everything…everything! Have you been angry and bearing a grudge for all this time? Will you refuse to forgive me…your sins? When I tell you that the joy of seeing you makes my heart turn upside-down? You had been very naughty, the last time I saw you…no, it wasn't you—there! It's me who was entirely in the wrong. I was brutal and nasty. Listen, Malvina, you're prettier, more fragrant, more delightfully innocent and graceful than ever, in spite of the time…"

"I don't know you, Monsieur, I don't know Malvina, and I beg you not to follow me!" cried the lady, turning around abruptly and presenting the umbrella to the Marquis's face.

"Impossible!" said the Marquis. "Do you remember the summer of 1828, Malvina?"

"1828! You're out of your mind, my good sir. Do I look like a grandmother?"

The lady fled. Chastelandry hesitated.

"Well, what about me—do I look like a grandfather?" he murmured, frustratedly. "Damn it! Malvina! Malvina! Is it Malvina? Isn't it Malvina? Am I mistaken? It's definitely her nose, it's definitely her dimple. Was I seeing things, or didn't she want to recognize me because…? Let's follow her!"

But the lady was already some way off, having crossed the road. A surfeit of carriages prevented Chastelandry from crossing as swiftly, and by the time he reached the other pavement he could no longer see the pink umbrella.

"That Malvina has always been a strange creature! Coquettish and fickle! No talent as an actress but so pretty, so mischievous! Let's see, how did we come to fall out in 1828? It was definitely 1828, I remember that—the year of the Martignac ministry. But of course! The Jardin Turc adventure—that was Malvina! It all comes back to me now—what I was trying to remember at the Laforcades. Yes, in the Jardin Turc! I must clear up that business—I'll run along to the Laforcades' house! No one laughs at me and gets away with it! I've lost Malvina again, but I still have the other one!"

Chastelandry felt his bad mood get worse. In addition to the refusals of his money-lenders and the scornful attitude of the false Malvina, life was full of annoyances and vexations. He chewed his cigar and did not find it very tasty. The hunting season was imminent and he knew that not a single invitation had arrived from anywhere, that he would not have the pleasure of taking aim at the smallest deer or the tiniest rabbit. If only he had been able to rejoin his old regiment, his company of black musketeers, and some nice riot somewhere—no matter what sort—had furnished him with an opportunity to work off some of his anger by kicking up a fuss, with noise and action!

He arrived, grumbling in this manner, at the Laforcade house and rang the bell vigorously.

The grandfather was alone, his son having gone to his crinoline factory, recovered some time before, and Robert not having yet brought back his grandmother, of whom there was good news, but who could not travel very rapidly.

The grandfather welcomed Chastelandry with his most gracious smile, although he did not like him at all. At that moment, full of joy, he found himself disposed to see everything—men and events alike—in the most favorable colors. Chastelandry as exquisitely polite. He had lost one of his ill humor, and he eyes were still glittering with wrath, but he had put on his finest airs and called upon all his gentlemanliness, in order to come down from a greater height on the wretch of a shopkeeper who had stolen Malvina's heart in 1828.

"Delighted to see you, Monsieur," said the grandfather. "Your health is still brilliant? And your amiable son? It's several days since we last saw him."

"My health is delightful, my dear Monsieur, and I hope that ours is no less flourishing," Chastelandry replied.

"Not bad, not bad," said the grandfather.

"By the way, your petty memories of 1828, have they come back clearly yet?"

"Of 1828? What memories?"

"But you know full well—the Jardin Turc? Rather bourgeois for me, the Marais, and the Jardin Turc, but I was tired of the Tivoli and I was looking for Malvina…"

"Oh, the Jardin Turc, about which we talked a little while ago… I'd forgotten about it again. Yes, on due reflection, I must have seen you at that time… One evening in the Jardin Turc. Oh, it was a long time ago. We must have had some little history together—you looked somewhat ill at ease, as I recall… I don't know any longer what it was about, doubtless some trifle, a quarrel between young men!"

"A trifle! Damn it! Try to recall that trifle, my dear Monsieur."

"I'm trying. I have a vague memory of an altercation, but the reason escapes me…"

"Malvina, Monsieur, Malvina! Whom I encountered just now, and the mere sight of whom was sufficient to remind me of everything…"

"Which Malvina? It might have been sufficient for you but not for me…"

"The Malvina you had on your arm in the Jardin Turc!"

"I had Malvina on my arm in the Jardin Turc? You must have been seeing things."

"My dear Monsieur, that statement gives me as much cause as everything else… I beg you, though, to deign to clarify your memory somewhat. I met you in the Jardin Turc—you were there?"

"I was there, certainly, I grant you that, as I've already said."

"You had Malvina on your arm."

"I certainly didn't have any Malvina on my arm. There is no Malvina in my life—not the slightest Malvina, my dear Monsieur!"

"Tell me that she has no talent, tell me that she sings off-key, tell me that she has her own ideas regarding orthography, but…"

"Very well, I'll tell you that—but…?"

"I am magnanimous, and might possible overlook those allegations, but if you dare to tell me that you do not remember Malvina, stop there!"

"I repeat, Monsieur, that I have no idea who your Malvina might be!"

"Are you claiming that you have completely forgotten Malvina, Monsieur?" cried Chastelandry, who was beginning to set aside his determination to remain calm and correct. "To forget Malvina, to forget her perpetually laughing eyes, her blonde hair, the dimple at the corner of her mouth, hr success at the Théâtre Montansier, to cast Malvina disdainfully into forgetfulness after having stolen her from me, is one insult more, and that makes, if I count correctly, three grievances: firstly, Malvina; secondly, your remark about seeing things; thirdly, obliviousness of the injury! That is more than sufficient for me to be desirous of granting you six inches of my sword in your abdomen, the abdomen of an impertinent lady-killer!"

"Lady-killer! Me, a lady-killer!" cried the grandfather. "Despite your six inches of steel, you're deluded, doubly deluded and triply deluded, as you were in 1828 if you saw me with a Malvina on my arm! In 1828, I was recently married, Monsieur!"

"Good! That's an aggravating circumstance! I shall, therefore, in washing away the insult to me with your blood, have the honor of simultaneously avenging the insult inflicted by you upon Madame your spouse! You will therefore receive a visit from my seconds, two of my comrades from the royal

183

guard! To the pleasure of seeing you on the dueling-ground, Monsieur!"

"Go to the Devil!" cried Monsieur Laforcade, furiously.

"And of skewering you, my dear Monsieur, in the honor and memory of Malvina!" said Chastelandry, bowing with exquisite politeness. He was on his way out and had already closed the door behind him, but he opened it again to add: "Besides, that's already happened to you in 1828. You won't escape! It's coming back to me now—I skewered three opponents the day after that business in the Jardin Turc. See you soon!"

This time he had gone. Grandfather Laforcade shouted for the maid and forbade her ever to let Monsieur Chastelandry in again.

"He's completely mad," the grandfather said to himself. "Malvina? Royal guards? We had an encounter, a little altercation, perhaps, but nothing more, so far as I can remember. What the Devil—if he'd skewered me already in 1828, I'd remember it!"

However, as he was slightly anxious, in spite of everything, he wrote to Palluel, who was fortunately at liberty and able to come to see him immediately.

"Bah, don't worry!" said Palluel, when the grandfather had told him the story of the row over Malvina. "That terrible old man, in whom all the instincts of life, carousal and relentless fighting of a strong family are being revived, won't cleave you asunder for so little. If he waits for his old companions in the guard to send them, his whim will have time to pass, for we haven't got there yet—he's still ahead of his time! In any case, I'll have a word with his son to see if he can be persuaded to see reason…"

"You see what an ugly business it would be," said the grandfather, "if he had come to pick a quarrel with me over his Malvina in two days time, when my wife will have returned! It's absolutely essential that the affair is settled before then."

"I'll take care of it."

Without losing a minute, Palluel leapt into a cab and was driven to Houquetot's domicile. As he arrived, he saw the tall figure of Chastelandry on the pavement outside the door. The latter seemed to be in conference with two burly fellows buttoned up to the chin, their hats titled over their ears and stout canes under their arms, and a third individual of a scrawnier appearance.

"What!" said Palluel to himself, as he jumped down from the cab. "Has he got his seconds already?" Advancing towards the group with a smile on his face, he said: "Bonjour, Marquis. Is all well?"

"Very well, my dear Monsieur Palluel," said the Marquis. "You find me with my two guards."

"What? Are you trying to tell me that you've already arranged your seconds for this ridiculous business from 1828. The worthy grandfather Laforcade has just told me about it—but Marquis, we need an explanation of it. What is this adventure concerning a Mademoiselle Malvina—very charming, apparently—who is still troubling your thoughts?"

"Malvina? It does indeed concern Malvina! Permit me to introduce you to these gentlemen, two excellent bailiffs assisting Monsieur the Guardian of Commerce here present, who has come to arrest me and take me to Clichy by reason of a few little promissory notes inscribed to a crooked broker—notes which I had, on my honor, completely forgotten. These gentlemen were waiting for me at my door and have pinched me without resistance—that is the reason why you find me in such amiable company."

"Ah! Very good!" said Palluel.

"But no—very bad!" said the Marquis. I know that I shall get very bored at the Hôtel de la Dette… I was already in a murderous humor, judge for yourself whether this adventure will help me see things in a rosy light. What ridiculous times we're living in! Imprisonment by bailiffs! Fie! A vile creditor, for the sake of a few miserable *écus*, can throw a gentleman into the dungeons of that Bastille! I request that you inform my son, Monsieur, and tell him that I shall burn Clichy down if I am left there any longer than it takes to effect a little rest cure!"

Imprisonment for debt had been re-established some years before, and the debtor's prison at Clichy rebuilt, along with the Hôtel des Haricots for refractory National Guardsmen. The passage of time had already brought back many things, among which these two prisons—precious resources for vaudevillians—were included. Although less terrible than the lead-mines of Venice or the dungeons of Spielberg, Clichy was not, however, as cheerful as vaudevillians and caricaturists depicted it.

"Escort me to my Bastille with these gentlemen," the Marquis continued, "and I'll tell you the story of Malvina. By the way, tell Monsieur Laforcade that there has been a case of mistaken identity."

"Ah!" said Palluel. "You were mistaken about Malvina?"

"No, not about Malvina. As I arrived here, deeply engrossed in reflection—which delivered me into the hands of my bailiffs without my seeing them—my memories became more precise. I did indeed argue with Monsieur Laforcade in the Jardic Turc one evening in 1828, in a fit of bad temper caused by the treason of the delightful Malvina, but Monsieur Laforcade is right; he had nothing to do with that treason. He did not know Malvina! The memory has returned completely: I was furious; I had just slapped the face of the real traitor— one of my friends, a lieutenant in the King's Rifles—but that was insufficient to discharge my fury entirely. While I was waiting for him there on the following morning, I soothed myself by picking fights right, left and center... I had no wish, you understand, to perish in the prime of life from a fit of apoplexy, which I felt to be imminent. I thus harvested a few duels, to be fought one after another. Monsieur Laforcade's face displeased me—I have no idea why—and I told him so, as I did a number of others; there was a dispute, tables turned over, an intervention of the guard, but I was soothed; I felt better and more light-hearted! Three duels the following morning, Malvina's accomplice paid out first with a nice thrust to the shoulder, but in the third, I sustained a cut myself…"

Chastelandry had taken Palluel's arm, while the bailiffs walked behind, sharing in Monsieur de Chastelandry's confidences; the latter was speaking in a loud voice, like a man who had nothing to hide of his life—nor that of Malvina, who had obviously been a very charming woman in her time, albeit somewhat flighty. Still chatting in this manner, they arrived at the Rue de Clichy, within sight of the prison gates, without having endured a minute's boredom. The bailiffs were charmed.

"Ah, Monsieur," said the Guardian of Commerce, "the job would be ideal if all our clients were like you! No sniveling or chicanery with you!"

"Hold on," said Chastelandry. "Since you are content with me, know, estimable functionary of the State, that I am delighted in my turn to have had the honor of making your acquaintance! You must be acquainted with money-lenders, businessmen, lenders at high or low interest, etc. Would you care to provide me with a little list of those that you can recommend to a man of the world whose tenants are sometimes considerably in arrears?"

In front of the sentry-box guarding the famous number 48, Rue de Clichy, Palluel bid farewell to Chastelandry and left him engaged in noting down the addresses that the Guardian of Commerce gave him.

"Make my excuses to Monsieur Laforcade for the little error I made just now," Chastelandry shouted after him. "I'm a veritable dunderhead. My most humble excuses, and most amiable civilities. If, however, he still bears a grudge against me, tell him that I remain, of course, at his disposal…"

"If he stays in Clichy for as long as possible," Palluel said to himself, "it will be a few months of tranquility for his son."

CHAPTER XV
Step By Step to the Honeymoon and the Engagement

Everyone admitted it; Palleul was right to proclaim the superiority of the new form of life unfolding in the inverse direction to the old, in every respect, but particularly that of marriage. Yes, everything is much better than it was before; yes, everything is going in a better direction; one extracts much more satisfaction from life now than then—especially in matrimonial life, which was formerly the butt of so many comic or furious diatribes, so much bitter mockery and joking.

All evils, like all benefits, and all sorrows, like all joys, have always been contained in that single word, marriage. We must to leave to the institution's accountants the obviously-diluted statistic that estimates at scarcely 20%-25% the espousals that formerly worked out fairly well. This figure is evidently adapted to the needs of their cause by sad bachelors in search of excuses. Let us invert the proportion and admit that 25% of unions turned out quite badly, adding to that 25% of stormy households, and we ought to arrive at a figure closer to the verity of the old times.

Would you like to know today's truth? It is quite simply this: 100% of marriages evolve in the direction of perfect happiness and all of them end up getting there! No wastage at all—not the pettiest pourcentage on the bad side![21]

This is the great miracle wrought by the force of events, by today's natural course of life, so extraordinarily superior to the former march of time. How often, in former times, did unions commenced in the rosiest of lights, amid joy and illusion, rapidly decline at intense and complete blackness?

---

[21] I have left the improvised word *pourcentage* as it is, italicizing it as Robida does; the pun is somewhat transformed by the different meanings of the French *pour* [for] and the English "pour," but remains a pun of sorts.

How many households, borne by tempests on to the reefs of misunderstanding and incompatibility, sank into the abysses of betrayal, hatred and despair? We no longer see that—or, at least, even the darkest situation works out happily. Everything sorts itself out. That is the eternal refrain of the new life.

Balzac once wrote a Physiology of Marriage. He could begin it again now; everything is changed, everything is reversed, to the extent that we even see people once divorced for the gravest of reasons, which we think it unnecessary to specify, recommencing their life, climbing up the descendant slopes again, and ending up rediscovering the happy times of cloudless skies.

These general considerations lead us to the particular case of Robert Laforcade and Berthe. They too had descended the fatal slopes, as you will recall, and had arrived, just as the old era came to an end, at the great crossroads of divorce, at which the various roads of the realm of marriage then ended rather frequently.

Since the beginning of the New Era, taking one more step every day along the road to the springtime of their young love, Robert and Berthe Laforcade, becoming younger and younger, have left behind them almost everything, even the memory, of what had once soiled their life. All the cares and sorrows brought by maturity, painfully exaggerated by the vicissitudes of life, are past and forgotten.

Step by step, they have arrived, as we have seen, at the first season of their marriage, the fullness of the honeymoon. One sole thought, one sole heart—to the great joy of the relatives who now follow their happiness with a tender and tranquil gaze, absolutely devoid of the uncertainties and anxieties that were ever-present before, even with regard to unions formed under the most fortunate auspices.

Father Laforcade, very busy, wrapped up in his business, is usually at his shop, absorbed by the fabrication and sale of his crinolines, but the grandfather and grandmother are still there, happy and smiling, their tender old hearts warmed up as in the dawn of their lives, experiencing all the sunlight and the joys of the past again, with long perspectives before them. For them, too, everything will come back; for them, too, life will bloom again.

This morning, Robert—the joyful Robert, whose mind knows only gaiety and insouciance—has prepared a little prank for his young wife. It amuses him to give her presents, and in order to have a pretext, he has dressed her up in all the saints' names in the calendar, forging new ones where the names of male saints cannot be feminized, calling her successively Pélagie, Clotilde, Médardine, Estelle or Scholastique—but today, Sainte Berthe reigns supreme on the calendar, and he has just brought her a little two-*sou* bouquet of violets wrapped in an enormous sheet of white paper, in the middle of which another piece of folded paper envelops a little gift, which Berthe is pretending not to notice.

"Well now," said Robert, pretending to be annoyed. "Aren't you going to unwrap it? Are you spurning Sainte Berthe's gift? Are you one of those spoiled, disdainful beauties? It's nothing but a little ring alas, very simple, an inexpensive little gift, to be sure, for one isn't rich!"

Berthe made as if to throw her arms around her husband's neck, but he stopped her. "A moment, Madame!" he said. "Is the little piece of paper in which the ring is rapped a symbol of your servitude?"

It is a rather thick piece of paper, quite crumpled by virtue of having been folded repeatedly. Berthe unfolds it and casts a glance over it while Robert bursts out laughing.

"A stamped paper! Since when does one wrap gifts for one's wife in frightful illegible documents? What is this lawyer's gibberish?"

Berthe read a few lines and suddenly blushed. "Oh the villain!" she said. "He has kept these horrid things!"

"Little souvenirs!" said Robert, taking back the paper. "Listen, it's pretty:

" '1901, day, etc.

" 'At the request of Madame Berthe Emma Palluel,[22] spouse of, etc., having Monsieur Ducoudray for her advocate, etc., etc....

" 'Presented to the Tribunal the following facts and legitimate complaints that she intends to weigh against Monsieur Robert Laforcade, her husband, in the petition for divorce presently introduced by the aforesaid lady...' "

Berthe snatched the piece of paper and rapidly tore it into little pieces, which she blew into her husband's face.

"There, see what I think of your document! What horror! Were we mad, though? Is it possible, my darling Robert, that we have been as close to the edge of the precipice as that? No, it wasn't us—it wasn't me, I swear it!"

"Nor me either!" said Robert. "It was two transformed and spoiled versions of us, two hearts withered by maturity, which made them do stupid things. You see, it's maturity that makes husbands gloomy and grumpy, wives irritable and cantankerous; it's maturity that brings necessities, true or false, and responsibilities, inevitable or artificial, and desires for luxury, worries about money, the endless torture of existence... It's maturity that spoils everything! Fortunately, we're cured of it now—long live the youth that will repair everything!"

Yes, long live youth, radiant and triumphant youth. Robert and Berthe are returning to the happy age of their beginnings in life. They are now a young couple at the beginning of their honeymoon, charming to one another, competing in attentiveness and graciousness. A delightful existence! How well made for one another those children are!

---

[22] The reader will observe that the full version of Berthe's name has apparently changed since the first time the divorce petition was excerpted in the text, as has the name of her lawyer. This is doubtless one of the tiny flaws in the scheme of things that crept in when the clock of time was set in retrograde motion.

How they love one another, as if the soul of each one were reflected the other's eyes!

Thus the days of that honeymoon continue to pass—too rapidly, in truth; time marches on, and here is the day of their wedding arriving, just as each of the spouses swears that the dreamed-of perfection is found, the husband truly ideal, the wife exquisite, the charm and poetry of life.

The next day, they are no more than fiancés, which is certainly still charming and procures marvelous states of mind. Everything is tender and rosy, sweet illusion and paradisal emotion.

And very gently, our two young people are moving towards adolescence, Berthe preceding her ex-husband by a few years. There will be a happy and joyful adolescence, then a childhood without cares, and a childhood even happier. And so it will be, henceforth, for everyone: individuals, families, nations.

CHAPTER XVI
By Reason of the Perturbations of the Commencement, A Few Extraordinary Cases of Returns Ahead of Time

By reason of the initial perturbations and irregularities following the abrupt reversal of the march of time, there were a few hazards for the new society to avoid and some rather considerable difficulties to negotiate.

A number of people emerged ahead of time, as we have seen in the cases of the Marquis de Chastelandry, grandfather Laforcade and others. Quite naturally, these irregular individuals, arriving with their own ways of thinking, aspirations and tastes, were manifestly impatient to recover the institutions and the milieux with which they had been familiar before, in order to take up their old habits more rapidly.

One could only preach the gospel of patience to these exiles, who were understandably discontented to have emerged amid the innovations of a generation that was not in any respect their own.

As the progression of things became increasingly regular, these cases of advance emergence became extremely rare. Among these exceptional and phenomenal rebirths, however, there were a few cases even more exceptional and even more remarkable than that of the Marquis de Chastelandry. These were produced in every country; a careful statistical survey revealed 100 in Europe and a few in America. As exact data were lacking regarding advanced newcomers in Asia and Africa, save for the Mediterranean coasts, these regions were not included in the statistics. We are not talking about advances of 30, 40, or even 50 years; those emerging from the 19th century had not been included in the survey. The 18th century and the two preceding it had furnished the greater number of these rebirths, but there were a few among them even stranger: amazing reappearances of people emerging from the past many hundreds of years in advance.

From this very detailed and analytical case-studies included in this exhaustive document—a document far too long to be reproduced here in its entirety—we shall be content to cite the most remarkable:

* Guyot Clairefontaine, deceased in 1250, minstrel in the court of the Comtes de Champagne, reappeared in Provins, where he wandered for a weak like a soul in torment, weeping at the sight of the ruined château and mourning his lord, the valiant Thibaut de Champagne, a courtly poet in his own right. "Has he gone on the crusade without taking me with him?" the poor man asked repeatedly. Brought to Paris, Guyot Clairefontaine has been lodged in the Collège de France, where a chair in Old French and Medieval Poetry has been created for him. Occupies himself in transcribing all the poems that he can still remember, and re-establishing the true text of the Chanson de Roland. Continues to versify, but instead of joyful or martial songs, composes melancholy rhymes, as in the following work, comparing his epoch with the present and proclaiming the superiority of the former. He speaks of the ladies of today and describes railways and machines, roundly castigating the impact of the modern era, which will happily soon pass away.

"Loyal lovers of remembrance/Ladies of noble family with soft skin, Valiant horses of Eastern France, replaced today by horses of iron and fire/Ladies who seem askew, betrayed! Engines of fire unfurnishable with lances/O my sweet time/Am exceeding doleful!" [23]

* Cornelius Vanderbroek, Lutheran minister of Harlem who was councilor to William the Taciturn, a violent preacher whose sermons were collected in a thick octavo volume

---

[23] The original of this passage is, naturally enough, written in mock-Medieval language, but there is no point in trying to render the translation into mock-Chaucerian English.

printed in Leyden; also distinguished himself in the great war against Spain, marching at the head of the burghers of Harlem in several combats, notably on one occasion when the town almost fell to a surprise night attack by the Duc d'Albe. Reappeared in a little town in Spain and almost immediately went raving mad. As he was taken to Madrid, he assumed, despite all the attentions that were lavished upon him, that he was destined to feature in an imminent auto-da-fé, in the sackcloth of heretics condemned to the fire. Must be sent to Harlem immediately, to prevent him dying too soon.

* Jehan Maulin, curé of Saint-Benoît-le-Bétourné in 1540, who delivered ardent harangues against the heresy of Calvin and, it appears, wielded an arquebus no less ardently on the night of Saint Bartholomew. Reappeared in Geneva in a Calvinist family bearing his name. Believing himself to have fallen into Calvin's hands, immediately fell victim to an illness from which he might not recover. Brought back to Paris immediately.

* Ali Yousuf, of the janissaries of Kara Mustapha, killed at the siege of Vienna in one of the first Turkish attacks, at the moment when he reached the top of the rampart. Reappeared in a Vienna suburb. Believed himself still at the siege, a prisoner of the Christian dogs. Well-treated, interrogated by the scientific commissioner of Vienna, with the aid of an attaché from the Ottoman embassy; refused to recognize the frock-coated diplomat as a Muslim. Immediately escaped from the apartment provided for him at the embassy, stole a horse and set off in search of the Pasha of Hungary's army; arrived in Constantinople more than half-dead, after awful misadventures in Hungary, Serbia and Bulgaria.

* Thomas Robiquel, keeper of an inn neighboring the convent of Saint-Germain-l'Auxerrois in Paris during the reign of Henri III, enthusiastic partisan of the Guises and the Sainte-Ligue; hanged by the neck from the sign-post of his inn on the

day of the barricades in 1588, for having stirred up the population of his quarter and having dared to establish a barricade directly in front of the Louvre, thus blocking the King's path.

This brave innkeeper had a poor understanding of his role as a popular agitator, for he defended his barricade himself and was captured at 10 a.m. This lack of prudence prevented him from seeing the triumph of the Ligue at mid-day; he returned furious, threatening to sack the house of his own descendant, a peaceful Parisian notary, if he did not immediately run up the Cross of Lorraine. It was necessary to take him to the Louvre, which he scarcely recognized, to force him to admit the reality of certain changes. Disappointed by no longer being able to take action against Henri III, became angry when he saw the statue of the Béarnais.

Entitled to a pension from the July government, elected president of the syndical chamber of wine-merchants and spirit-sellers of Paris, and honored member of the Societé des Combatants des Trois Glorieuses.

* Pierre Brigaille, little-known poet of the 17th century, died of indigestion in 1668 following a series of banquets in the homes of financiers and aristocrats. Reappeared in the home of a descendant, a bailiff's clerk; did not wish to live on the produce of this labor and has returned fervently to work. Ten thousand rapidly-written lines of verse having procured him no more than a dinner and a pair of shoes, Brigaille immediately produced 10,000 lines of verse cursing the stupid and vilely utilitarian epoch into which he had so sadly fallen. Has fortunately been awarded a pension by the Societé des Gens de Lettres.

* Jacob Manassé, money-changer, carried off by a plague that ravaged the Mainz ghetto in 1580. Suddenly re-emerged in the home of Monsieur le Duc de Marcoucy—a descendant of the illustrious Marcoucy of the Crusades, eight centuries of warrior nobility, 120 consecutive Marcoucys dead on

battlefields, two constables, seven Maréchals de France, but also descended from Manassé via his mother, heiress to the Manassé fortune, an accumulation of millions harvested in various crashes or industrial enterprises enjoying great success…for their founders.

Monsieur le Duc is very embarrassed by his ancestor, who refuses to understand anything and believes that he has come back to negotiate a little loan. Proposed at first two deniers per livre by way of interest, or 43% per annum—legal interest authorized by the ordinances of Louis X of France—but came down to 30%. The Duc established the ancestor in a remote room at the very end of one of the Château de Marcoucy's wings and is keeping him carefully locked up, but Manassé, gradually brought up to date by he servants, is kicking up a fuss. Great aristocratic scandal.

* Geoffroy, knight, Comte de Campigny, Vicomte de Mauvezin, Seigneur de Chamarans, patron of the most holy Abbaye de la Trinité-sur-Loire, slain while attacking the English defenses at Orléans with Jehanne la Pucelle in 1429. Suddenly returned in a room at the Château de Campigny and fell very quickly from his initial amazement into a state of fury closely akin to madness. In the first place, his beautiful château, which he had left almost new, solidly built, surrounded by deep moats and furnished with engines of war, munitions and skilled mercenaries in order to make war with the English, has been demolished—he does not know when or by whom—save for the keep, whose ditches have disappeared and which could not be held for two hours against a band of free archers. New and very ugly buildings have been constructed in place of the fine towers and walls; the chapel has vanished. Of the Abbaye de la Trinité-sur-Loire, nothing remains but three or four ivy-covered arches; the town of Campigny has lost its walls and has grown at the expense of the château's projections!

Moreover, this false Campigny is inhabited by Barons de Campigny who are neither his heirs nor his kindred—which is to say, by felonious usurpers. And Geoffroy, Comte de Campigny, Vicomte de de Mauvezin, Seigneur de Chamarans, who found himself in good health and strong in body, having already been in a mad mood at the moment of his accident at Orléans, did 100,000 francs' worth of damage to the property of his successors at Campigny in the first few hours of his return. Fortunately, the new Campignys, from a large Jewish bank, have the means to sustain this petty loss. It required a dozen of their gamekeepers to prevent the old warrior from doing any further damage, and the new branch of the Campignys was generous enough to award him a pension of 1200 francs.

* A patrol from the Egyptian army of year VI in the Revolutionary Calendar, massacred by the mamelukes on the eve of the battle of the Pyramids, named Pierre Beadu, Jean Crapotte, Joseph Bellart and Jean Lecoq, returned to the light of day in an Arab village and made their way back to Cairo with weapons and luggage. The four-day old—or rather young—soldiers were repatriated by the first available boat and are lodged at Les Invalides, not yet comprehending anything of their adventure and anxiously awaiting news of their comrades.

* Claude Forquin, burger of Paris, sworn Great Warden of Hosiery-Drapers, merchant at the sign of the Agneau-d'Or, choked by anger in 1702 on learning, during his supper, of the 15th deferment of a lawsuit that the guild had brought against the braid-sellers. Returned to the home of his several-times-great-grandson in the same profession, a minor employee of Deux Magots, the biggest emporium of the latest fashions in Paris. When he had pulled himself together so far as was possible on that same day, Claude Forquin hastened to the superb offices of the guild in the Rue des Déchargeurs, which, to his great indignation, he found occupied by a cheese-merchant. He ran thereafter to the home of the guild's bursar in the Rue Barredubec, where he found no one, the last bursar

having ceased to practice 50 years before. It was impossible to obtain any information on the suit against the scheming braid-sellers, haberdasher and ribbon-makers!

On his way, Claude Forquin passed the Deux Magots and went in to inform his grandson of his frustration. Horror! Within the shop were, all together, woolen cloths, silks, cottons, textiles, gloves, furs and made-up garments! These infamous mercers were, therefore, infringing the rights of the drapers' guild, and usurping those of the glove-makers, fur-dealers, hat-makers, merchant tailors, etc. Had they, therefore, won a conclusive victory in the lawsuit? The grandson, interrogated, knew nothing. Other subjects of indignant amazement: instead of three apprentices at most, according to the regulations of the Guild, there were more than 30 employees.

"Thirty?" said the grandson proudly. "No, 45! We're the largest shop in Paris."

"Forty-five! The owner must have 42 sons, then? And look at these fabrics! Do you have Calmande, Espagnolette, Dauphine, frieze-cloth, baracan, wincey? Yes, these fabrics! Your drugget is nothing but a drug, my lad![24] What about the rules of mastership and wardenship? What have you done with them? And the wise ordinances of the King? Everything is lost!"

* Jeanne Verdure, wife of Louis Goget, merchant butcher of the Rue Montmartre, departed for a less troubled world in '93 at the age of 24. The ci-devant curé of the church of the ci-devant Saint-Eustache having been arrested and his church transformed into a sort of public house, she dared to manifest an unpatriotic disapproval in the street. Was included in a batch condemned by Citizen Fouquier-Tinville and found herself in a tumbrel with her curé, a market-porter guilty of the

---

[24] I have transcribed this pun (*droguet/drogue*) directly into English, although the word "drugget," meaning a type of cloth made from mixed yarns, is unfortunately somewhat obsolete.

same crime, a former Maréchal de France, two former provincial ladies, a drummer from the ex-Gardes Françaises who, while drunk in an inn, had spoken ill of Robespierre, an ex-monk, a girl from the Palais-Royal[25] and a carpenter who had complained that he had no work.

Returned in the home of one of her great-nephews, an opposition deputy, a Voltairean and Freemason, an admirer of the Great Revolution and its immortal principles—the regenerators of modern nations—and of Napoléon and his no-less-immortal method of rejuvenating Old Europe by means of a large bloodbath and the repeated application of 500,000 bayonets, and, on top of that, an old bachelor, a member of the Caveau and a bon vivant in private.

* Messire Aubin de la Marre, equerry. Mayor of the little town of D***, which he quit at a ripe old age in 1625. Returned to the home of a petty coppersmith, his descendant, in the same town, rather embarrassed by this important magistrate. Messire Aubin's heart is distraught with bitterness; in addition to the decadence of his family, which could look back in his own time on three or four centuries of haute bourgeoisie, he observes too many dire changes in his fine town, formerly so lively and very proud of its eight churches, its bishopric and its collegiate church, its four convents, its old belfry, its royal château, its ramparts, its privileges, its town council, etc., etc. None of that remains; everything has been erased. There are only two churches left, one of them the rather poor parish church, whose bell-tower is scarcely holding up, the other converted into a pump-house and feed-store. The belfry has

---

[25] The girl from the Palais-Royal is not a princess but a whore, the streets surrounding the edifice in question having become Paris's most notorious "red light district" in the late 18th and early 19th centuries. The Caveau to which Jeanne Verdure's descendant is subsequently said to belong was a singing club, the not-so-subtle implication of the whole description being that the reader is free to doubt his heterosexuality.

collapsed, the bishopric has been suppressed and market-gardeners are growing salad vegetables on the site of the château; there are silly little houses where the majestic ramparts and terraces once stood, and silence reigns in the dismal streets. Cleared of all monuments, vestiges of superstition and barbarism, the disgraced and disgruntled town vegetates, forgetful of its past. Of old and important families, extinct or vanished, no trace remains but names on crumbling headstones in the cemetery…

In addition to these authentic reappearances, there are several doubtful cases, among which it is appropriate to cite that of a fallacious individual who dared to present himself one day at the prefecture in Poitiers, representing himself as a free Comte, grandmaster of Charlemagne's cup-bearers, sent by that Emperor to inspect the Administration of Aquitaine. It was soon established that this extraordinary revenant had not come from such a distant past and was none other that a celebrated trickster named Romieu.

To the mild public astonishment occasioned by these reappearances so far in advance of their times, young Doctor Montarcy, with the great authority derived from his long career, replied with reasonably strong considerations. What do we really know about natural laws? Almost nothing. It is necessary to admit that we are subject to them, and that we try with more or less success to work out what they are. There are phenomena that will always remain incomprehensible to us, mysteries that will remain eternally impenetrable, and before which thought must always retreat. Was it not the case before, in the former order of things, that one saw people veritably in advance or behind their times, in respect of their character, their ideas, and the entire-make-up of their personality?—people who had strayed into a century that was manifestly not their own? That happened continually. These irregularities of the former order furnish, by analogy, the only possible explanation of the troubling irregularities of today.

CHAPTER XVII
First Specimens of the 18th Century

Our already-old acquaintance, the Marquis Houquetot de Chastelandry, who was getting younger every day, could pass for a very young man by comparison with Antoine-Claude Le Coq de la Bénardière, departed in 1788 at the age of 72, and Lady Etiennette Barbé, his wife, younger than he by 15 years, who had lived until 1815—both of whom were thrown back by an error of destiny into an absolutely unfamiliar society in a world transformed, to which they could not reconcile themselves.

Antoine-Claude Le Coq de la Bénardière, in his time a bourgeois of Compiègne, lieutenant of the Administration of Rivers and Forests for the population of Soissons for Compiègne, Senlis, Beaumont-sur-Oise, Clermont en Beauvois, Noyon, Laigue, Villers-Cotteret, Coucy and Grurie du Valois, had found himself replanted in that region, considerably in advance of his time, with neither relatives nor friends—understandably—in the midst of a generation completely unknown to him. The initial pleasant surprise of this worthy old married couple in finding one themselves on Earth again, in seeing the green trees and the blue sky, in once again feeling the warm caress of the sunlight on their old bones, quickly changed into a confusion from which they would have had considerable difficulty in extracting themselves if Palluel and Montarcy had not enthusiastically seized the opportunity to collaborate to some degree with Providence.

The young and savant Doctor Montarcy and the spirited Palluel, editor of the journal *Backwards* and champion of the past, were highly honored to arrange things on behalf of, and put themselves at the service of, the worthy old couple from Compiègne, welcoming them into the journal's offices and venerating them as the first examples of the 18th century that was scheduled to return and was already almost on the horizon. They were lodged in a quiet little apartment above the journal's offices, far from the noises of the street, in order to shelter them from indiscreet inquiries and from excessively violent mental shocks, as they were still somewhat startled by their return to life and their abrupt disembarkation in an unknown century.

Monsieur Le Coq de la Bénardière was a tall, strong man, whose full and florid features radiated the benevolent tranquility of an optimistic temperament. His chin and lips were those of a man sensitive to the pleasures of life; he had the bright and intelligent eyes that one sees in bourgeois portraits of the 18th century, absolutely lacking in the vague anxiety or rather insolent irony of the eyes of 19th century portraiture.

A rather marked tendency to plumpness gave Monsieur de la Bénardière's flowery waistcoat a pleasant amplitude and a rather cheerful appearance, which completed the impression given by the general character of his physiognomy. Monsieur Le Coq de la Bénardière must have been a good, brave, honest and very happy bourgeois, a worthy man with well-developed faculties, a very healthy constitution and an open mind, satisfied with living a healthy and expansive life in which everything was happily equilibrated, with work and duties conscientiously accepted and distractions enjoyably accepted in both occupations and pleasure—a life facilitated by honest ease, due as much to personal endeavor as to an honest portion of a inheritance, representing the supplementary fraction of the accumulated labors of several good bourgeois generations, in commerce, in trade and in the king's service.

Monsieur Le Coq de la Bénardière was quite cheerful at first, disposed to accept philosophically the immense changes and upsets that confronted him. Open-minded and curious, he saw before him a new world to discover, a true journey into the unknown. His wife, however, who was still rather weak, did not appear to accept the situation as well; she spent every day ensconced in a large armchair, silent and sad. Monsieur de

203

la Bénardière accused her of being childish, and became impatient with not being able to draw anything from her but vague replies when he questioned her on very important personal matters—family matters with which he was preoccupied.

CHAPTER XVIII
How the Difficulties of Doubling Awkward Cases
Sorted Themselves Out Better Than Was Feared.
Follies of Old Age of Some Young Political Men

As time marched on and brought a modification of ideas and things, the political machine, especially in our country, did not function without a certain amount of friction and grinding of gears. There were two Chambers, the Chamber of Deputies and the Chamber of Peers, continually occupied in unmaking laws—a process which would have been subject to almost as much empty verbosity and vain agitation as that with which the previous era had made them, had not a few wise and alert minds, profiting from the lessons of life, been continually striving to calm the turmoil with appeals to reason and to stifle the prattle of parliamentary oratory.

The existence of Chamber of Peers, which we mentioned above, suffices to indicate that certain political capes have already been doubled for a second time on the return journey—stormy capes, the first time around, whose reefs had broken several ships of State, the flagship of the July monarchy and the imperial galley.

It was inevitable that the approach of certain fateful dates caused many people considerable anxiety, spreading a malaise of anticipation everywhere, from which commerce and industry suffered greatly. Then, when the day of the inverse revolution arrived, to everyone's astonishment and relief, a truly amazing facility was observed in the event, a sort of simple gliding transition. 99 out of every 100 Frenchmen were suddenly satisfied, quite happy and content, for the great majority no longer remembered that they had imposed, acclaimed or accepted the opposite. With sentiments inverted in all sincerity, several groups of political men sat down at a new trough, ready to defend it as if they had never previously sought the exercise of their unbreakable convictions and the satisfaction of their appetites.

Everything has, therefore, gone smoothly. Historians must surely have worn spectacles with excessively strong lenses, which made them see double or even triple, greatly exaggerating our little events. What exaggerations there are in the chronicles of our civil discords! It makes no difference whether it is a small matter of un-executing a few of those naïve individuals who, during the game of the Revolution, knew no better than to catch a dozen bullets in the head, or a simple opportunity for a voyage from the colonies at the expense of the State.

It is, in all probability, much the same in the other countries of Europe or America; people everywhere must see things sorting themselves out quite well, thanks to the new progression of time.

Thus, with the unfortunate capes negotiated and orderly life resumed, the Chambers were able to occupy themselves in unmaking the laws that had formerly been concocted, one by one—and, which may seem rather surprising at first, in the abrogation of laws inevitably called laws of progress, which were no longer making things go badly.

Are we bound therefore, to concede that Palluel, the champion of the past, was right? Does true progress really consist in going backwards? The seasons of political perturbation that we have relived, the returns of social squalls, have not passed, however, without leaving some anxiety in certain minds that are agitated and muddled by nature, which cannot find, in the new order of things, either the philosophical joys of superior minds or the good and simple satisfactions of the host of good folk who live quite naturally.

The danger, or rather the difficulty, comes from those malcontents by temperament, who never think that things are moving quickly enough—the same ones who, in the old order, under the pretext of going forward, were seized by vertigo, overturning institutions and customs and precipitating populations towards a chimerical and utopian future. Have they not assassinated the present sufficiently before, with the threat of a future that they claimed to be inevitable, forging unnecessary sorrows and creating enormous artificial currents in the indolence or panurgism of large numbers of people: veritable mental illnesses of the social organism? Now, these men who are always in too much of a hurry want to run too rapidly backwards, and are working to bring back too soon old institutions for which people were not ready, whose time has not yet come.

The journal *Backwards* has found itself under pressure, and Palluel, considerably worn down by the good cause, has had to struggle hard against the impatient individuals who—just as before, when they claimed to be making the world march in an opposite direction—name themselves the sole representatives of Progress. They have been trying to buy Palluel, and today we find the valiant editor of *Backwards* in his office, in the process of resisting an assault by these excessively hurried progressives.

From general considerations like: "Don't encroach, gentlemen, on the work of the returning generations; let us prepare their task by softening the sometimes difficult transitions, but not hurry precipitately along the road of Progress!" it has reached the point of personal arguments. Pushed to the limit, Palluel does not hesitate to mete out rough treatment in his turn to the ambassadors—or, rather, the leaders—of the party of excessive hurry.

One of them was a young millionaire financier, the son of speculators from the troubled times. Enriched by clever gambles during public disasters, or in the equipment of armies, the young financier had, in the old era—when socialism had appeared to have a chance of seizing power, with all its advantages—undertaken to serve as the financial backer of the party's newspapers, in order to take a hand in their direction. The other was a historian, one of those writers who, from generation to generation, work to confuse the few truths that can still be discovered in various narratives of events taken from contemporaries and eye-witnesses.

"My dear Monsieur Bouquigny," said Palluel, taking a sheaf of old newspapers and pieces of paper, yellowed by age, from a box, "it's useful to have these archives in order. Here's a certain little document that you seem to have forgotten, and which I propose to publish some day or other, to edify the salons enthusiastic for your pleasant follies of old age! What a delightful little program it is, dating from your pre-New-Era career:

" 'Abolition of property and reversion of land, of built property and all industrial equipment to the collective, scientific organization of social collectivism.

" 'The citizen owes his labor to the collective.

" 'In return, the collective owes the citizen shelter, nourishment, plus an indemnity whose amount is fixed.

" 'No more taxes, no more rents, etc.

" 'Division of citizens into several classes: period of activity until (age to be decided), semi-activity thereafter or reserve, inactivity for old age.

" 'Directors, inspectors of labor—national, regional, municipal—sub-directors, sub-inspectors, secretaries, overseers, etc, indispensable cadres furnished by the workers' syndicates which have led the class struggle to triumph, and, of course, national recompense to these valiant combatants, or to other citizens for services rendered. Allocation of suitable residences in the seized domain to the profit of the collective. Regional and municipal houses of discipline for those refractory in performing social duties, etc.'

"Have you forgotten, my dear Monsieur Bouquigny, these little kindnesses, which society has only avoided by reason of the complete change in the march of time? I appear, do I not, to be reading you a set of prison regulations…?"

Monsieur Bouquigny took up his pince-nez, took the piece of paper, turned it over and gave it back to Palluel. "Astonishing," he said. "Truly curious. There were times when the world was positively insane… and that is exactly why I say, since we are now heading in the right direction, that it is necessary…"

Palluel stopped him with a gesture. "Dear Monsieur, and very eminent historian," he said, turning towards Bouquigny's acolyte, "in desiring a more rapid march backwards, have you also forgotten your own writings, your historical works on the ancient régime, your civic manual for young citizens, your great History of the use of maternal schools and wet-nurseries? What will become of you, unfortunate plebeian? According to you, in France prior to 1789, there was nothing but a population of miserable slaves, submissive to the most oppressive reign of pitiless and ignoble tyrants! Twenty-none and a half million serfs attached to the soil or trades, atrociously exploited by 5000 lords or monks! Before 1789, manual workers in towns and peasants in the fields toiled all day without pay for the nobles and the priests, beating the ponds by night to prevent the frogs from keeping the aristocrats awake; their wives and daughters were subject to the *droit du seigneur*. The noblemen of town and country could, for the slightest trifle or by simple caprice, throw any honest citizen into the dungeons of their châteaux or hang them from the gibbets with which the land bristled, etc., etc. Dismal images and vile atrocities everywhere, the frightful hardships of prisons crammed with these unfortunates. The towns, as everyone knows, were mere molehills without monuments of any sort, without art and without beauty, populated by ignorant manual workers performing thankless tasks they hated, surrounded by gross superstitions, turpitudes and ignominies. The sad and wretched rural areas were where the poor serfs vegetated, scratching the soil under the aristocratic whip...

"That was what our country was and what our unhappy ancestors endured before the wind of 1789 came to regenerate the nation, giving it consciousness of itself and creating the Fatherland that had been non-existent before, along with the arts, sciences, letters, industry and everything else—everyone knows that! There, according to you, is the rightful and true picture of these frightful times; there is the *Ancien Régime* of serfdom, ignorance and misery—and yet you are in so much of a hurry to get back to it?"

The ex-eminent historian opened his eyes wide. He too, in going backwards, had forgotten many things. Forgetfulness: a precious faculty given to men, without which they would be victims of torments and hindrances of every sort! He had completely forgotten.

"Wait, don't protest," said Palluel. "I can hear someone now who lived through those olden times before the Deluge of 1789, and who will be able to tell you about it, knowing whereof he speaks."

The sound of voices was audible in the office of the journal—not a dispute, for the voices seemed to be in agreement, but something akin to a duet of exclamations redolent with bitterness. It was the man of the 18th century ahead of his time, the venerable Monsieur Le Coq de le Bénardière, who was talking to an editor of *Backwards* about the 19th century, about which, for the moment, he was still learning. It was necessary to conclude that his impression was not very favorable, for he appeared at present to be developing a veritable indictment of the century of light and science. The editor, perhaps by way of equipping himself to write an article, like any good journalist, was agreeing completely with his conclusions and echoing them.

Monsieur Le Coq de la Bénardière was a sanguine man, even a trifle violent and authoritarian by nature; when he had something on his mind and felt himself touched by conviction, he spoke loudly and clearly, without forsaking his bourgeois politeness.

"Misery of my life!" he cried. "Pretentious and presumptuous generation, look what you have made of the house that we, your ancestors, founded, built, decorated and rendered as agreeable as possible to live in, which we left to you without any suspicion that that you, wretched and naughty children, would overturn everything, change everything, demolish everything, insulting your fathers and treating them as inept barbarians enmired in darkness and filth! With the absurd idea that humanity began with you, and that you alone have been capable of saying, doing or thinking anything reasonable and acceptable! Ah—were we monkeys, then, your ancestors?"

"In truth, Monsieur de la Bénardière, you're quite right—but did you not also have some of these same ideas relative to the century that preceded yours?"

"Never!" said Monsieur de la Bénardière, striking the table. "Look out for your writing desk...never! Entirely to the contrary, we were full of respect for the 17th century, the great century; we bowed down to its great men, its great ideas, we took shelter in its shadow. While you, our children, are not content to merely treat all your ancestors as blockheads; you attempt to make a *tabula rasa* of their works, to erase them, so to speak, and with an obstinate ferocity, to behave as if they had never lived, thought and worked—which they did more than you, perhaps, and in any case, infinitely better!"

"You're getting angry, Monsieur de la Bénardière," said Palluel, "with good reason, I admit—but be patient; your time will come again."

"And how, Monsieur, shall we recover the house that we have abandoned? Nothing remains standing of that which we loved, of that which we respected, or merely of that which we knew. Everything has been suppressed, materially and morally; you have destroyed it all! Is anything left of the France that I knew? The four centuries' worth of edifices that constituted her face in 1788, in Paris as in our provinces, has disappeared, and I search for their sites in vain. The picks and spades of sons have overturned the work of fathers, ferociously and stupidly persevering in obliterating its traces, like parricides murdering a progenitor and burying the body! Oh yes, stupidly, one can shout it out, in looking at what they have put in place of the grandiose monuments in the midst of which we lived, in contemplating their dismal, vulgar, ostentatious or gloomy buildings! Can I recognize it, your Paris of immense and cold rows of cages for rent, replacing the 500 edifices that the religion, charity wealth or power of

211

fathers raised, the thousands of more modest houses with their own character? Can I recognize my little town, stripped in the same fashion of the attire that the work of centuries had designed for it?

"Around me, instead of all that might embellish and ornament life, elevating it by the contemplation of those beautiful things that make the eye and the mind negligent, oblivious to stains and vices, I see nothing but the aggressive collection, accumulation and overcrowding of all that may, in the moral order as in the material, contribute to making life uglier, baser and sadder! Have you instituted a cult of ugliness? Or have you, degenerate children, acquired a taste for that which is base, trivial, odiously flat and banal? Go then to ask for lessons in good taste, not from your builders of palaces or cathedrals, but from the simple village peasants constructing the hovels of our era! What is there to look at now in your era? What fodder have you left for the gaze of the worthy man possessed of eyes? Nature alone! Nature eternal, which you have not yet spoiled!"

"But…but…" the eminent historian stammered, "you are utterly scornful, Monsieur, of modern taste!"

Monsieur de la Bénardière disdained to hear, or even to look at the eminent historian, thus demonstrating that he put him on the same footing as the productions of modern taste.

"Oh, yes," he continued, "I have just been reading your history; I have emerged from your history since 1789 as from a nightmare! You might have economized on all your revolutions, since all the modifications really necessary, the progress demanded by experience, we either had in 1788 or would have acquired peacefully, in the natural way of things. A transformation of the fiscal system, wrought entirely by a process of useful liberalization, and the entire management of France would have been ameliorated! In 1788, we had an aristocracy that was an ornament, the stout remnant branches of the old oak of French monarchies, sustained everywhere by the growth of its roots… It was a force, as in the past, and a decoration, the nation in flower! And the aristocracy was open—ever open, whatever you may say, to the accession of everyone, but accession that had to be justified by good reasons! Deign to take up the Royal Almanac and see whether, in the highest functions of plebeian names, new names are not proudly intermingled with the oldest names of the most ancient French annals! Your equality would make me laugh, if it did not make me weep! It is in everyone's interest that there should be several layers in society, several ranks—that is the margin of advancement so necessary for the emulation of all. Evidently, the greater number, the mass will remain lower down, but if they do not distinguish themselves with any particular merit, that is, and always will be, justice.

"We did not expel the souls from our bodies. We did not have hearts like desiccated sponges, empty of all ideals and aborted of all religious sentiment! Above the highest interests and the great purely human things, we still perceived the superior regions and the immense mystery towards which the steeples of bell-towers directed our hearts! Superstitions, you say? I even admit superstitions; they are good, they are the parasitic ivy of religion, the humble ivy that attaches itself to old edifices but does them no harm, adding, on the contrary to their beauty. Take it upon yourselves to recover them, those superstitions! Better the exuberance of vegetation than desiccation and withering. The intelligence of encyclopedist brains cannot be found therein—fortunately!—but the fine and brave intelligence of rustic brains, solidly founded and entirely human!

"Your liberty, as we saw before you came to understand it, is oppression and violence, a brutal and disordered tyranny leading inevitably to the establishment of regulated tyranny. Your impossible equality will be a stupid abasement of all to a sub-normal level by a roller-press! Your liberty of 1789 ended in the prisons of 1793, where everyone found themselves equal before the guillotine, the supreme and final expression of that sweet word 'fraternity,' which was never so misunderstood as it was on the day when such a scaffold was made—yes, the fraternity of aristocratic and plebeian heads in the bran of the basket.

"Goodbye, Monsieur!"

"Wait a minute. You wanted to have a chat? Let's chat...yes! In the bran of the basket, I tell you...the great carnage and the sound of the cannon..."

"A thousand apologies! I'm in a hurry..."

The ex-collectivist millionaire and the eminent historian had picked up their hats and sidled backwards to the door, but they were grabbed and held by the old and worthy bourgeois. Holding one by his coat-button and the other by the back of his collar and shaking the a little, he continued to put upon their heads, beneath the torrent of his vehement indignation, all the aberrations of a pretentious and culpable century.

CHAPTER XIX
The Grand Council For the Prevention
of the Errors of the Past

Monsieur Le Coq de la Bénardière had been ill for some time. He had learned too many things in too short a time, consuming the entire course of modern history in a single draught, overloading his mind. He had heaped surprise upon anger, joy upon fury, indignation upon melancholy. Moreover, his wife, who had seen the whole immense drama personally—and had, like all mothers, been particularly subject to its sorrows—had decided to speak.

His heart, still bleeding, overflowed then, and the worthy bourgeois, the father of a happy family in 1788, found out in the space of an hour what the formidable tempest had done to his family in the space of a few years—throwing some into prison and to the scaffold, condemning the others to the endless carnage of the Empire, to the bloody fields of battle, to the fields of snow and mud, to the hospitals ravaged by typhus and surgical infection.

Young doctor Montarcy had to look after the poor wounded old man. Meanwhile, a group of people came together in the offices of Backwards, composed of men of good will like the valiant writer Palluel, veteran of the good cause—thinkers both young and old, the young armed with the experience of a long life already unfolded and the old newly returned with the comprehension of the epoch to come.

Backwards, with the authority acquired in its already-long career, had succeeded in instituting a Grand Council for the Prevention of the Errors of the Past. This Council was universal; all the civilized nations were associated with the project. Sections in each country would only occupy themselves exclusively with their own country, but delegates would come together at three-monthly intervals in an international conference to discuss questions relevant to the community of nations.

At Monsieur Le Coq de la Bénardière's bedside, the two initiators of the Council for Prevention, Palluel and Montarcy, were debating the final questions relating to the formation and functioning of the Council. Numerous difficulties of every sort could certainly be anticipated, and in its work of social defense, the committee would have much to do, but obstacles and difficulties had to be overcome—the immensity of the cause demanded it.

Montarcy and Palluel re-read the list of Council members, still debating certain names before the definitive official sanction of the government of return—which is to say, informed—would be given to it.

"First and foremost, no politicians!" said Palluel.

"Understood—not under any pretext!" agreed Montarcy. "Anyone having been involved in politics, in any manner whatsoever—and, in consequence, having the pitiless and noxious virus in his veins—cannot be part of the Council, which is intended, above all else, to attenuate in the largest measure possible the often-disastrous effects of politics."

"That's the principle! From generation to generation, the Council will only recruit members from among those men who are entitled, by their intelligence or their character, to have an influence on the march of events and the destiny of populations—and who, more often than not, have been left or cast aside, and have lived without even getting close to the means of world government."

"Very good!" said Monsieur de la Bénardière.

"Let us ameliorate the times! Let is work courageously to repair, to the greatest possible extent, the innumerable errors of the past! It is inadmissible that the generations, returning along the beaten track, should carelessly step into the same puddles; the Council for Prevention will be there to post lanterns at the most dangerous corners…"

"Of which there will be no lack along the road," said Monsieur de la Bénardière.

"But which will be known, and which it will be necessary to negotiate better than before."

"How? By what practical means?"

They will be sought out and discovered! It is sufficient, to put our hopes of amelioration into action, for each generation to bring together a company of fine minds, supported by the good will of governments."

"Hmm!" said Monsieur de la Bénardière, still in the grip of his deep pessimism, for reasons that were all too justified.

"The History we have to hand, uncertain as it is, will permit the Council for Prevention to act effectively on governments. The Council will guide, in every possible fashion, by warnings or actions, good governments, kings, ministers and statesmen, helping them to extract the maximum number of satisfactions from the good situations and happy period traversed, which they can combine in order to shower them down on populations—satisfactions which, alas, ever since there have been governments and populations, have hardly piled up under that relationship. And when the difficult times come, the periods of misfortune and desolation, the Council for Prevention, permanently constituted, will search for the most efficacious ways and means of getting out of those calamitous periods with the best possible results. To anticipate, to strive, to ameliorate! It is a superb role that the committee will play in operating a sort of revision, day by day, of the history of the world, in trying to weaken evil and fortify good, favoring good and useful actions and neutralizing, so far as it might be possible, the bad ones."

"If harmful individuals could be seized as soon as they show their faces, and hanged without further ado, I'd have more confidence," said Monsieur de la Bénardière.

"My dear Monsieur, let's not forget that we cannot suppress the past as we please. We must inevitably submit to time's backward march; we can only try to soften and organize things."

"The time of perturbations is getting close now," said Palluel. "The Council for Prevention only has a few years in hand for consideration! Brrr! What other epoch can manifest such a fine collection of harmful individuals? There's little time to devote to the question of the imminent return to Earth of those who will see once again the great upheaval of nations, shaken by a fit of political epilepsy that will grip all Europe. What they know of their sins in old age will render the harmful, the evil and the injurious less offensive, I hope. We shall soon see again the old tremblers of the Plain who, out of laxity, replied in the affirmative with their votes—their *pollice verso* [26]—to all the demands for heads, the ex-guillotiners who subsequently became the undistinguished courtiers of the Empire and the excellent prefects furnishing conscripts for the imperial hecatombs. Afterwards, we shall see those who devoured one another in the struggle: the great wild beasts; the terrorists who plied the guillotine's blade so freely.

"Let us wait for them with a firm stance: the talkers and the fighting-men, the hypocritical and the ferocious, the rogues and the madmen, and let us work for their amelioration…"

"What will you do with them? What?" demanded Monsieur de la Bénardière, raising his arms in the air.

"My dear Monsieur," said Montarcy, "you only arrived recently; you are still ignorant of the new order of things. The backward progression of life is favorable to the amelioration of the human race! Already, the thinkers and the observers have been able to establish real progress. No, man is not the imperfectible and irreducible animal that we thought; people are beginning to recognize that today!

"Having to retrace a life already lived, proceeding backwards towards naïve and candid youth, forgetting painful phases, trying, by virtue of an understandable interest, to avoid faults and falls—that enormous circumstance has enormous consequences! And one has a better sense of the connection between generations, the solidarity between them and the cousinly relationship—so as not to abuse that beautiful word

---

[26] A turn of the thumb.

but besmirched word fraternity—the cousinly relationship binding everyone together. Look, here's a very simple calculation. Every one of us has two grandfathers and two grandmothers, which makes eight for the preceding generation and 16 for the one after. At four generations per century, we arrive in 200 years at 512 grandfathers and grandmothers. Which is to say that the man without a home, the unfortunate who has no family and no place in the world, nor shoes on his feet, who wanders starving through inhospitable streets, would, if he were suddenly transported to the time of Louis XV, have 256 paternal houses. Imagine this: the rich man of today, who looks down from the height of his luxury without sympathy, might encounter him at the hearth of a communal ancestor!"

"And as for all those wild and bloody revenants of the Revolution who are beginning to return," said Palluel, "some of them sinister bourgeois forgotten in little towns, mulling over their terrible memories by the firesides of old pensioners, others corpulent lords strutting ostentatiously about vast estates or opulent church properties, members of the Chamber of Peers, still meddling in politics, do you imagine that the thought of finding themselves petty lawyers again, as before, mere provincial attorneys or needy novelists, will not incline them to be a little more easy-going and gentle during the hard period, when they will pay the leading roles in the great tragedy? For in the end, having passed through his great days again, Monsieur de Robespierre, to his great detriment, will have to go back to pleading petty cases at the Arras bar; the terrible Danton will put away his thunder and plead at the Châtelet. 'Monsieur Danton,' the judge will say, 'it is useless to strike us down with your eloquence; all that is at stake now is a mere trifle of a case, a shopkeeper bringing an action for 100 *écus*!' Barrère too will plead and fill in forms for minuscule fees; Carrier, the executioner of Nantes, will return to pressurize the pleaders of Aurillac; and Fouquier-Tinville, the public prosecutor, will again become the shyster of the Châtelet, embezzling money from his clients and serving as a police spy. Hébert, Père Duchêne,[27] will have to go back to selling tickets to make a living; the frightful Marat will go back to work as a veterinary physician in the stables of His Royal Highness the Comte d'Artois, who will have been Charles X. Collot d'Herbois, the proconsul-executioner of Lyon, will reappear in the theatre as an actor and writer; people will whistle at him again in *La Journée de Louis XII*, a heroic comedy in four acts, *L'amant loup-garou*, *Rodrigue et Séraphine*, etc., etc. One can, I think, rely on that certainty of returning one day to their own particular humble origins to give these gentleman cause for some reflection!"

"By the same token," observed Montarcy, "I imagine that, for the Great Emperor, the prospect of one day finding himself merely a lieutenant of artillery might trouble him slightly upon his imperial throne!"

"Most certainly! And what thoughts will that inspire in him? Will his politics not feel its effect, and will not the populations over which he trampled, and the victims of his cannon, and his own soldiers, old veterans or young conscripts, gain something therefrom?"

"We shall see!"

"Say rather: it must be!" said Palluel energetically. "It is in the great crises that the Council for Prevention will demonstrate all its finesse and ingenuity, deploying all the resources on which the international association of the most noble intelligences permits us to count."

---

[27] Jacques Hébert was known as "Père Duchêne" because that was the title of the celebrated radical periodical he published.

CHAPTER XX
The Cycle of Generations

The years continue to pass—or, rather, to re-pass. Yet more changes in everything, in mores and ideas as well as the material conditions of life!

The Chambers continue to work feverishly at their task—which is to say, unmaking a large number of laws that have ceased to be necessary and indispensable, and bringing back the old ones, almost always to everyone's great satisfaction. This legislative work is not very exciting for Parliament and the electors, although there is always discussion, and even sensational discussion; this is, after all, the epoch of great parliamentary eloquence.

Certainly, one can sometimes observe rather violent currents in public opinion—but such violence gradually dies away; anger and bitterness decrease; everything becomes calm. Parliamentary eloquence becomes increasingly considered and polished, more classical in form and content. Its effect is primarily soporific, except upon the true amateurs of the genre. Never has it been so easy and so comfortable to sleep in the Chamber. There are still, of course, contests of personal ambition, portfolios that are disputed, ministers to topple, interests, jealousies and hypocrisies in conflict, programs to defeat, promises to break, friends to betray and oaths to violate—but much less bitterness is brought to bear in such matters. Everything is accomplished and supported more easily. Besides, one knows now that, for all annoyances that become manifest, as to all diseases of the body, tomorrow will unfailingly bring the remedy.

Alas, one must expect a terrible revenge of parliamentary eloquence and an enormous reflux of malevolent, damaging and destructive power from the heyday of the Revolutionary Assemblies, which will mark the epoch when the venom of speech, overheated by streams of vitriol, brought France—

seemingly at least—to its maximum of virulence and noxiousness.

In the meantime, all is calm and full of *joie de revivre*. We once knew *joie de vivre*, but it is that of *revivre* that we savor now. Fine and mild weather! It really does seem that the seasons are more beautiful and that the Sun shines more brightly. March is certainly now less cold and more discreet in its sudden storms, and more flowers bloom in the fresh April greenery. Springtime's festivity is visible in the towns, as in the country, galaxies of daisies speckling all the meadows, white dresses and trousers adding to the gaiety of streets and promenades. Does it still rain sometimes, and does winter still bring its snows and frosts? Yes, certainly—but in sensing the march towards youth, the world passes through these tedious little intervals more easily.

And what modifications in ideas! Truly the 19th century, with its abrupt orientations and disorientations caused by rapid changes of every kind, moral and political alike, in customs and conditions of life—a convulsive century full of passion and folly, which turned all ideas on their heads and whose heart ended up almost petrified by lamentable and gross materialism—marked the end of a human era: an era after which, with all hopes disappointed and all illusions dead, there was nothing better to do than retrace its steps in search of the tracks and grooves of preceding ages.

Each generation that reappears corresponds to change in the social ideal. It is, for each one successively, the finest ideal—the one glimpsed in the days of the first existence.

What astonishing small changes have been observed within the great change! One no longer hears talk of feminism or of feminine resentments against unjust and long-standing masculine spoliations; there is no longer any question of the famous Madame Y*** or the tempestuous Madame Z***, who dream of overturning these ancient and obsolete ways, the abolition of masculine monopolies and the accession of women to all social roles. These ladies are becoming wise little girls who study the petty catechism and baptize their

222

dolls; their mothers or grandmothers, presently, are very considerate individuals, very calm, even timidly bourgeois, who embroider slippers for their husbands and whose minds, when they are not occupied with jam-making, wax indignant for three months over some petty infraction in the ordering of the chairs and the prie-Dieu at high mass, or over the slightly extravagant hat worn by a certain flighty individual about whom there is a great deal of gossip in town.

These ladies would of course, be even more indignant, and would make their husbands party to their indignation, if they had ever been able to believe that at a certain moment, as rumor has it, women had dared to adopt masculine manners subversive of the natural order—a cavalier tone, as the slang of the time put it, I am assured—while, on the other hand, men, descending in their turn from some nook or canny of low society, would match their thoughts with the tone of their words and reel off uninhibitedly, in respectable drawing-rooms, jokes and expressions that a sapper of the 1820s would scarcely have dared risk in conversation with another sapper in a guard-room.

It is also said, and is just as difficult to believe, that young ladies were quite fluent in slang learned while roaming freely in the fields, schoolboy slang reported to them by brothers, and the truly excessive language of contemporary soldiers. No, all these obviously-exaggerated tales are impossible to credit.

It is certainly preferable that grumbling parents should sometimes to cry out impatiently: "Birdbrain! How little it needs to occupy the mind to a young girl!" than that people should say, with justified suspicion: "What's behind those pretty eyes, and what troubling thoughts are rolling around in that head?"

It is the general feeling, and there is no longer any question of irritated and unbalanced women. The fashion has passed; one no longer sees these 'hysterical states of mind,' as the jargon of the end of the 19th century put it. Ladies and maidens are generally sweet, reserved and very romantic, and sometimes remain romantic for quite some time. At the end of the day, comparing the fashions, this one is preferable.

CHAPTER XXI
The Principle of the Steam Engine Is Finally Forgotten!

The railways are entirely decrepit and forgotten; people are no longer intent on scorching and burning vertiginously through life. Members of the public are less and less inclined to risk themselves in these dangerous conveyances, with which, for the illusory benefit of a needlessly exaggerated speed, one must risk terrors, bruises, grazes, chills and all kinds of death. One after the other, the lines have been abandoned; day by day, agriculture is reconquering the vast tracts of land formerly monopolized by railways and other abolished industries.

Our beautiful royal roads have recovered their cheerful movement, their circulation of stage-coaches, diligences, berlines, mail-coaches, poste-chaises, carts, etc. Monsieur Laforcade, whom we knew as a grandfather, is the post-master at Auxerre, on the road to Lyon and Italy. Despite the concurrence of river-borne transport, there is a diligence every day containing ten people who are traveling to Lyon—a journey taking four days in summer, five in winter.

A beautiful road, perpetually ribboned with carriages and travelers of all sorts, amid the joyful racket of bells, horns and the cracks of postillions' whips. It is a perpetual procession: trader's carts carrying large bales of merchandise, very numerous and coming from every country, especially when the great fair is held at Beaucaire; poste-chaises bearing English lords to Italy; mail-coaches; horsemen; pedestrians; regiments changing garrison; peasants going to the nearest free market; companions on the Tour de France with their packages of personal belongings on their shoulders and ribbons in their hats.

A little blond boy is playing by the roadside with his brothers and sisters; it is father Laforcade, who has scarcely donned his first pair of trousers.

What changes in science, industry, commerce and everything else!

Finally! Finally, the principle of the steam engine is on the point of being forgotten. It is already no more than a curiosity that scientists demonstrate to one another in their laboratories.

Here is the last gasp of murderous and brutalizing mechanization, the closure of the last large factories, the disappearance of enormous industrial agglomerations draining life away and depopulating the countryside in favor of black cities of sad labor, and giant factories whose innumerable inconveniences have finished up sowing alarm in all minds not closed to reflection. Those ferocious machines, so long triumphant and dominant, have been cast down at last! Only the economists and statisticians, with hearts as dry as figures on balance-sheets, were able to contemplate them without shivering—and even to congratulate one another on their industrial and financial returns, uncaring about what the tons of manufactured products or the gold heaped up in coffers represented in terms of tears, misery and evils without number.

For too long, mechanization and large-scale industrialism have crushed free and healthy individual work, erasing all that small-scale concurrence, bringing forth immense warehouse-barracks, industrial and commercial centralization—which is to say, the suppression of small and medium-sized independent situations, the servitude of human beings: slaves of the monster of iron and flame, workers reduced to mere hands, or tools!

In addition to material harm, the immense factories brought promiscuity and its perils, eroding the family little by little, if not destroying it.

All that is now finished, though! The creature of iron and steel, the work of man that became his ferocious tyrant, expired with the death-rattle of its extinguished furnaces and the sinister grindings of its moving parts. The last blasts of its strident whistles and the last gasps of its cranks and pistons gave the impression of an exhausted fortress expending its last cartridges. The iron cog-wheels stopped, and the formidable monsters—so long victorious, harsh suzerains whose flamboyant keeps overlooked vast black regions—have collapsed one by one, becoming immense cadavers of rusty scrap iron, which the dust and the grass of the fields will transform into strange hills: the tumuli of the extinct Iron Age.

This evolution accomplished, liberated humankind will be able to utter a long sigh of relief; entirely returned to old and sane ideas, it has already forgotten everything. To factory work and machine labor, people much prefer the more flexible work of the hand and traditional methods.

Thus, everything that the 19th century called its achievements, all that it proudly proclaimed as its conquests, in the scientific context as in the political and social contexts, has fallen or vanished. We have seen all those so-called conquests rejected, one after another, in the name of true progress: that which must have for its goal, above all others, the true happiness of human beings and the real embellishment of life—good and simple truths too long misunderstood or lost to view.

And in consequence of this return to good and simple ideas, one can foresee in the near future—after a temporary phase of definite difficulties—the re-establishment of guilds, traditions rediscovered with all their former authority. After a lapse more painful than genuinely long, old abandoned habits will be reborn and will rule life as they once did—which is to say, open and organized guilds, as much for the advantage and progress of the craft as for good regulation, apprenticeship, protection, foresight and help for the sick and the old.

Small towns, which were emptied to the profit of congested Paris or a few great industrial centers, feel the life-blood returning to them now, and are beginning to recover their own life; the deserted countryside is being repopulated, and agriculture, our good old nursing mother, is recovering her arms.

One no longer hears talk of the bitter and ferocious struggle for life, the idea of which has generated sorrow since its inception and ravaged all advanced minds towards the end of the ancient era. Strife still exists, naturally; life is perhaps inconceivable without strife—do we not see a struggle for existence even among mollusks clinging to a rocky promontory?—but one is not always talking about it; one does not have the notion obsessing and tormenting the mind. Moreover, thanks to the new mode of life, the majority of anxieties that the notion brought with it are no longer features of existence in the present march of time, so joyous and novel, towards youth and the morning!

We have mentioned that with the return of active life, Monsieur Laforcade, the grandfather, has become a post-master again. Our friends, the famous Doctor Montarcy and the illustrious Academician Palluel, are very young now. One is beginning to study his ABC with a tutor in his native town, in a tranquil corner of Saintonge. The other plays with his top or runs through the woods with other vigorous urchins, enjoying himself, while his father, a country doctor, gallops over the roads for ten leagues around his village.

Messire Houquetot de Mont-Héricourt, Marquis de Chastelandry, whom we left in the debtor's prison at Clichy, emerged therefrom a long time ago. Having become again a lieutenant in the Company of Musketeers of His Majesty Louis XVIII, he dazzles the salons of the noble faubourg and those of the Chaussée d'Antin with his luxury, and fills the chronicle of Paris with a thousand adventures and a thousand follies...

CHAPTER XXII
Last News

As for the other characters in the story, all of them have long since been replaced by their fathers or grandfathers. Listen! Soon the last blast of the cannon of Waterloo will sound, opening the difficult period. The past is on the march...

Thus goes the world. Beyond each epoch another reappears; beyond each generation, another marks time, and makes its entrance when its hour sounds—or, rather, re-sounds—on the Clock of the Centuries, which the Great Clockmaker has re-set and regulated in a fashion so very different from before.

Come back to the world, centuries already spent!

THE END

BLACK COAT PRESS

Gaston Leroux. *The Phantom of the Opera*
Jean-Marc Lofficier. *The Katrina Protocol*
Jean-Marc & Randy Lofficier. *Edgar Allan Poe on Mars*
Jean-Marc & Randy Lofficier. *Robonocchio*
J.-M. & R. Lofficier (eds.). *Tales of the Shadowmen 1: The Modern Babylon*
J.-M. & R. Lofficier (eds.). *Tales of the Shadowmen 2: Gentlemen of the Night*
J.-M. & R. Lofficier (eds.). *Tales of the Shadowmen 3: Danse Macabre*
J.-M. & R. Lofficier (eds.). *Tales of the Shadowmen 4: Lords of Terror*
Xavier Mauméjean. *The League of Heroes*
Frank J. Morlock. *Sherlock Holmes: The Grand Horizontals*
Marie Nizet. *Captain Vampire*
C. Nodier, Beraud & Toussaint-Merle. *Frankenstein*
Charles Nodier. *Lord Ruthven the Vampire*
Henri de Parville. *An Inhabitant of the Planet Mars*
John William Polidori. *Lord Ruthven the Vampire*
P.-A. Ponson du Terrail. *The Vampire and the Devil's Son*
Eugène Scribe. *Lord Ruthven the Vampire*
Brian Stableford. *The New Faust at the Tragicomique*
Brian Stableford. *The Stones of Camelot*
Brian Stableford. *The Wayward Muse*
Brian Stableford (ed.). *News from the Moon*
Villiers de l'Isle-Adam. *The Scaffold*
Villiers de l'Isle-Adam. *The Vampire Soul*
Philippe Ward. *Artahe: The Legacy of Jules de Grandin*
David White: *Fantômas in America*

NON FICTION
Jean-Marc & Randy Lofficier. *Shadowmen: Heroes and Villains of French Pulp Fiction*
Jean-Marc & Randy Lofficier. *Shadowmen 2: Heroes and Villains of French Comics*
Randy Lofficier. *Over Here: An American Expatriate in the South of France*